Praise for

My Vampire and I

The love between Andrew and Tommy is beautiful as either is willing to give up everything for the other...Marcus is wise enough to use Dakar's own ambitions to trip him up, but will it be enough? Only time will tell. ~ *Fallen Angel Reviews*

Total-E-Bound Publishing books by J.P.Bowie:

My Vampire and I Volume One
My Vampire and I
My Vampire Lover

My Vampire and I Volume Two
Duet in Blood

My Vampire and I Volume Three
Blood Resurrection

My Vampire and I Volume Four
Bound in Blood

My Vampire and I Volume Five
Blood Lure

Single titles
Ride Em Cowboy
Ride 'Em Again Cowboy
The Set Up
Personal Trainers
Halloween Angel
The Officer and the Gentleman
With a Little Help From My Friends
Blood Relations
Nowhere to Hide
Trip of a Lifetime
A Ghost Story
Happy Ending
A Highlander in L.A.

Anthologies:
Heatwave: Summer Bliss
Naughty Nooners: Lunches in Laguna
Friction: Cruising
Fabulous Brits: Under the Law
Saddle Up 'N Ride: Ride 'Em Hard Cowboy

Seasonal Collections:
Homecomng: Blueprint for Love
Christmas Spirits: A Present Christmas
Yule Be Mine: A Special Christmas
Immortal Love: Night Wing

MY VAMPIRE AND I
Volume Six

Blood Lust

Blood Talisman

J.P. BOWIE

My Vampire and I Volume Six
ISBN # 978-1-78184-573-8
©Copyright J.P. Bowie 2012
Cover Art by Posh Gosh ©Copyright 2012
Interior text design by Claire Siemaszkiewicz
Total-E-Bound Publishing

Published in 2013 by Total-E-Bound Publishing, Think Tank, Ruston Way, Lincoln, LN6 7FL, United Kingdom.

.

BLOOD LUST

Dedication

For the readers who asked for more of Tommy and Andrew's story — this one's for you — and for Phil, always.

Chapter One

Tommy Cordain was depressed. He knew he shouldn't be, but for the life of him he just couldn't shake the feeling of despondency he'd woken up with, and now couldn't dispel.

"Damn it," he muttered, pouring himself the third cup of coffee of the morning. His mood might have been lighter if his lover, Andrew Berés, was there with him, but Andrew wouldn't be up and about until later in the day — and therein lay the problem — or at least, one of the problems.

Since Andrew had left New York and moved in with Tommy their relationship had grown stronger than Tommy had ever dreamed it would. He'd never been in a monogamous relationship before, had never felt like committing himself to only one person, until he met Andrew. And Tommy had never been happier.

So what was the problem?

Andrew was a vampire.

But that wasn't the problem. Well, if Tommy was really honest with himself, hell yeah, it *was* the problem. Because, until Andrew had come into his life, Tommy had been okay with the prospect of growing older. Not that he'd really thought about it that much. His parents were older, and they still enjoyed an active life, taking trips, even going line dancing every week. Somewhere in the back of his mind he'd figured that when he was their age, late fifties, he'd probably still be going to the gym, take the occasional hiking trip, go swimming, jogging, all the things he did now. He'd look older, but that didn't matter, did it?

Well yes, it kinda does, 'cause Andrew won't look older – will never look older.

Andrew would always look like he was in his mid-twenties, the age he'd been when he was changed – younger than Tommy was now. Andrew was over two-hundred years old, yet sometimes Tommy felt older than him, and in reality, at twenty-nine, he was. Andrew had told him that with regular infusions of vampire blood, he would age much more slowly than a normal human – he might even live to be a hundred, perhaps a hundred and fifty years old without much change in his physical appearance. And in the ecstasy of their love making after Tommy had discovered what Andrew really was, all of that had seemed just fine – fantastic even – but now, he wasn't so sure.

Tommy had been drained almost to the point of death by Lazlo Marek, Andrew's devious uncle, and he'd been saved by drinking Andrew's powerful blood. That rich essence had already added several years to Tommy's life, something he'd thought incredible at the time, but now, it didn't feel right.

What about his parents, his friends, those he would lose over the years – and wouldn't they at some point wonder why they were aging and he was not? How could he explain that away? There was also the fact that Andrew couldn't meet any of his buddies for lunch, couldn't go to the ballpark with him, couldn't go for a swim in the ocean, unless it was a moonlight swim.

And those were definitely great. The two of them under a starlit sky, swimming out as far as they could, then floating in each other's arms, buffeted by gently rolling waves. Sometimes Andrew would hold him and they would skim over the surface of the ocean, locked in an embrace, their naked bodies fused as one. Oh God, yeah, the sex was always the best. Each and every time better than the time before, if that was possible. Andrew was beautiful, his body perfect in every way, his face one that any artist would long to capture on canvas, his hair like black silk, his eyes...

Yeah, he's the hottest guy I've ever been with. I'm so damned lucky to have him in my life, but I can't overlook the fact that one day he's going to leave me behind.

Tommy wasn't arrogant, but he knew he was no slouch in the looks department. He'd been told numerous times he was hot. He kept his quarterback physique in shape with regular workouts — the rigours of his job as a firefighter demanded he be at his best, physically and mentally at all times. Yet he knew the day would come eventually when all that would fade.

I'll become baggy and saggy and my vampire boyfriend will start lookin' around for the young and the hung...

"Tommy?"

The sudden call from the bedroom made him jump. Andrew was awake?

"What's wrong?" he asked, pushing the bedroom door open. "Did I wake you?"

"Yes. Your anxious thoughts entered my consciousness. Come sit by me."

Tommy walked quickly through the darkened room and sat on the edge of their bed. "Sorry," he mumbled.

Andrew reached up and cupped Tommy's face with a cool hand. As always, Andrew's touch induced a shiver of ecstasy in Tommy and he turned his face into Andrew's palm and kissed it gently.

"Sorry I woke you."

"I am sorry that you are so troubled by what you see as the consequences of our blood bond, Tommy." Andrew sat up and kissed Tommy's cheek. "I am aware that a relationship between a mortal and a vampire is not easy, even when love is involved. And I do love you, Tommy."

"And I love you," Tommy said without hesitation. "I've never loved anyone as much in my whole life..."

"Yet my immortality is an obstacle to your complete happiness."

"When you put it like that, it sounds like I'm a selfish ingrate." Tommy leaned in and brushed his lips over Andrew's. "I don't want there to be tension between us. Yes, I admit that sometimes the thought of you living forever – without me – gets me depressed. The thought of you finding someone else to replace me when I'm dead..."

"Hush." Andrew put his arms around Tommy and pulled him down on top of himself, covering his face with feather-light kisses. "What on earth has brought this on? You are still a young man. Why talk of death when you are in the prime of life?"

"Oh, I don't know. I guess I'm just in a shitty mood." He pressed himself harder against Andrew's naked body. "I was up and wishing you were sharing the day with me, then I started thinking about all the things we can't do together and I just depressed the hell out of myself. See? I told you it was me being selfish."

Andrew fell silent, gently stroking Tommy's thick, blond hair. "You know that I will never tire of loving you," he said finally, quietly. "That no matter what I will love you until death." He managed a small smile. "I will not go looking for 'the young and the hung'."

"Oh my God, you heard that? Now I'm embarrassed."

"Don't be. Just be assured my love for you is real and lasting."

He kissed Tommy's mouth, his lips lingering on the warm flesh, opening to Tommy's questing tongue. Their kiss was long and sweet until Tommy tried to pull himself free of Andrew's embrace.

"I should let you rest," he mumbled into Andrew's mouth.

"No, don't go." Andrew slid his hands under Tommy's T-shirt. He ran his fingertips up and down the length of Tommy's spine, sending sensual shivers all through his body.

"But it's still daylight."

"I know, but that doesn't mean that I must sleep." He smiled into Tommy's eyes. "I can still be... active."

Tommy grinned. "I can feel you being active." He brushed a hand over Andrew's erection. "Mm-mmm...*very* active." He lowered his head and nipped at Andrew's nipples, taking each one lightly between his teeth then scouring it with his tongue. The vampire shuddered beneath him, making Tommy smile. It always filled him with a certain pride that he could bring pleasure to this beautiful man—a man who had lived for more than two centuries, who had loved and been loved by many men, and yet had chosen him,

Tommy Cordain, ordinary guy-next-door, to share his life and love with.

Just the thought of that made Tommy moan softly as he skimmed his lips over Andrew's cool, smooth skin until he reached the hard, throbbing flesh that pulsed against his mouth, the copious pre-cum leaving a glistening kiss on his lips. He opened to take the velvety crown into his moist warmth, his tongue lapping at the salty essence that sent his senses flaring. He slipped his hands under Andrew's butt, easing his lover's slim hips up, at the same time as he slid his mouth down the entire length of Andrew's rigid cock. His throat muscles clenched around the head and Andrew groaned, his body bucking in ecstasy, his hands caressing Tommy's hair and the sides of his face.

"Gods, Tommy, you'll have me coming in record time if you keep doing that."

Tommy chuckled wickedly as he gazed up at Andrew's face. *"That's my intention…"* He knew Andrew could read his thoughts so there was no need to stop what he was doing in order to speak. He grasped Andrew's cock at the base, pumping and sucking for all he was worth until Andrew's normally slow breathing quickened and rasped in his chest.

"Oh yeah, lover, come for me. Wanna taste you now…"

He felt Andrew grow even bigger, harder in his grasp, cum racing up the throbbing shaft, exploding into Tommy's mouth with such force he had to swallow quickly to avoid gagging. He pulled back just a little so some of the creamy seed flowed over his taste buds, then he sighed, savouring the spicy tang that was Andrew.

Strong arms pulled him up so they were lying chest to chest and Andrew's lips closed over Tommy's in a long and passion-filled kiss.

"Bite me," Tommy whispered when he could breathe again. "Drink from me."

* * * *

Andrew nuzzled Tommy's neck where the carotid artery pulsed. He inhaled the rich scent of his lover's blood, his vampire senses reeling from the anticipation of the sweet, heady taste he knew that at any second would flood over his tongue, filling his body with renewed vigour. He also knew his bite would bring Tommy a sexual rush like no other, and as he bit down, sinking his fangs deep into Tommy's neck, the moan that was torn from Tommy's lips was one of pain overlain with sensuous pleasure.

"Oh God, yeah..." Tommy writhed in Andrew's arms, forcing his neck into the pressure of Andrew's sucking, pressing his now rock-hard erection against Andrew's abdomen. With reluctance, but also with a loving care, Andrew pulled back from the sweet taste of his lover's blood then swept his tongue over the smooth flesh, sealing the wounds.

He claimed Tommy's lips again and the young firefighter moaned his need into Andrew's mouth. Andrew tumbled him onto his back and lay over him, their eyes locked on one another's. He reached for the lube and coated his fingers liberally with the cool gel before inserting one then two fingers deep inside Tommy, gently massaging his prostate. Tommy's body arched upward in ecstasy and Andrew withdrew his fingers, replacing them with the head of his cock, then pushed slowly forward, burying himself in Tommy's lush heat. Tommy threw his legs around Andrew's torso and their bodies moved together to a slow, sensual rhythm.

Andrew smiled into Tommy's hazel eyes as he levitated them off the bed. He knew Tommy loved this—loved this feeling of weightlessness as they floated above the bed while Andrew fucked him with long, deep strokes. Tommy's muscular arms wound tightly round Andrew's neck, his lips claiming Andrew's in a kiss that brought them both over the edge. Gasping into each other's mouths, they climaxed together, Tommy's hot semen jetted over both their chests, while with a strangled groan of pure pleasure, Andrew emptied himself into Tommy.

As they settled once more on top of the bed and Tommy's breathing returned to an almost normal pace, he murmured, "You know just how to put a guy in a good mood."

Andrew chuckled and kissed Tommy's chin. "I'm glad I can be of some use."

"Oh, babe, you have no idea how useful you are."

"Have I managed to drive those worrying thoughts from your mind?"

"Totally. See...?" He gazed into Andrew's ice-blue eyes. "Nothin' in here but love for you and the happy feeling I get when we're together."

"Good..." But Andrew was glad that Tommy could not read his thoughts.

* * * *

The following night Tommy was pulling a late-night shift at the fire station and Andrew took advantage of that to visit Marcus Verano, the renowned Master Vampire to whom Andrew owed his survival, and more than usually powerful vampire blood. Several months ago Andrew had been attacked by hired killers and left for dead, his blood being slowly poisoned by a net of silver barbs.

Tommy had been the one to find him in a smoke-filled hotel room, but it was the quick actions of Marcus and his friends that had ultimately saved Andrew. Infusions of vampire blood had cleared the poison from his system and had given him even greater strength—something he had needed when faced with his treacherous uncle, Lazlo Marek.

But now he came to see Marcus about a completely different matter, hoping the ancient vampire could give him the answer he sought. He knew his question would be met with surprise, but he hoped not with condemnation.

Marcus himself opened the door to Andrew's knock, and as always he looked amazing. Andrew was certain that Marcus Verano was the oldest vampire in the world. Neither he nor any other vampire he had spoken with knew of anyone older, although the man appeared not yet thirty years old. His mane of black curly hair was devoid of any grey strands, his body still fit and muscular as in the days when he was a Roman centurion, and his emerald green eyes still bright with humour and knowledge.

"Welcome, Andrew." His voice was deep and melodious—just one more attractive feature of the many the man possessed. "Come along in. It's just you and I tonight. Roger and his friends have gone over to La Fortuna to visit with Jean-Claude and Ron. Tommy is working?"

"Yes..."

"You are troubled, Andrew. What is the problem?"

It was the measure of the man that he had not read what was in Andrew's mind, though he could have done so easily. Vampire etiquette, Andrew thought, with a soft smile.

"But before you begin, shall we have a glass of wine? I have an extremely fine French Burgundy you must sample."

"Thank you." Andrew followed Marcus into the massive living room, the veranda of which overlooked the glittering lights of Los Angeles. "Thank you also for allowing me to intrude on your privacy without giving you more than a few hours' notice."

Marcus slipped behind the oaken bar and took down two crystal glasses from a rack. "It is no intrusion, Andrew. You are welcome here anytime." He withdrew the cork from the bottle and inhaled the wine's bouquet. "Mmm... I think we shall enjoy this." He poured a small amount into Andrew's glass. "Tell me what you think."

Andrew lifted the glass to his lips and took a small sip. "Excellent," he murmured in appreciation.

"Joseph brought me two bottles back from France. He and Micah were there last week." He poured a larger quantity into Andrew's glass, then his own. "Salud."

"Salud."

"So now, tell me what is at the front of your mind that I am sorely tempted to simply read. It must be weighing heavily on you, my friend."

Andrew sighed. "This may be something that even you do not have the answer to, Marcus, but I know of no one else I could ask. You have lived longer than any vampire, have seen things, have done deeds of which we younger vampires can only dream, yet...what I am about to ask may confound even you."

"You are intriguing me."

Andrew squared his shoulders and looked Marcus directly in the eyes. "Is it possible to undo what we are — to become mortal again?"

Chapter Two

For a long moment Marcus said nothing, simply stared back at Andrew with a thoughtful expression on his handsome face. Then he said, "Would you care to tell me what prompted this question?"

Andrew grimaced. "I am in love with a mortal who is having second thoughts about our relationship."

"I am sorry," Marcus said, frowning. "I thought that you and Tommy were happily bonded."

"We are, to a certain extent. Tommy loves me, I know that. I hear it in his thoughts, see it in his actions, but he worries about his friends and family. How they will react to his not aging as quickly as they. Yesterday morning his mind was filled with doubt as to the wisdom of being bonded to a vampire. He seems to think I will tire of him as he ages and will look for a new companion. Of course, I would do no such thing..."

"And you have told him this?"

"Yes, but he is human, and as you know only too well, they are not always easily persuaded, not always rational in their thinking. Human emotions can be like quicksilver at times."

Marcus smiled wryly. "This I know, and their actions can be just as irrational. Before Roger became vampire, his spontaneity could sometimes be alarming. Even now... But you did not come here to listen to tales of Roger's unpredictable nature." He took a long sip of his wine then put his glass down on the bar. "Let me ask you this. Have you considered the consequences of becoming mortal?"

Andrew stared at him with widening eyes "You mean it's possible?"

"I did not say that. To be honest, I have never heard of any vampire reverting to mortality. But if it were possible, the fact that you are over two hundred years old would have some effect on your physiology. The human body is not designed to live forever. I imagine that you would age overnight, perhaps even crumble to dust in an instant. Hardly the result you intend, Andrew."

"But if it could be done over a period of time. Perhaps if I stopped drinking human blood..."

"Then you would simply grow weak. You would not become mortal, Andrew — and imagine how Tommy would react to seeing you in such a state. No, my friend, such a thing is not possible, I'm afraid. Relationships with mortals are tenuous at best. However, they are not impossible — Ron and Jean-Claude seem to manage well. Perhaps Tommy should talk with Ron or Christopher, Carlos' lover."

Andrew nodded. "I expected that such a thing was not possible. I just thought that if anyone would know of it, it would be you."

"Have you heard from Jared recently?" Marcus asked, changing the subject none too subtly.

"He and Joey are in New York."

"There again, another mortal-vampire union." Marcus smiled and motioned Andrew towards the plush wingback chairs by the fireplace. "I really do think you are worrying needlessly, Andrew. Tommy and you are in love, and love makes all things possible."

They spent the rest of their time seated by the fireplace, engaged in small talk until Andrew felt he had wasted enough of Marcus' evening and rose to take his leave, thanking him for his time and patience.

"There is an alternative," Marcus said as he walked Andrew to the door.

"One that you do not fully approve of."

Marcus acknowledged this with a slight nod. "It is my belief that humans should be changed only after understanding all the consequences, and only if they are completely willing—even if their mortal life is in danger."

Andrew smiled sadly. "I think that is a choice Tommy would never make. It would put him even more at odds with the doubts that already cloud his mind."

* * * *

It was a quiet night at the fire station. Tommy and his friend, Alex Benson, had worked out, eaten a large pizza between them, and now Tommy was reading a magazine while his buddy lay on a bench gently snoring. The rest of the crew were sitting around likewise napping, reading or gabbing. Some nights were like this—no alarms, no distress calls from pet owners trying to get their cat down from a tree, no vagrant wandering in looking for a cup of coffee and a handout.

Quiet. Too quiet. Tommy tossed his magazine aside with a soft sigh. Times like this when he didn't have enough to occupy his mind and body were when he thought about his relationship with Andrew, and just where the hell it was all heading. He loved the guy — loved him more than he had ever believed it was possible to love, but there were just so many obstacles in their way, and with each passing day those obstacles seemed to grow larger and more difficult to ignore.

Why the hell did he have to be a vampire?

Tommy knew he should never have allowed it to get this far. He should've thanked Andrew for saving him from his son-of-a-bitch uncle, and run for the door. Well, maybe it was okay that he'd stayed and shown Andrew how grateful he was, had that unbelievably fantastic sex with the guy — then he should have run for the door.

But, of course he hadn't, because the sex had been so damned fanfuckingtastic that he'd wanted it over and over, and now look where he was. In love with a 'mysterious boyfriend' as Alex called Andrew, and filled with so many conflicting thoughts that sometimes he thought he'd go nuts from the pressure.

Maybe he should take some time off, go visit his folks in Oklahoma. Yeah, that might help clear his head. Would Andrew be pissed? Somehow he didn't think he would be. He was always so understanding of his *mortal lover's* doubts and fears that it made Tommy feel like a shithead anytime his jumbled thoughts spilled over into Andrew's consciousness. Like yesterday when he'd been dithering about and had woken Andrew from his rest. Yeah, the sex had been as wonderful as always, for both of them, and it had allayed his qualms and uncertainty for a time, but they never really went away—and somehow he was going to have to do something about it all. If he could just figure out what.

"Whatcha so deep in thought about, buddy?"

Alex's voice, though sleepy, was enough to startle Tommy out of his reverie. "Huh? Oh, nothin' in particular. Just thinking."

"You've been doing a lot of that lately." Alex sat up and swung his long legs off the bench. "Wanna share?"

"Thanks, but that's okay. Just some stuff I have to work out by myself." *Yeah, like I'm gonna share with you the fact that my walking wet dream of a boyfriend is a vampire!*

"Trouble in paradise?"

Tommy gazed at Alex's tanned, wholesome face and couldn't help thinking how much easier it would have been if he'd fallen for this guy. Alex and Tommy were the only two openly gay members of the fire crew and they'd palled around in the beginning when they'd found out about each other two years ago. After one less than satisfying attempt to fool around—they'd started laughing in the middle of their first kiss—they had opted to be friends. And they were—good friends.

But not *that* good.

"Nothing that can't be fixed," Tommy replied, hoping that what he'd just said was somewhere close to the truth.

"Well, if I can be of any help..."

"Thanks." Tommy couldn't quite ignore the look of concern on Alex's face, and it made him feel good that someone actually cared if he was happy or not. "Let me ask you something, Alex. Do you ever wonder about the future? You know, where all this is going. How long you might be here, that kind of thing?"

Alex shook his head. "Can't say I do. I'm a one-day-at-a-time kinda guy."

"Yeah, I used to be too, but lately I've been thinking about, well, the bigger picture, I guess. Know what I mean?"

"You're talking about your relationship with Andrew, right?"

Tommy sighed. "It's some of that." *God, but I wish I could open up at bit more about this…* "We're tight, but I wonder about the long term sometimes."

"So go have your fortune read or something."

"What?"

"Yeah, you know, tarot cards, channelling…"

"How the heck do you know about that?"

Alex grinned. "My sister Lorna. She's heavy into that stuff."

"Lorna is? I'd never have guessed."

"I told you she was a bit weird. Calls herself and her friends wiccans or something like that."

"Wow —"

Their conversation was brought to an abrupt halt at the sound of the klaxon going off and the crew jumping into preparedness for action. Tommy made a mental note to question Alex more about his sister when they got back to the station.

* * * *

As luck would have it, the fire they were called to was a big one and by the time they'd controlled it, finished with the reports and returned to the station, the new shift was checking in.

"Don't know about you, but I'm beat," Alex said, pulling off his boots. "Think we'll have to make it tomorrow for that beer you promised me."

Tommy grinned at his buddy. "I thought it was your turn to buy. But you're right, I'm bushed too. Catch you later. Oh, and don't forget to find out some more about Lorna's tarot reading—I think I might just be interested in that."

"Really? It's probably just so much bullshit."

"You never know, there might be something to it."

I live with a vampire, so how could I knock anything to do with the supernatural? For all I know we could be rubbing shoulders with werewolves and demons every time we go out for a drink – or maybe even right here…

He took a long look round at the guys he worked with as they climbed out of their heavy gear and pulled on jeans and T-shirts. He forced out a quiet chuckle at the thought that some of them might be creatures of the night.

Nah, not a chance. Right?

* * * *

Andrew was waiting for Tommy when he got home. He was glad to see the tiredness he knew Tommy had been feeling dispel as they smiled at one another.

"Hi…" Tommy let himself be wrapped in Andrew's embrace, visibly shivering when Andrew's cool lips nuzzled at his neck. "You make me hard so fast," Tommy murmured, slipping his hands inside Andrew's shirt. "No matter how beat I am you always get me goin'."

"You had a difficult night." Andrew released him and stepped back. "I wanted to talk about something — something that concerns us, but it can wait if you are tired."

"No, no, it's okay. Lemme just grab a beer and I'll be all yours. Sounds serious."

"It might be."

Andrew followed Tommy into the kitchen and poured himself a glass of wine while Tommy pulled a beer from the fridge and popped the top of the can. He watched as Tommy tilted his head back and gulped at the can's contents. His cock stirred as he gazed at the smooth but strong column of Tommy's neck, the gentle pulsing under the skin near the carotid artery. With an effort he dragged his eyes away from the sensuous sight and took a long sip of his wine.

"So..." Tommy wiped his mouth with the back of his hand. "What's up?"

Andrew regarded Tommy's boyish face with affection. "Straight to the point, eh, Tommy? No bullshitting, as you would say."

"Best to come right out with it. Especially if it's bad news." He gave Andrew a lop-sided grin. "You leaving me?"

"Would you mind very much if I did?"

Tommy stared at him for a long moment, his eyes wary and glistening. "Of course I would mind, Andrew. I love you. I've told you that a million times."

"Yet, there are times when our relationship troubles you — when you wish I was not vampire, but human like you, so you would not have to hide me from your friends."

"That's not fair. I don't hide you from my friends. It's just that you're not always *available* when they are. I work crappy hours, but you knew that, and I know better than to expect you to join us in the daytime. It's difficult, yeah, but it's not an impossible situation. Certainly not a reason for us to break up."

"I don't want us to break up, Tommy. But there are times when I feel you would be better off without me. Perhaps then you would meet another man more suited to your way of life."

Tommy gave out a wry laugh. "And who might that be? I'm almost thirty years old and you're the first guy I've ever really felt anything for. We've been together almost six months now, and if you must know they've been the best six months of my life. I thought you felt the same way."

"I do." Andrew put his wineglass on the counter and took Tommy in his arms. "These months with you have been wonderful. After Jared, I never thought I would love again, but you changed all of that with your excessive charm, your down-to-earth ways—and your kisses." He brushed his lips over Tommy's. "Have I ever told you that you have the most beautiful mouth of any man I have ever met?"

"You're makin' me blush," Tommy murmured, wrapping his arms around Andrew's waist and holding him close. "And very hard..."

"Oh, and I forgot to mention your one-track mind." They touched foreheads and laughed softly together. "So... you're not leaving me?"

"Do I look like a fool?" Andrew kissed him again, then stood back with a soft sigh. "But I should tell you that I went to see Marcus tonight and asked him if he knew of any way to reverse my immortality."

Tommy gaped at him. "Why the hell would you do that?"

"Because I know what has been on your mind recently, and I wanted to ascertain if there was a way to become mortal again, to live a normal life span — with you — so that we would grow old together."

"You would do that for me?"

"I would do anything for you, Tommy." Andrew cupped Tommy's face between his palms. "Anything. Unfortunately, Marcus knows of no such process."

"And wouldn't it kinda, you know, make you age real fast?"

"He did point out that aspect of it too."

Tommy shuddered. "Well then, there's no way I'd want that to happen. I'm glad you can't reverse it." He pulled Andrew close. "I love you the way you are, vampire or not. I can't imagine my life without you now."

"Marcus did mention that Ron, Jean-Claude's lover, might be able to help."

"Help?"

"You know, come to terms with our differences. They've been together for almost five years — granted, not a long time in the span of things — but he may be able to tell you how he overcomes the day-to-day problems."

"Andrew..." Tommy tightened his arms around his vampire's body. "I am sorry, so sorry I've let this worry you. I should be more careful what I think about when I'm around you. And those thoughts? They're not really worth you giving them the time of day."

"Nevertheless, I — "

Tommy put a finger on Andrew's lips and pushed his crotch against Andrew's. "Enough talking. I'm going to take a shower, then we are going to go to bed and you are going to do weird and wonderful things to my body. Okay?"

"Okay. But why must we wait until we're in bed? We could start in the shower."

Tommy chuckled. "A very good place to start. Let's go."

Chapter Three

Tommy leant back against his vampire lover's chest and sighed with contentment as Andrew ran soapy hands over him, caressing his defined pectoral muscles, teasing both nipples before sliding down the length of his torso to fondle his cock and balls. He pressed his butt into the pulsing heat of Andrew's erection, thinking that before Andrew he'd never really liked being fucked, but now he longed for it, craved it almost every time they made love.

Probably because his vampire lover did it better than anyone he'd ever been with, he thought with a wry smile.

"Thank you," Andrew murmured in his ear.

"You..." Tommy chuckled and turned to kiss Andrew's lips. "Is nothing sacred?"

"Many things..." Andrew nuzzled Tommy's earlobe. "But you thinking I'm the best fuck you've ever had hardly comes under that description." He slipped a soapy finger into the cleft between Tommy's butt cheeks and pushed in enough to make Tommy squirm.

"Oooh, yeah...that's it." Tommy wriggled over the length of Andrew's finger and let his head fall back on Andrew's shoulder. "They say there's more to life than just sex, but when you're around I don't believe a word of it." He gasped as Andrew inserted another finger. Turning his head, he sought Andrew's lips again with his own, joining them in a hot and hungry kiss. He pumped his aching erection held fast by Andrew's soapy fist, his orgasm building in his balls, the slow churning causing his heart to speed up and his breathing to grow harsh in his throat.

He whimpered with anticipation when Andrew withdrew his fingers then replaced them with the head of his cock, his broad girth pushing hard into Tommy's tight heat.

"Ungh..." Tommy's breath exploded into Andrew's mouth and he clenched his ass muscles around the base of the pulsing flesh that had penetrated him to the hilt with one long, slow glide. He pushed back against Andrew's thrusts, matching the rhythm his lover had begun, the steady, strong movement back and forth over Tommy's prostate bringing him closer and closer to the brink.

"*Oh God, Andrew...*" Tommy clutched at Andrew's taut butt cheeks, pulling him in even deeper if that were possible, grinding his own ass over the length of Andrew's cock. Feverishly he gave himself up to the incredible sensations that swept over him, his orgasm blinding him momentarily with its intensity. He shuddered, falling back against the hard wall that was Andrew's chest, then arched again in ecstasy as his lover's scalding semen surged inside him. They stood under the hot spray, silent and unmoving but for a tender kiss or brush of fingertips over wet skin. Once again, Tommy's fears were swept away, if only for the time being.

* * * *

"Hey!" Alex greeted Tommy as they clocked in for their shift. "I didn't forget to ask Lorna about her tarot sessions. She said they're having one tomorrow night as luck would have it, so if you want to join in give her a call."

"Oh, yeah." Tommy had forgotten all about that particular conversation. It just didn't seem all that important anymore. Still... He was kind of curious about what lay ahead, and he wondered now if the cards would pick up on him having Andrew in his life, and what they could possibly have to say about their future together. One way to find out. "Okay, I'll give her a call."

"Don't expect me to hold your hand through it," Alex said in a teasing tone. "I don't go for that bullshit myself."

"I'm not sure I do, but I like to think I can keep an open mind about most things—unlike you!"

He laughed as Alex lunged at him and they started wrestling, giggling like schoolboys, then someone yelled, "Get a room, you guys!" That made them laugh even more until the alarm sounded and they went on full alert.

* * * *

The following night, Tommy and Andrew had an invitation to join Ron and Jean-Claude at the restaurant Ron managed, after closing hours.

33

"Can I meet you there?" Tommy had asked when Andrew mentioned the invitation. "I told Alex's sister Lorna I'd pay her a visit. Haven't seen her in a while…" With an effort, he'd deliberately kept his mind off the reason he was going to see Lorna. He had a feeling Andrew wouldn't care for it. He'd tell him about it later — if there was anything interesting to tell.

Lorna's apartment in Silver Lake was in an old building, one that both Alex and Tommy had let her know was not up to fire code. But Lorna loved the old-fashioned architecture of the exterior and the art-deco panels that decorated the lobby walls. The elevator was an original with a set of folding metal gates that seemed to resist any attempt to open or close them. Tommy wondered how some of the little old ladies living there managed, and sure enough, as he entered the building after parking his motorbike alongside Lorna's car, he spotted one of the old biddies struggling to slide open the uncooperative outer door. Although, at a second and longer look, she appeared to be doing just fine.

Must be a wiry little thing, he thought. "Here, let me," he said, gripping the handle of the ornate ironwork and sliding it open the rest of the way.

"Why thank you," she simpered. "My, aren't you the handsome one." She batted her eyelashes and touched Tommy's arm as she entered the elevator.

Tommy smiled despite the uneasy shiver from her touch. "How d'you manage this on a daily basis?" he asked, keeping his voice light and steady.

"Oh, I don't live here. I'm visiting Lorna."

"Oh yeah? Me too… I'm Tommy Cordain, by the way." He held out his hand and it was taken in a surprisingly tight grip.

"Sylvia Holloway." The old lady gave Tommy a long, speculative look. "Are you Lorna's boyfriend?"

Tommy chuckled. "No, I work with her brother, Alex. You know him too?"

Sylvia tutted impatiently. "No, he doesn't come to Lorna's séances. Doesn't approve, she says."

"Séance?" Tommy felt a prickle of apprehension on the back of his neck. *Oh boy, I have a feeling Andrew's not going to like this... Maybe I should bow out...* "I thought this was going to be a tarot reading."

"Oh yes, that too, but I really come for the séance. I'm a medium, you see."

The elevator stopped with a bump and Tommy pulled the gate open. As Sylvia passed in front of him, Tommy was very tempted to say goodnight and press the 'down' button. He didn't like the idea of a séance. He'd never been to one and had always considered them a scam, but since he'd met Andrew he'd changed his mind about a lot of things.

Pull yourself together. What can happen? It's only Lorna and her cronies...

He stepped out of the elevator and followed Sylvia down the hallway to Lorna's apartment door. What was it about her that made him so...so *wary*?

She's just a little old lady, for Chrissakes.

Chapter Four

Sylvia rapped loudly on Lorna's door and it was immediately swung open, a tall, dark-haired man framed in the doorway.

"Welcome, Sylvia." His beaming smile was wasted on the old lady who swept by him as if he wasn't actually there. Dark Hair gave Tommy an appraising look. "And you are?"

"Tommy. I'm a friend of Lorna's. I work with her brother, Alex."

"Oh yes. Lorna said you were coming tonight. I'm Arturo." He held out his hand and Tommy shook it, trying not to show his annoyance at the blatant way Arturo prolonged their handshake.

"Yeah, pleased to meet you."

Not. Jeez, who the heck are these people Lorna's got herself mixed up with?

He entered the apartment, twitching his nose at the strong aroma of incense. Lorna was talking to Sylvia but waved and smiled when she saw him. There were one or two other people standing around.

"Like a drink?" Arturo was at his side, a hand on his shoulder.

"Uh, yeah..." Tommy didn't want to appear rude so he resisted the impulse to shake off Arturo's hand. The guy creeped him out. "A beer if you have it."

"Sure thing."

Arturo disappeared, presumably to get the beer, and Tommy walked over to where Lorna was listening intently to whatever Sylvia was telling her. They broke off their conversation as Tommy approached.

Lorna hugged him. "I was surprised when Alex said you wanted to come to one of these," she whispered close to his ear.

"Well, I didn't know it was going to be a séance. Don't know if I'm into that stuff. I told Alex I was just kinda curious about the tarot thing, but if you're not doin' that I can come another time."

He really wanted to get the hell out of there. Lorna appeared different tonight, and she looked...*unfocussed* was the only word he could think of to describe her. Her eyes didn't quite meet his and she seemed to be preoccupied...worried.

"Are you okay?" he asked.

Alex hadn't mentioned his sister was sick, but then Alex didn't see her on a regular basis.

"Too many weird friends," Alex had told him once.

And they all seem to be here tonight...

"Fine, just fine." She gave him a smile that didn't quite reach her eyes. "You've met Sylvia, I understand, and Arturo." She waved the other couple over. "This is Amy and Caleb. Meet Tommy Cordain. He's a firefighter—works with my brother, Alex."

Amy and Caleb murmured some kind of greeting then drifted away again as Arturo showed up with a bottle of beer. Tommy had the distinct impression from the way Arturo was hanging around him that the man wanted to get a whole lot cosier than Tommy would ever allow.

"Shall we begin then?" Arturo seemed to snap to attention when Sylvia's voice, her demanding tone belying her age and frail appearance, sliced through the room. She marched over to the table covered with a dark green cloth and surrounded by six chairs. "We'll start with the reading since that's what our handsome firefighter has come for—then we shall see."

See what? Tommy frowned. *Soon as this reading's over I'm outta here.*

Lorna handed Sylvia a pack of cards which she expertly fanned out in front of her, face down.

"So, Tommy, place your forefinger on five of these cards."

Tommy reached out, hesitated for a moment then placed his fingertip on one card, following quickly with four more.

Let's get this over with…

Sylvia picked up each card after he'd touched them then shuffled the cards without looking at them. While she moved the cards back and forth in her hands, she stared long and hard at Tommy for several moments, her eyes seeming to bore into his. He shifted uncomfortably in his seat. He could feel small beads of sweat breaking out on his forehead.

God, but it's hot in here!

"You have chosen interesting cards, young Tommy," Sylvia muttered, placing the first one face up on the table. "Are you aware that these cards are older than those associated with the Book of Thoth?"

Tommy shook his head. He hadn't a clue what the Book of Thoth was.

"Dakar, an important demon of the Underworld, second in command to Lord Kardis himself, is represented here. He is the one who holds your future in his hands."

Tommy peered at the image of a handsome man — a demon? — with long, flowing blond hair. His breath caught in his throat. He could have sworn there for just a second that the sapphire blue eyes — eyes that so closely resembled that of the woman opposite him — had narrowed slightly as they stared up at him from the table. He sat back quickly and glanced around the table. Everyone was focussed on the card, but no one else seemed surprised or startled.

Must've been my imagination.

Sylvia laid the second card down. "The Sword of Damacian. This represents coming conflict in which you will have to choose between your life, and the life of someone you love, deeply."

Everyone's gaze lifted from the card to Tommy. Lorna gave him a knowing smile and Tommy wondered just how much Alex had told her of his relationship with Andrew.

"The third card represents your hopes and dreams." Sylvia laid down the card that depicted a landscape of verdant green, the sun shining through tall pines in golden shards of light.

"That's beautiful," Tommy murmured and a glimmer of hope ran through his body. *Maybe it's not going to be all darkness and conflict.*

"But I must place the fourth card on top of the third."

And Tommy's heart sank as Sylvia covered the card with one that was totally black.

"Wait," he croaked. "Why d'you have to cover it with that, that *thing*? There's no picture on it. It's just a black card. What does it represent?"

"It represents struggle—you, Tommy, struggling to find your way out of the darkness and into the light."

"What?" He forced out a derisive laugh. "This is bullshit, just like Alex said. Sorry Lorna, but I have to go."

Sylvia gave him a wolfish smile. "I don't think so, Tommy. You will stay until I have finished with the reading, and then we'll see."

"We'll see? Listen, lady, I have a date and—" He started to get up and found he couldn't move. His legs felt paralysed. "What the hell?" He tried again, and again he could not move.

Arturo rose and walked over to stand behind Tommy, placing his hands on Tommy's shoulders—hands that were much stronger than he remembered. Hands that were holding him down with such force that despite the excellent physical shape he was in, even squirming was impossible.

"What the hell are you people doing?"

Across the table from him, Lorna turned to Sylvia with a worried expression. "What are you doing, Sylvia? I've never seen that black card before, and there's no reason to hold Tommy here against his wishes."

"There are many things you haven't seen before, Lorna dear." She laid down the fifth card and Tommy gaped at the image of a vampire, his fangs exposed in a silent scream of anguish, hands grasping at a long stake protruding from his chest. "The death of a loved one." Her sniggering laugh chilled Tommy's blood and had Lorna leaping to her feet.

"What the hell, Sylvia?"

"This night brings more promise than I ever thought possible," Sylvia said, ignoring Lorna's reaction. "I thought merely to enslave these others to my bidding. Such a twist of fate that brought you to me, Tommy, but I knew from the moment you got on the elevator with me that you had lain with a vampire. His blood is in you. There is no mistaking that scent of spice — an aphrodisiac to humans — alluring even to me."

Tommy stared at Lorna's stricken expression, then at the other two seated at the table — Amy and Caleb, was it? They looked dumbfounded, frozen in place by the drama unfolding before them. He knew he had stumbled into something intrinsically evil. Whatever Sylvia was, she was no little old lady. Something lurked inside her, and Tommy could only guess at what it might be. His time in Andrew's company had exposed him to some pretty amazing stuff. But while Andrew's friends, apart from his creepy Uncle Lazlo, had never made him feel unsafe — this, whatever Sylvia represented — was definitely scary. And from the immobility he felt in his arms and legs, he wasn't at all sure he was strong enough, either mentally or physically, to deal with it.

He sent out a silent plea to Andrew, but he had no way of knowing if he would hear him and realise he was in imminent danger. Their connection was strong, but he was way on the other side of town from the restaurant in West Hollywood where Andrew was meeting with Ron and Jean-Claude.

Sylvia sniggered again. "Useless to appeal for help, Tommy. I have shut down your ability to communicate with your vampire lover. I can tell from your silence that you cannot deny your association with the vampire. What is his name?"

"If you know so damned much, how come you don't know that?" Tommy snarled.

"There are a great many vampires out there. Some are known to me, many are not, but in your mind, Tommy, I can hear the name Andrew. Yes, he is your lover and foremost in your thoughts. And wait, so many others... *Marcus.* Ah, would that be Marcus Lucius Verano himself? Master Vampire? You travel in exalted company, young Tommy. Exalted and *useful* company. And how marvellous that, through you I can infiltrate this vampire echelon and destroy them once and for all."

Sylvia rose from her chair. Her head fell back, her body began to vibrate, and a long plume of black smoke spilled from her open mouth. It rose into the air, hovering over the table, then dived towards Tommy. With every hard muscle in his body straining against Arturo's grip, Tommy tried to get up, knock the man out of the way and get the hell out of the room, but it was not to be. He yelled as Arturo forced his mouth open, then gagged as the black smoke entered him, filling him, taking him over with its sentient power. For only a few seconds Tommy had the will to fight, then...

Okay, this isn't so bad... Feels good actually... Powerful. Wow. Yeah...bring it on!

Without any effort whatsoever, Tommy rose to his feet, freeing himself of Arturo's iron grip as if it had been a mere nuisance. The big man backed away in obeisance while the others stared at him with something approaching awe.

"Tommy," Lorna whispered, a flicker of fear appearing on her pale face. "What happened to you?"

He leaned over and picked up one of the cards. He glanced at it, twisting his lips in amusement. He showed it to Lorna.

"*He* happened to me," he said, his voice a deep rumble. "Or rather, this vessel pleases me more than *that*."

Lorna gaped at the image of the demon, Dakar, then at Sylvia who was slumped, unmoving in her chair.

"She's dead," Tommy said with apparent indifference. "Without me to sustain her, her body was beyond its endurance."

"Oh my God!" Lorna looked at the others for help. "What are we going to do?"

"Dispose of her body, of course. Arturo, see to it."

Without hesitation, Arturo picked up Sylvia's body and left the apartment.

"As for the rest of you..." What had once been Tommy swept a hand over Lorna and the couple who had not moved from their places at the table. "You remember nothing of what took place here." Another move of his hand and the cards disappeared. "You were gathered to share a quiet evening, share some wine – and shame on you Lorna, your guests' glasses are quite empty."

"Right," Lorna muttered and headed towards the kitchen for the wine bottle.

With a grim smile of satisfaction, the man who looked like Tommy turned on his heel and left the room.

* * * *

When Dakar exited the elevator, Arturo was waiting for him in the lobby.

"What now, my liege?"

"You will await my orders. I will contact you when I am ready to move against the vampires." Arturo nodded, then followed Dakar as he strode through the lobby and out into the parking lot. As the demon sat astride Tommy's bike he smiled at his minion. "Never would I have thought this could be so easily done. The gods of the Underworld must have sent this vessel to us."

"A very pleasing vessel, my liege," Arturo said, smiling and licking his lips.

"Yes, one that should have no problem getting what he wants in life, although..." His brow puckered in a small frown, "I sense a naivety in his persona that I must remember to affect if I'm not to raise too many questions from his friends, especially his vampire lover." He chuckled. "That should be an interesting coupling." He revved up the bike's engine. "Goodnight, Arturo. I'll be in touch."

Arturo watched him speed away, a scowl replacing his smile. Dakar's mention of "coupling" with the vampire had not pleased him. Arturo, a sub-demon, knew he was considered unworthy of anything more than assisting Dakar in the task set him by Lord Kardis, but that did not stop him from wanting more.

As foolish as he knew his longing to be, Dakar remained foremost in his desires. Just the thought of having the handsome demon in his embrace, in his *life*, was enough to inflame Arturo's blood with passion so intense and dizzying, his vision blurred and his cock grew hard as steel pressing against the denim fly of his jeans to an almost painful degree. Dakar should be his, not some cursed vampire's! If Lord Kardis knew of Dakar's wish to have sex with a vampire, he would be furious. Such unions were forbidden, although the scent of a vampire was known to act as an aphrodisiac, even on demonkind.

But Arturo would not, could not, betray Dakar. Occasionally his liege allowed him some intimacy, always brief and always one-sided, but it gave Arturo hope that Dakar would look on him with more affection, and perhaps one day, even with love.

* * * *

When Dakar entered the restaurant, the vampire, Andrew, was sitting at the bar talking with the manager. Another mortal. *How interesting…* Ron.

"Hey, Tommy." Ron gave him a wave.

The man they knew as Tommy returned Ron's smile and ambled over to the bar. He gave Andrew's cheek a peck and sat on the stool next to him.

"What'll it be?" Ron placed a bar napkin in front of him.

"The usual."

"Comin' up."

"How was your friend's sister?" Andrew asked.

"She's good. We hadn't seen each other in a while so there was quite a bit of catching up to do."

"Am I keeping you from your friends, Tommy?"

"No, of course not." He leaned over to kiss Andrew on the lips. "There's no one I'd rather spend time with, you know that."

Andrew started back in surprise.

"What's wrong?"

"You are usually shy about showing such affection in public." Andrew's smile was teasing. "And you've just kissed me twice. Have you already had something to drink?"

"Just a beer earlier." Dakar filed away that piece of information then picked up the glass Ron had set in front of him. "Cheers." He took a long sip and grimaced.

"Something wrong?" Ron was frowning at him. "It's your usual brew."

"No, no…it's fine." He took a longer sip and put the glass down.

Gods, but this stuff is vile. Would it seem too strange if I asked for a glass of wine instead?

"Well, you will insist on drinking it, even though you've been invited to join the wine club," Ron said.

"Yeah, well maybe I'll give it a try."

Both Andrew and Ron chuckled at his remark. "Have you forgotten? You have already given it a try." Andrew squeezed Tommy's shoulder. "And you told us there was no way you'd give up your beer for it."

"Right…" *I'll have to be more careful of the little things.* He was aware that Andrew was watching him, a speculative expression on his face.

"Are you all right, Tommy?"

"Yeah, never better."

Something is wrong.

Andrew knew instinctively that Tommy was not himself. They teased each other about Andrew's mind-reading ability, but he never took advantage of that ability, only using it if he felt Tommy was out of sorts, or when they were making love and he could playfully banter with his lover's lustful thoughts.

This was different. He had gently probed Tommy's mind and found a barrier there that had never existed before. As if he was deliberately blocking his thoughts from Andrew—but why?

Is he still upset about the conversation I had with Marcus?

"Is Jean-Claude in the back office?" Andrew asked Ron, knowing exactly where his fellow vampire was.

"Yeah, he's double checking my figures before I make the night's deposit. You need him?"

"Just a word before we go home." He picked up his wine glass and slid off the stool. "Be right back," he told Tommy, who smiled and nodded.

As Andrew walked into the small hall separating the restaurant he heard Ron ask Tommy, "You okay?" and he paused to hear the mumbled reply of, "Yeah, fine..." before knocking gently on the office door and slipping inside.

"Jean-Claude, I need your help."

"Of course." The slim, fine-featured vampire rose from the desk. "What is it, Andrew?"

"I'm not sure, but I grant you permission to try and read Tommy's mind."

"What—but why?"

"Because something is not right with him, and when I tried a mental pulse it was immediately blocked—almost as though he had suddenly become resistant to my searching his thoughts. Not something I ever do for idle enjoyment. I respect his privacy, but something is definitely wrong with him tonight. You can do it from here if you like."

He watched with apprehension as Jean-Claude concentrated for a moment or two, hoping he was mistaken, but then Jean-Claude shook his head.

"I cannot," he murmured. "You are right. He is deliberately blocking all our thoughts, and he is very strong, very determined that nothing breaches his mind."

"What can it mean?"

"Where was he earlier?"

"Visiting a friend. Lorna, the sister of a fellow firefighter, Alex..."

"Nothing very sinister about that."

"No, but he has not been the same since he returned."

"I'll come out to say hello. Perhaps I can determine something more if I am face to face with him."

Andrew nodded. "Good idea. I know you will agree that something is troubling him."

Dakar shifted uncomfortably on the stool. He had made a mistake by blocking his thoughts from the vampire. In doing so, he had caused him to be suspicious and it was too soon to alienate him. He needed to get to know these vampires better, discover their strengths and vulnerability, particularly Andrew's. He could not afford to lose Andrew's trust before he had formulated a plan—and before he had succeeded in taking the vampire for his own needs.

Concentrating, he pushed his darker thoughts to the back of his mind. When Andrew, accompanied by Jean-Claude, came back into the restaurant he gave them both a big smile.

"Talking about me were you?" he asked in a teasing tone. He felt the mental pulse as both vampires searched his mind.

"*Can't wait to get you home and have you fuck me silly...*"

He almost laughed aloud as Andrew and Jean-Claude exchanged surprised glances. Jean-Claude's expression was one of embarrassment mixed with titillation.

"*Wanna join us Jean-Claude? You and Ron?*"

Andrew's chuckle was a little forced. "Tommy!"

"Well, serves you right for readin' my mind, guys." He was letting Tommy's persona take over and it seemed to be working well.

"Glad to see you're more like your old self," Ron remarked with a grin.

"Oh, I was just kinda depressed. Lorna's got herself tied up with some weirdos. They're into tarot reading and séances and the like. I couldn't wait to leave, to be honest."

"Does she know what she's doing?" Jean-Claude asked. "Séances can sometimes be dangerous."

Pleased that he seemed to have averted any more mind probes, Dakar said, "She says she does, but I don't believe in that stuff anyway. Do you?"

"Absolutely." Jean-Claude raised an eyebrow. "You, who knows what we are, does not believe in the supernatural?" he added, lowering his voice so that the few remaining diners could not hear their conversation.

"Well, yeah… I believe in you guys, of course. Seein' is believin' as they say."

"Séances can be quite remarkable," Andrew said, "depending on the strength of the medium, of course, and their ability to control the situation. But amateurs can sometimes get more than they bargained for."

Isn't that the truth…? Dakar controlled the smirk that almost flitted over his face, and pushed the thought away, just in case…

"Well, what say you and I head home, Andrew?" He slipped off the stool and put an arm around Andrew's waist. "My chariot awaits."

"And now that you've informed Jean-Claude of your intentions when you get me home, I see no reason to hesitate," Andrew said, chuckling.

"Yes, well…" Was it possible for a vampire to blush? If not, Jean-Claude was doing a fair imitation of it. "Goodnight, and uh…sweet dreams as they say."

"They'll be sweet all right." Turning on Tommy's mega-watt smile, Dakar guided Andrew towards the door.

"G'night guys," Ron called as he made his way to the back office. "See ya!"

Chapter Five

Dakar studied Andrew as the handsome vampire strode across to the living room window and pulled the drapes closed.

He is beautiful, without a doubt... He licked his lips as he took in the sleekly muscled body under the form-fitting white T-shirt and black jeans. The round fullness of Andrew's butt made his mouth water with the anticipation of plundering that sweet ass, first with his tongue, then with his cock that now swelled inside Tommy's chinos. He wondered what vampire blood tasted like, what it would do for him. He knew what he was intending was forbidden, but being with Andrew, breathing in his alluring scent made his blood seethe with a lust he had seldom experienced.

The blood lust. He had heard of it—heard that it could take over a vampire's senses, drive him or her mad with desire. Dakar shivered at the thought, his need to taste Andrew, to own him, rendering him almost dizzy from the craving he felt building inside him.

Andrew turned to face him, a small smile touching his lips. "Are you going to tell me what's troubling you?" he asked. "What can be so bad that you felt you had to hide your thoughts from me?"

Dakar returned Andrew's smile with what he hoped was suitably sheepish while he searched Tommy's thoughts for the answer. "Well, I hadn't told you the real reason I was going to see Lorna—see, I wanted her to do a tarot reading for me, give me an idea of what the future held for me, and you..."

"Tommy, was this because of my confession earlier?" Andrew moved nearer and put his hands on his lover's broad, muscular shoulders. "I don't want you to worry about that again. We will find a way to make things work. Whatever you want, I will try to make it so."

Quite the romantic fools, these two... Too bad there can be no future for either of them.

But first, he would enjoy fucking the vampire.

He pulled Andrew into his arms. He cupped Andrew's butt and ground their groins together, relishing the feel of Andrew's hard cock against his own. Their bodies writhed in unison while their lips locked in an almost brutal kiss. Dakar fisted his hand in Andrew's silky hair and tugged hard, forcing Andrew's head back.

Andrew gasped, a bemused smile on his handsome face. "So suddenly aggressive," he murmured.

"Want you—want to fuck you..." The growl rumbled out, so unlike Tommy's deep but gentle voice and, alarmed, Andrew wrenched himself completely out of their embrace.

"What is it, Tommy? What's different about you?" Andrew's steel-blue eyes searched the familiar face, grown suddenly hard and hostile. He probed Tommy's mind, gently at first, then with more determination when he felt the resistance he'd experienced before. His body tensed in self-protection mode as his mind encountered a darkness he knew didn't belong in Tommy's mind. The man he knew as Tommy stared back at him, his green eyes holding a strange blue gleam Andrew had never seen before.

And then he knew. "*Demon,*" he whispered, trying hard not to show his distress.

"You are too clever, vampire," Dakar said, his voice devoid of any real surprise or admiration. "You have the blood of the ancients in you. It has sharpened your senses, made you an interesting foe."

"Have you killed Tommy?" Despite his determination not to show weakness in front of the demon, Andrew heard his voice crack with the emotion he felt building inside him. *Tommy dead — no it cannot be!*

The demon chuckled. "So in love, are you, with the mortal? He still lives, but for how long depends on you."

"What do you want?"

"I told you, I want you."

"Out of the question," Andrew snapped. "Next?"

Dakar shrugged. "I could take you, you know."

"I doubt that. You may look like my lover, but I know now you are a long way from being anything like him in nature. Who are you anyway?"

Dakar reached inside Tommy's bomber jacket and withdrew the tarot card he still carried. "I am the demon, Dakar, second in command, and answerable only to Kardis, Lord of the Underworld, Himself." He waved the card in front of Andrew's eyes. "The task I have been set is to take down Marcus Verano, your leader, the self-proclaimed Master Vampire, and any other vampire who gets in my way."

Andrew's laughter was tinged with derision, but at the same time he sent out a silent warning to any and all vampires within reach of his mind.

"I would wish you good luck, but it would be a wasted one. Marcus has survived countless attempts to destroy him. Nor is he a self-proclaimed master vampire. He is revered among those who know and love him. You will be torn to pieces should you so much as attempt to harm him."

"Well now, brave words." Dakar's lips curled in a sneer. "But you have to admit I hold the ace, Andrew. As long as I will it, Tommy lives. If you do not assist me in my task, he will die."

"Assist you? You must be mad."

"Not mad, merely insistent. Assist me or your mortal lover dies—horribly, I might add. Without me to keep his body alive, he will become a hollow husk. He will shrivel up before your eyes, screaming in agony all the way."

"Monster," Andrew hissed, baring his fangs.

"Ha, look who's calling the kettle black. Sophisticated, and oh so gentle when you drink mortal blood, but you are still vampire, still abhorrent in the eyes of most humans, still a *monster*."

"Why do you wish to do Marcus harm?" Andrew knew that if he could play for a little more time his thoughts he sent out would be intercepted and a vampire, perhaps even Marcus himself, would come to his aid.

Dakar shrugged. "I am simply carrying out the task set before me," he replied with a nonchalance that Andrew found remarkable.

Surely even demons as powerful as this one knew that a confrontation with Marcus and his loyal vampires would not end well. Dakar might be strong enough to inflict damage, but Andrew could not imagine that even demon power could overwhelm Marcus. And the thought of the wounds that might be inflicted on Tommy's beautiful body sent a fury through Andrew he found hard to control.

Dakar grinned. "Kardis, the Lord of the Underworld, finds you vampires, and especially *Master* Vampires like Marcus Verano, to be too arrogant beyond your worth. Some time ago, Marcus and his cohorts thwarted Lord Kardis' plans to rule this earthly realm by placing a demon of his choice on the Papal throne. For that insolence he and all those who abetted him, must perish. It's as simple as that."

"Simple is hardly the word I would choose for the task set for you." Andrew stared at Dakar, remembering that he had heard of this story from his friend Jared. "My friends told me that one of those who abetted Marcus was a demon like you."

Dakar sneered. "*Constantine*, a half-breed spawned in a petri dish and a traitor to his own father. He is to be dealt with, never fear."

"I don't think you have any idea of the kind of power Marcus wields," Andrew said quietly. "I promise you, you will not walk away from the confrontation unscathed. But let me offer you this solution. Release Tommy, forget about the task Lord Kardis has given you and I will ask Marcus not to harm you."

For a long moment, Dakar gazed at Andrew as if he could not quite believe his ears. Then his laughter filled the room. "*Fool*," he bellowed, reaching for Andrew. "You will—" He reeled back, the blow from

Andrew's fist connecting squarely with the demon's jaw. Andrew hated striking what looked like his lover, but he knew Tommy was now a mere shell, unable to free himself from the demon's possession.

Dakar spat blood from his cut lip and cursed at Andrew. "Now you will wish that all I wanted was to fuck you," he snarled, ready to attack Andrew, but sprang back, startled, as the door to the apartment was flung open and four men rushed into the room.

Andrew blew out a sigh of relief as he recognised Marcus, Roger his companion, Joseph, Marcus' right-hand man, and his companion, Micah.

"Marcus," Andrew exclaimed, "a demon inhabits Tommy's body and—"

"I understand." Marcus stared steadily at Dakar and Andrew's eyes widened as Dakar took a step backwards.

Is he already afraid? Andrew watched with some amazement as Dakar hesitated. *Does the power Marcus exudes give the demon pause as to the wisdom of meeting Marcus face to face?*

Dakar seemed to pull himself together. "So, vampire..." The smug sneer, so alien-looking on Tommy's face, was back in place. "Had to bring reinforcements, eh? I thought you would be vampire enough to meet me *mano a mano.*"

"Fuckin' demons!" Roger interrupted before Marcus could reply. "Anyone of us could take you—shithead."

"Roger." Marcus held up a hand to silence his hot-headed companion. "I believe Andrew has not tried to 'take him' because of the danger to Tommy."

"Oh yeah...right...that," Roger muttered.

Dakar snickered. "It seems you know all, Marcus. So then, how do you intend to save the mortal?"

"There are many ways," Marcus said calmly. "The most obvious would be to force you to release Tommy before I kill you—and mark what I say, Dakar, if you do not listen to reason, I *will* kill you. You and your kind cannot be allowed to walk about freely, taking over mortal bodies and using them to wreak revenge on your supposed enemies. And if your death results in more demons being sent against us, they will also die. I would suggest you return to your Lord and tell him what I have told you. But before you go you will release Andrew's lover. If you do not, you will die here, in this room."

Andrew curled and uncurled his fists in frustration. If Marcus killed Dakar then Tommy would die with him. Dakar had to exit Tommy's body and seek a new host if Tommy was to live. *But Marcus knows that,* Andrew reasoned. He would not deliberately endanger Tommy's life. His eyes darted back and forth between Marcus and Dakar, then Joseph stepped forward and Andrew knew that all three were engaged in a silent mind struggle for dominance. He sent out a mental probe and quickly wished he hadn't. Pain, as sharp as a hot knife, seared through his skull, causing him to stagger back with shock.

"Let them do it," Micah said, grabbing Andrew's arm to steady him.

"I could hear Tommy calling to me." Andrew looked at Micah in anguish. "He has to let him go!" Cursing in his native Hungarian and before anyone could stop him, Andrew launched himself at Dakar, taking him to the ground.

The demon was weakened by the power exerted by Marcus and Joseph yet he still managed to croak out a warning. "You will never get him back now. I have killed him!"

"No!" Andrew screamed as the other vampires pulled him off Dakar.

Marcus lifted the demon to his feet as if he weighed no more than a child and pinned him against the wall. "You will release him," he said, his voice low but commanding. "He is not dead. I feel his life force still. Release him, Dakar, or suffer the consequences for the rest of your vile existence — short though it might well be."

Dakar squirmed in Marcus' grasp, but his eyes blazed with defiance. "No, I will not!"

"So be it. Joseph, open the door to the balcony."

"What are you going to do?" Andrew asked him as Joseph opened the glass sliding door.

"You will see. You may follow, if you wish."

"I wouldn't miss this for all the tea in China," Roger said, with a grim smile.

Marcus locked his arms around Tommy's body, strode over to the window and out onto the balcony before lifting off and disappearing rapidly into the night sky. Andrew and the others took off after him as fast as they could. Andrew could see Marcus and the struggling figure he held hovering hundreds of feet above the earth.

"Now, Dakar," Marcus was saying as Andrew drew close to them. "We all know demons cannot fly. The human body you now inhabit will not survive the fall. So the choice is yours, release Tommy now or I will drop you. What do you say?"

Andrew saw the fear in Dakar's eyes change to a look of cunning. "Then drop me," he growled, "but you will only kill the human!"

Marcus opened his arms. A scream of terror was involuntarily dragged from the demon's throat, but at the same time a plume of black smoke erupted from his mouth and spiralled off into the darkness. Andrew dived down through the night air towards Tommy's body as it hurtled earthward. He grabbed Tommy's arm with one hand then his jacket collar with the other, pulling him up and into his arms.

"Tommy, Tommy..." Andrew peppered his lover's face with kisses. "Tommy, can you hear me?"

"'Course I can hear you," Tommy groaned. "You're yelling in my ear somethin' fierce! What's going on?"

Andrew grinned at him. "Look down."

Tommy looked. "Yikes! What the heck are we doing way up here? You know I can't stand heights, 'less there's a ladder under me."

Andrew kissed him again. "You have no memory of what has happened?"

For the first time Tommy noticed the other vampires hovering near. "What the heck is happening? Is this some kind of vampire party?"

"I'll tell you all about it when we get home."

"We'll leave you to make the explanations," Marcus said. "I want to make sure Dakar isn't hanging around trying to find another human host. Goodnight, Andrew, Tommy..."

"G'night," Tommy muttered. "Get me down, will you please?" he whined as the vampires laughingly left Tommy and Andrew still hundreds of feet above the ground. "This explanation better be good!"

* * * *

Tommy stared wide-eyed as Andrew related what had happened that evening. "Jeez, the last thing I remember is a little old lady reading some cards over at Lorna's place. Sylvia, I think her name was. Then everything else is a blank. You mean some kind of *demon* was inside me?"

Andrew nodded. They were sitting on the couch, arms round one another, Andrew gently stroking Tommy's hair. "If it hadn't been for Marcus and Joseph gaining dominance over Dakar's mind, the outcome might have been very different."

Tommy shuddered and laid his head on Andrew's shoulder. "I'm just glad I can't remember what that felt like. Wait..." He lifted his head as part of what had taken place in the restaurant came back to him. "There is something. You and me in Ron's restaurant. You were trying to read my mind. Jean Claude was there too."

"Yes, you were acting strangely, being bolder than you generally are in public."

"What d'you mean?"

"Well, usually you are reticent about showing me too much affection in front of strangers, but you kissed me, twice, in the restaurant."

"I did? Were people watching?"

"Everyone," Andrew said, teasing him. "You were all over me, and I knew then that something was very wrong."

"Huh. All over you?"

"Yes, your reputation is ruined, I'm afraid."

"You're joshin' me, aren't you?"

Andrew chuckled, then his eyes became serious. "Yes, I'm trying to make light of a situation that could have been extremely ugly. I can only thank the gods that Marcus and Joseph are as powerful as they are. Also that the demon Dakar is a bit of a braggart. He may be cunning and devious but I think he weakened himself by taking over your body. He might very well be stronger in demon form—however, I have a definite feeling that when he returns to his Lord, having failed in his mission, he will not be kindly received."

"I'd like to punch his lights out, the son of a bitch."

"That was my inclination also." He laid a gentle kiss on Tommy's lips. "But now, having you safe in my arms, I'm somewhat else inclined..."

"Oh, yeah?" Tommy's eyes sparkled with mischief. "And what would that be?"

"Guess," Andrew whispered before his lips took Tommy's.

Chapter Six

Dakar strode through the cavernous halls of Lord Kardis' palace with a great deal more bravado than he felt. His imposing height and appearance hid the nervous flutter in his stomach as he approached the throne room where he was to make his report. Of course, Lord Kardis would already know Dakar had failed in his mission, and failure was not something Kardis particularly cared for. Dakar's punishment would be either death or exile — death either way, for exile meant he would be cast out of the Underworld with no place for him to go. Demons were not welcome in any other realm, and the idea of a half-life of hiding and disguising himself, was not one Dakar could stand.

However, there was, perhaps, just one ray of hope...

After Marcus had dropped him and he had escaped only by leaving the mortal body everyone seemed so intent on saving, he had hidden in his essence-like existence trying to find a suitable human shell to inhabit. He had waited several hours until he was sure Marcus and the others had given up their search, then he found a vagrant sleeping with his mouth wide open. He had entered him, but even a demon has standards. The stench inside the vagrant was unbearable and Dakar had exited the drunken man, cursing. He'd decided the best move was to descend to the Underworld and regain his own form.

Perhaps he should have changed back earlier, shown his true self to Andrew, instead of using the vampire's lover's shell as a disguise. It was Dakar's immodest opinion that in his demon form he was extremely handsome—able competition for the mortal, Tommy, any day. He still wanted Andrew, even knowing that such a union was forbidden and that he would most likely have to take the vampire by force. Not an easy task, he knew, but the rewards would be worth the struggle—and time spent with him would most likely change Andrew's mind about fighting him. He felt a rush of heat to his groin as he imagined Andrew's sleek and supple body under his. The thought of capturing the essence of the blood lust while they mated had kept him hard since his return to the Underworld.

Approaching Lord Kardis' throne, he quickly dispensed with his thoughts of carnal pleasure. As he bent his knee in front of Lord Kardis he was glad he had taken the time to assume his own likeness and dress accordingly. He knew he looked good.

"So, Dakar..." Kardis stared down his long nose at the demon that knelt before him in obeisance. All around the pillar-lined throne room inquisitive eyes watched from the shadows, eager to see Dakar's punishment. "I sent you on a simple mission. Take out Marcus Verano. I understand you were even in the vampire's presence, yet you failed to kill him."

Dakar stood and struck a pose that was obeisant with just a trace of his usual arrogance. "The vampire is powerful, Lord."

"And you are not, it seems."

Dakar swallowed his growl of protest. "He had his cohorts with him. Joseph Meyer, his right-hand man, who is almost as powerful. Their mind dominance is tremendously strong. I had no defence against the two of them combined."

"I find these excuses pathetic, Dakar." Kardis ran a hand through his thick, dark hair that hung about his shoulders while he stared at Dakar with brooding eyes.

Dakar bowed. "Lord, I ask of you one more chance to prove myself worthy in your eyes."

"An insurmountable task, I'm afraid," Kardis said with a sneer. "You have already proven yourself useless. Death will be your punishment."

A hiss of approval went up from the onlookers, the sinister sound echoing through the enormous room and seeming to sear into Dakar's brain.

"Lord," he blurted with a recklessness that silenced the crowd. "I claim the right to challenge by Damacian's Sword!"

Now another mixture of sounds filled the room. Derisive laughter and chuckling.

Dakar glared at the assembly. "It is my right!"

"It is your right only if I sanction it," Kardis said, sneering yet again. "Challenge by Damacian's Sword is granted only in very special circumstances. I see nothing special about *your* circumstances, Dakar. You were given a mission, you failed. Anything more *un*-special than that, I can't imagine."

More laughter greeted Kardis' words and Dakar's body shook with fury. "I have served you well in the past, Lord Kardis, and you would dispose of me so easily? I demand trial by Damacian's Sword. I repeat — it is my right!"

"Very well, Dakar, if you wish it." Kardis' eyes took on a vicious gleam. "As you know you must defeat my champion in armed combat, and — "

"But I am your champion, Lord Kardis," Dakar said with a self-satisfied smirk. "I can hardly meet myself in armed combat."

"Insolence!" Kardis all but jumped out of his throne in anger. "You thought to trick me with this devious ploy? Well, you are no longer my champion. Your failure to kill Marcus Verano deems you unworthy to be my champion. In your absence I have chosen a new man — one worthy of the title 'Champion'." He gestured towards the assemblage. "Step forward, Barca, and be recognised."

From out of the crowd strode a demon so huge that Dakar had to swallow quickly in order to hide his gasp of amazement. Heavily armoured, his face hidden by a visor in the shape of a hawk's eyes and beak, he marched towards Dakar, sword drawn.

"Sire," Dakar blustered, "I have not had time to prepare. I am weary from the journey back to the Underworld — "

"Oh, stop whining, Dakar." Kardis gave a wave of dismissal. "You wanted challenge by Damacian's Sword. You've got it, now get on with it. Frankly, I don't think you have much of a chance against Barca, but nevertheless, proceed."

Dakar had no choice but to draw his own weapon as the huge demon bore down on him, sword slashing the air in front of him. The crowd now chattered with excitement, no doubt at the thought of seeing Dakar split in two. Dakar knew he had no chance against

Barca in a fair fight, so he did what he had to in order to survive the duel.

Barca was still about twenty feet away when Dakar hefted his sword into a spear-like position and threw it, with all his strength, at his opponent. The sword flew straight and true, piercing Barca's visor and penetrating his brain. The demon fell in midstride, crashing to the ground like a granite rock.

The sound of a collective gasp filled the room, followed by cries of "Coward", "Cheat", and other more derogatory calls until Kardis stood and held up his hands for silence. He did not look pleased with the outcome. Indeed, he looked as if he was about to spit on Barca's corpse.

"Dakar has won, although I cannot add, 'fair and square'. Nevertheless, he is the winner and as such will be granted the chance to redeem himself." He ignored the mutterings of disgust from the crowd and fixed his eyes on his reprieved champion. Dakar returned his stare with studied arrogance. "Meet me in my library in one hour, Dakar. That should give you enough time to *prepare* yourself after your long journey back home." With that he swept from the throne room followed by his retinue of soldiers and courtiers.

Well... Dakar couldn't quite hide his grin of satisfaction as he turned to go to his own quarters. *That went better than I thought it would. Lucky for me Barca had such a big head. Couldn't miss really...* Throwing a look of contempt at those who had hoped to see the end of him, he strode with an exaggerated swagger from the throne room.

* * * *

High up in the Hollywood Hills, Marcus stood on the veranda of his mansion and gazed down at the lights of Los Angeles. He had known that this day would come, when the demon world would want to exact revenge for the lost opportunity of ruling the earth and all its inhabitants. The demon Pope they had set upon the throne in Rome had been destroyed by Marcus and his friends, and their plans smashed beyond repair.

He had sent a message to his friend Bernard Fournier, a vampire, who along with his lover, Pietro Dante, worked in the archives of the Vatican library.

"Warn Constantine and Gustav that the demons have begun a bid for revenge upon us for our part in taking down the demon Pope. Tell them to be on the lookout for anyone they do not know trying to get near them — and Bernard, I know I do not have to say this, but safeguard yourself and Pietro most closely..."

Bernard would always have a special place in Marcus' heart. They had been friends and lovers hundreds of years before Marcus had even dreamed of meeting Roger, and their bond, both mental and physical, had never weakened over the centuries. Just as his bond with Joseph was one he would defend with his life, so it was with Bernard.

He smiled as he felt two arms encircle his waist and cool lips caress his nape. "Problems?" Roger murmured.

"Demon problems." Marcus turned to his lover, his smile replaced with a more sombre expression. "I'm afraid we haven't seen the last of Dakar or whatever other demon Lord Kardis might use against us. Kardis is nothing if not prideful, and the fact that we ruined his plans to rule the western world through a demon pope obviously still sticks in his craw. I have apprised Bernard of the situation."

"You think Kardis will try again?" Roger looked sceptical. "Doesn't he know by now you can't be beaten by demons? I would think after what happened here the other night, and in Rome when you took out old Pius, he'd have received the message loud and clear—vampires, or at least *my* vampire, can't be taken down by demons."

Marcus smiled again. "Your belief in me is touching, but I worry sometimes that the inhabitants of the Underworld might one day seek an alliance with the Dark Forces. That would be tantamount to an all-out war—one that I will do my utmost to prevent."

"You think it's that serious?"

"It could be. Dakar's honour, if he possesses such a thing, but most certainly his ego, is at stake here. My best guess is that he will want to try again. Perhaps now that he knows he cannot do it alone, he will bring reinforcements."

"And once you beat the shit out of him again?"

Marcus chuckled. "Ah, Roger, you are so good for my self-esteem."

"Except that it's not misplaced." Roger pushed himself into Marcus' embrace. "You are the best, Marcus. There isn't another vampire or demon or wizard, for that matter, who can put you down. Or if there is, we haven't met him yet."

"Still..." Marcus tightened his arms around Roger. "I don't like what happened with Tommy and Andrew. How easy Dakar found it to take over Tommy's body. If Andrew hadn't been so quick to see through the ruse, who knows how much damage Dakar could have done. We all need to be alert—all of us."

* * * *

"So, how'd it go over at Lorna's the other night?" Alex grinned at Tommy as he stowed his packed dinner in the station's kitchen fridge. "Haven't had a chance to ask her myself."

"Oh, it was okay..." Tommy had already rehearsed his answer knowing Alex would be curious. "There was some old lady there who ranted on about luck and money and love—the usual kind of thing. They don't want to tell you anything bad, so from the sounds of it I'm going to lead a charmed life."

Alex chuckled. "So just the regular bullshit."

"Right. 'Course, when black smoke started pouring out of her mouth and her voice dropped a couple of octaves we all sat up and took notice."

"What?" Alex stared at him, his brown eyes wide.

"Just kiddin'. You're right, it was all bullshit."

"That's what I thought. I don't know why Lorna keeps getting mixed up with all that looney toon stuff. So what did you tell the boyfriend?"

"That the cards said I was the best and he better never let me go."

"Ha! But did he believe you?"

Tommy smiled. "He said he knew that all along."

Alex gave him the raised-eyebrow look. "So things are good with you and him? When do I get to meet him?"

Tommy thought quickly. "Uh, I have the day shift tomorrow. We can be at the Blue Moon tomorrow night if you'd like to join us." He'd have to do some fast persuading...

Alex frowned. "I don't get off shift 'til ten."

"We'll still be there. Stop by when you get off and I'll buy you a beer...or two."

"Okay, sounds good."

* * * *

Arturo paced restlessly across his living room floor. He had received the message that his liege lord—as Dakar liked to be addressed—was returning. A part of him was glad, another part apprehensive. He knew Dakar had been thwarted in his attempt to bring Marcus Verano the final death, and because of that failure he, Arturo, would have to work hard to soothe Dakar's battered ego. Not that he minded. Truth to tell, being allowed intimacy with Dakar was one reason Arturo stayed loyal to his demon lord, even though he knew Dakar only used him for pleasure when he couldn't get what he really wanted.

He watched, a slow smile quirking his lips, as a wraith-like column of smoke appeared in the living room of his apartment. It grew dense, took on the shape of a tall figure, then Dakar stepped out of the smoke, his long blond hair streaming behind him. He was wearing a polo shirt, blue jeans and cowboy boots. Arturo gasped. He had never seen Dakar so dressed down when in his own form.

"Surprised?" Dakar asked with a smirk.

Arturo's eyes swept over Dakar's toned chest and arms, and he licked his lips. He had always admired Dakar but had never acted on the impulses that would most likely earn him a sharp rebuke, if not exile from Dakar's service. He had learned to wait for Dakar's invitation.

"You look…"

"Handsome—strikingly so. Yes, I know, Arturo, but do I look like I might fit in, in human society? Or will people look at me and say, 'Demon'?"

"No, I can assure you, my liege, that no human, man or woman, would think that. Devil, perhaps," Arturo added with some humour. "A handsome devil."

"Ah yes. The human penchant to equate their baser side with the inhabitants of the Underworld. You devil, you naughty imp, etcetera… If they only knew that imps and devils really do exist and would love to show them what delights they can bring. Perhaps I will have that opportunity even yet—with Andrew, Tommy's vampire lover. I came so close while in Tommy's shell, but my eagerness betrayed me, more's the pity."

Arturo swallowed the reply that had almost sprung to his lips. It would not do to tell his liege that he would do anything to prevent Dakar coupling with the vampire—any vampire, human or any other demon for that matter. Seeing Dakar in his present mode of dress was giving Arturo many forbidden sensations, but he could barely quell them. The way Dakar's polo shirt was stretched across his broad chest, defining his pectoral muscles and making visible the tiny hard nipples, while the tight jeans showing Dakar's ample bulge was enough to make Arturo salivate. But as a sub-demon he was allowed only certain privileges and making the first move was not one of them.

"Arturo!" Dakar barked at his lieutenant. "What is the matter with you? You look dazed. Wake up, man!"

"Yes, my liege, I'm sorry." Arturo gave himself a shake. "So, what is the plan?"

"Lord Kardis has given me a second chance at Verano's assassination. I had to claim the right of Damacian's Sword in order to gain this second chance," he said with a prideful inflection in his voice.

Arturo gasped. "Damacian's Sword! But that meant…"

"Yes, and I sent the puffed-up fool to the fires of Hades forever. Kardis had chosen a new champion in my absence — can you imagine such a thing?"

"No, I can't!"

"Quite right. But Lord Kardis changed his mind and reinstated me. Still, there is the matter of the task at hand. Marcus Verano must meet his final death. He must not be able to rise again. If I fail this time, Arturo, Kardis will sentence me to execution — and all those closest to me."

Arturo shuddered at the implication. He would die too, if Dakar failed. All right then, failure was out of the question. "You have a plan in mind then, to kill the vampire?"

"Not yet. It will take time to formulate any plan that is foolproof. Marcus Verano is more powerful than Kardis ever suspected, plus he is surrounded by vampires and mortals who regard him as some kind of vampire demi-god. But even gods have been known to fall from grace…"

"And he has instituted a *code of honour* that could work to our advantage," Arturo said with a deal of sarcasm.

"Yes, the vampires who follow him have sworn not to kill the mortals they feed from — but make no mistake, Arturo…" Dakar still could not quite eradicate the memory of being held in Marcus' arms hundreds of feet above the earth, and how Marcus had shown no compunction whatsoever about dropping him to his death. "…Marcus Verano is a killer. He may show compassion to mortals, but his enemies cannot expect that same consideration. When we go against him we must be fully prepared—and we'll need reinforcements. Send out a message to those demons among us you can trust and who have the stomach for fighting. Only the strongest will do, Arturo."

"Yes, my liege."

"And we will have to recruit from among the humans. It will take a little time to get a sufficient number of them in my thrall, to do my bidding, but of course, I can do it."

Arturo smiled. "Yes, indeed you can, my liege."

"Now..." Dakar popped the metal button at his jean's waist and pulled down his zipper. "Fulfil your other duty to me."

"My pleasure," Arturo murmured. He dropped to his knees in front of Dakar and gripped Dakar's flaccid cock at the base. He lapped at the head then licked and sucked his way up and down the prodigious length, bringing the shaft to an almost instant hardness. He moaned as he savoured the copious pre-cum that spilled over his tongue.

As dangerous as his job might well soon become, Arturo would definitely remember this moment as one of the perks that made it all worthwhile.

Chapter Seven

Tommy had a 'movie date' with Roger and Micah, something he wouldn't have believed possible six months ago. Going to see a horror movie with two vampires. Weren't they the very subjects of most horror flicks? And here he was getting ready to meet two of them outside the movie theatre. Tommy gave a half chuckle as he stood in front of the bathroom mirror, rubbing a little gel between his palms, then running his fingers through his blond hair, spiking it into the style Andrew liked.

"I wish you were coming with," he said, turning to look at Andrew who was leaning on the bathroom doorframe watching him get ready. "You like a good movie now and then."

"The operative words there, *édesem*, were 'good movie'," Andrew said with a slight smile. "What you and your aficionados of horror are going to see tonight could hardly be described as good."

Tommy stuck his tongue out at Andrew. "What's Hungarian for snob?"

"*Sznob*," Andrew replied dryly.

"Oh, almost the same. Well, that's you—when it comes to movies anyway."

Andrew stepped behind Tommy and put his arms round his waist, his chin on Tommy's broad shoulder. "*Szeretlek*, Tommy."

"Love you too," Tommy said, pressing his taut butt into Andrew's crotch. "So what are you goin' to do tonight?"

"Marcus wants to talk to Joseph and me about future problems with Dakar. He wants to have a plan of action should Dakar try another assassination attempt."

Tommy widened his eyes in alarm. "Why does he want to involve you in this?"

"Because I asked him if I could help, Tommy. I owe Marcus and Joseph my life—you saved me from the fire where I would surely have met my final death had you not found me, but even then the silver poisoning would have killed me if Marcus and Joseph had not given me their blood to overcome it."

Tommy shuddered and he turned in Andrew's embrace to tighten his arms around his lover. "Don't think I'll ever forget that time. But grateful as I am to Marcus and Joseph I still don't like the idea of you getting mixed up in some sort of counterattack against a freaking demon!"

"Dakar is powerful, but his weakness is his over-inflated belief in himself," Andrew said, his lips brushing Tommy's cheek. "But he is cunning and will certainly use underhand methods against us. For example, what he did to you, he may try a similar ploy again."

"So while Roger, Micah and me are kicking back at the movies, you three are going to be working on strategies?" Tommy shook his head forcefully. "I'm gonna cancel and go with you. If you guys are planning dangerous stuff I want to know what it is."

"Tommy…"

"No arguing, Andrew. Roger and Micah should be there too—in fact, the whole gang should be involved. Shit, we've all got something valuable invested here. Don't they know what's going on?"

"Yes, they do…" Andrew kissed Tommy's lips tenderly. "I am happy you consider me valuable, Tommy."

"You know I do." Tommy groaned, feeling Andrew's erection press against his own stirring cock. "You're just tryin' to change the subject…"

"Have I succeeded?"

"If you mean, do I want to jump into bed with you, yes, you've succeeded." Tommy gave his watch a quick peek. "I do have an hour before I meet the guys, but Andrew, I don't feel good about this meeting. Promise me you won't agree to anything rash."

"I promise, but Marcus and Joseph never do anything rash, Tommy. That's why they have survived for centuries longer than most vampires. They have beaten the odds in battles against the Wizard Brotherhood, the Dark Forces, and they have faced demons before."

"Right, but still—"

"Ssh… come with me…" Andrew took Tommy's hand and led him to their bed. "You said you have an hour to spare. Let's not waste it."

* * * *

Despite the euphoria that making love with Andrew always brought him, Tommy still didn't feel good about his lover's meeting with Marcus, and he said as much to Roger and Micah while they waited in the movie complex foyer for the next screening.

"It's not that I don't think Andrew can handle himself in a tough situation—he's already proven to me he can—but *demons*, guys. Shouldn't we be included in whatever they're planning?"

"Oh, we will be," Roger said. "At least Micah and I will, and Marcus' other loyal vampires. I don't think Marcus wants to endanger you mortal guys."

"Well, darn it..." Tommy wondered what Ron, Chris and Joey would think of that. He guessed they wouldn't want to be left on the sidelines when their vampire lovers could possibly be in danger.

"We know what you're thinking," Micah remarked with a grin.

"I *know* you know," Tommy said a deal more abruptly than he'd intended. "Look, I also know we *mortals* won't be as strong or as quick as you guys if it comes to a fight with these demons, but we're not wimps either. Even Joey... I bet for all his fey ways he could be a tough little fucker when the chips are down."

"But fighting demons is a whole different game," Roger said, rubbing Tommy's shoulder affectionately. "We know you'd jump in if Andrew was in danger, and that's the problem, quite frankly. The demon that possessed you now knows what he's up against. If he plans on coming at us again, he knows he's going to need help—a lot of help."

"What kind of help?" Tommy asked.

"A small army, I'd guess. More demons, humans he has under his control, more demons..."

"Demon spawn, "Micah added.

"What the heck is that?" Tommy asked.

"Half demons, born of demon and human," Micah told him. "Not quite as lethal as the real thing, but pretty formidable in a fight."

"Strangely enough we have a friend in Rome, Constantine, who is half demon, half human," Roger said. "For a while there he was on the side of the bad guys, until he met Gustav, a mortal, and fell in love, then couldn't go through with his father's plan to rule the world through the papacy."

Micah chuckled at Tommy's wide-eyed expression. "It's all unbelievable, we know, Tommy, but after what you just went through, you have to admit it's all really possible."

Tommy groaned. "Guys, it seems *anything's* possible, and as hard as it is for me to get my head round some of this stuff sometimes, I know the danger is real—that's why I don't want to be left out. I want to help!"

"Okay, okay..." Roger glanced quickly around the crowded foyer to make sure no one was eavesdropping on this strange conversation. "We'll talk to Marcus and Joseph after the movie. Just get a grip for the next couple of hours."

* * * *

Andrew smiled as he accepted another glass of an excellent red wine from Marcus then walked over to stand by Joseph in front of the fireplace.

Joseph touched his glass to Andrew's. "It would seem Tommy is not at all happy about this meeting," he said with a rueful smile. "He is very protective of you."

Andrew nodded. "He feels he should be a part of anything we plan against Dakar and Kardis, especially as it was his body Dakar inhabited in order to infiltrate our ranks."

"Tommy is a brave young man," Marcus said, joining them. "He faces danger every day in his line of work, but I'm afraid even he would not be able to defeat a demon in mortal combat."

"I have tried to tell him that." Andrew shook his head, remembering Tommy's aggrieved expression when they'd had words about the situation. "I had hoped that Roger and Micah would be able to persuade him to back off."

Marcus chuckled. "According to the message Roger communicated to me, Tommy feels that our respective mortal lovers should be given the opportunity to help us. Impossible, of course, but I admire his eagerness to defend you, Andrew."

"He is a wonderful man," Andrew said quietly. "I am honoured by his love for me."

"Well, we must ensure that he and our other mortal friends are kept very safe when we take on Dakar and his demon cronies." Joseph's smile was wicked. "Of course, we have many crafty ways of keeping them out of the danger zone. Ways they will never even be aware of."

Andrew nodded his understanding, then said wryly, "We will only have to deal with their resentment when they realise what we've done."

"But they will be safe, and in the end that's all that matters." Marcus refilled their wine glasses and gestured that they sit in the tall wingback chairs by the fireplace. "I have it on good authority that Dakar has returned, this time in his own form, and is actively seeking recruits for his next campaign against us."

"You know this already?" Andrew asked with surprise.

"It helps to have a demon on our side," Marcus said. "I contacted our friend Bernard in Rome who in turn spoke with Constantine. Constantine, who is half demon, told Bernard that demons everywhere are excited about what happened between Dakar and Kardis. Apparently, Kardis was ready to execute Dakar for his failure to assassinate me, and had already replaced him with a new champion."

"No love lost there," Andrew remarked.

"None, but Dakar is nothing if not cunning. He has managed to get Kardis to give him a second chance, and is here even now, working on a plan to bring me, and all vampires loyal to me, down. Retribution not only for our success in foiling Kardis' power play attempt to place a demon on the papal throne, but also for Dakar's own humiliation at our hands. Constantine will keep me apprised of further developments as he hears them."

"A useful man to know," Andrew said. "But are you sure you can trust him? He is a demon, after all."

"He owes Marcus his life," Joseph told him. "And he loves a mortal for whom he almost gave his life. So yes, we think he can be trusted."

"He is also a tad sharper than most demons, partly due to his human mother, I would guess," Marcus continued. "In my opinion, demons have proven themselves to be notoriously slow-witted at times, a characteristic that gives us an advantage, of course."

Andrew smiled. "Slow-witted?"

"Yes, but one cannot overlook their slyness, nor the easy way their loyalty swings back and forth. Constantine says that some demons see Kardis' leniency towards Dakar as weakness. Apparently there is a faction eager to take Kardis down. This can only work to our advantage. If the demons are divided in their loyalty it could prove to be their Achilles' heel."

"Do we know who Kardis' rival is?" Andrew asked.

"No name has yet been mentioned, but would it be so much of a surprise if it was Dakar himself?"

* * * *

"Okay..." Tommy looked at his vampire friends as they left the multiplex. "What d'you think?"

"Of the movie?" Roger quirked an eyebrow. "Not the worst I've ever seen."

"I liked it," Micah said, hiding a smile. "I really liked that scene where the elevator doors opened and that huge—"

"Not the movie!" Tommy yelled. "Jeez, for mind readers you're really slow, you know?"

Roger and Micah laughed together and Roger punched Tommy on the arm. "Oh, sorry," he said when Tommy winced. "Forget sometimes..."

"Yeah," Tommy muttered, rubbing his biceps. "I know...vampire strength. So okay, you knew I wasn't talkin' about the movie. I repeat, what do you think we should do about this demon threat? I'm not going to back down about helping, guys. You better let Marcus know that, and when I tell Ron and the others, they're going to be just as pig-headed as me about it."

"*If* you tell them about it..." Roger gave him an exaggerated stare.

Tommy immediately closed his eyes, tight. "Oh no you don't! You're not gonna do any of that vampire voodoo on me!"

Micah chuckled. "How are you going to drive that big Harley of yours with your eyes closed?"

"Come on guys," Tommy whined, not opening his eyes. "No fair!"

"If you knew how dumb you look right now." Roger sighed loudly. "Everybody's staring at you, Tommy. Give it up."

"We won't zap you," Micah said.

"Promise?" Tommy opened one eye carefully.

"Promise, now come on..." Roger grabbed him by the arm "We're going back to my place and Marcus will fill you in on what they've discussed."

"I'll ride with Tommy," Micah said.

"Okay." Roger grinned at them both. "Guess I'll just have to fly home alone."

"See you later." Tommy fell in step alongside Micah. "Sure you want to take the long way there?" he asked.

"I love motorbikes," Micah told him, "and it's not often I get the chance to ride one."

"You wanna drive?"

"No, no, I'm happy riding pillion."

Tommy handed Micah the passenger helmet from the top box then sat astride his black Harley. "I know you guys don't really need one, but..."

Micah grinned. "I know. I don't want to get you pulled over." He settled himself behind Tommy and placed his hands on either side of Tommy's waist. He hoped Tommy wouldn't wonder why he was holding on. He had no need to out of safety, but for what he had to do, he needed the contact.

Fortunately, Tommy didn't seem to notice, even yelling "Hold on!" as they cruised out of the parking garage. So Micah held on, inching closer so that his chest was pressed to Tommy's back. He rested his chin between Tommy's shoulder blades and initiated a subtle thought transference.

By the time they reached Marcus' home up in the hills, Tommy had completely forgotten the reason for Andrew being there, but he did remember with a start that he'd promised Alex he and Andrew would be at the Blue Moon so Alex could finally meet Andrew.

"Shit," he muttered, glancing at his watch. Almost ten. "Uh, Marcus, this is going to sound rude..." His host smiled at him while Andrew and the others waited for him to continue. "Uh, I kinda promised Alex — you know, the guy I work with at the station — that we'd meet him at the Blue Moon. He's been buggin' me forever about meeting Andrew and now if we don't show he's going to be royally pissed, so would you mind if we, uh... left?"

"Not at all," Marcus said, gracious as ever.

"Hey, why don't we all go?" This from Roger, and Tommy could see right away he had devilment in his eyes.

"Uh well," Tommy muttered, hedging, "Alex is kinda shy. I don't know, all of you at once..." He knew his excuse had sounded lame but hoped they wouldn't see through the lie. Alex was anything but shy!

"Shy, eh?" Roger was laughing. "You'll have to do better than that, Tommy."

Damn. This is right up Roger's alley. He's gonna tease the hell out of Alex and he won't have a clue what's happening — or will he? The thought of Alex actually realising that Tommy's boyfriend and the other guys there were vampires made his blood run cold and his face flush with heat.

"Roger..."

Marcus to the rescue, thank God...

"I think for Tommy's friend's first meeting with Andrew it should be as low key as possible," Marcus said in a tone firm enough to bring even Roger to heel. "Don't you agree?"

"I suppose so." Roger's pout brought chuckles from the others. "Marcus, you really are a party-pooper at times."

"Some would see it as diplomacy, Roger, and perhaps even tact."

"*Whatever...*" Roger shrugged. "Well, have a good time, you two," he said, "though it won't be nearly as much fun without Micah and me there to supply the laughs."

The Blue Moon was crowded when they arrived a little after ten-thirty. Tommy could see Alex through the press of people standing at the bar talking to two men. Tommy stiffened with shock when he recognised one of them.

"What's wrong?" Andrew asked.

"That tall dark-haired guy talking to Alex... He was at Lorna's the other night. Arturo or something. Yeah...he was like helping the old lady." Tommy had to admit that his mind was fuzzy when it came to remembering just what had happened at Lorna's, but Arturo he remembered very well. "He tried to put the make on me."

"And the other?" Andrew was looking across the bar at the two men, a wary expression on his aquiline features. "Something about him doesn't seem quite right."

The man in question was also tall with long blond hair that hung about his shoulders. He had a loud laugh and his gestures seemed exaggerated. From the look on Alex's face Tommy could tell his friend wasn't entirely enthralled by the blond man.

"Looks like Alex needs rescuing," Tommy muttered, pushing his way through the crowd. But by the time he reached Alex the two men were gone.

"Hey, Tommy..." Alex beamed at him. "Thank fuck, I thought I was going to be stuck with those two all night."

Tommy gave Alex a quick hug. "Yeah, I saw you looking less than interested in whatever they were laying on you."

"Bullshit mostly..." Alex's eyes strayed over Tommy's shoulder and fastened on Andrew. "Oh, now...*now* I know why you've been keeping him all to yourself. You lucky dog, you." He thrust his hand past Tommy's arm. "I'm Alex, and you have got to be Andrew!"

"I am very pleased to meet you," Andrew said, taking Alex's hand in his.

Tommy didn't miss the slight shiver that coursed through Alex's body when he made contact with Andrew's cool flesh. *Never fails*, he thought, watching Alex fall under the spell of Andrew's charisma.

"So, did the dark-haired guy tell you he was over at Lorna's the other night?" Tommy asked sharply, dragging Alex's attention away from Andrew with some difficulty.

"Huh? No, he didn't mention that, but then why would he? We didn't get around to exchanging family names." Alex stared at Tommy. "He was there?"

"Did he at least tell you his name?"

"Yeah, Arthur or something."

"*Arturo*. He's not on the up and up, Alex. I hope you didn't agree to meet him later..."

"Are you kidding? He hardly said a word. It was the other one did all the talkin'. Yak, yak, yak, and all about himself."

"What is his name?" Andrew asked quietly.

"You know, that's the one thing he didn't tell me, and sorry, but I wasn't interested enough to ask. The guy was built and good-looking and all, but getting past all that self-adulation would be way too much hard work."

Tommy and Andrew exchanged glances and in that look Tommy knew Andrew was on the alert. Arturo's nameless friend was not likely to be on their buddy list anytime soon.

* * * *

Alex's apartment was only two blocks from the Blue Moon, an easy walk. He'd done it hundreds of times. But tonight, the darkened streets appeared even darker, the streetlamps dimmer, and no matter how fast he walked, the distance to his apartment building never seemed to diminish.

"Crazy," he muttered to himself. "Must have had one too many beers. Now I'm imagining things."

A few yards ahead two men waited, motionless, their body language, while not exactly threatening, still aggressive enough to put Alex on the defensive. They were blocking the narrow sidewalk, and it meant either Alex would have to step out onto the street to avoid the two men, or he would have to pass between them—something he didn't like the idea of one bit. Still, he wasn't about to back down.

Within a few feet of them he recognised them. The guys from the bar—the one who couldn't shut up. What the hell did they want?

"What's up, guys?" he asked, his voice steady and friendly enough.

"We wished to talk more with you," the mouthy one said with a faint smile.

"Why'd you leave the bar then? Seemed to me you were in an awful hurry to get outta there."

"Your companions were not to our liking."

"You didn't even meet them." Alex eyed the men warily. "Anyway, it's late and I have to work tomorrow, so if you don't mind..." He stepped to the side to pass by, but the one called Arturo gripped his arm and swung him round to face the blond man.

"Hey!" Alex tried to wrench his arm free. *Jesus, this guy is strong.* Alex was no weakling. His job as a firefighter and his daily workouts kept him in superb shape, but he couldn't remember ever feeling quite so helpless as he now did in Arturo's grasp. "What the hell do you guys think you're doing?"

"I told you we wish to talk further with you. But I am being rude. I haven't introduced myself. My name is Dakar."

"*Lord* Dakar," Arturo growled. "Kneel before your master."

"What?" Alex almost laughed, but instead had to bite back a cry of pain as Arturo twisted his arm and forced him to his knees. Alex couldn't believe how strong the man was. He felt like a wimp—something he'd never experienced before. "What the fuck kind of asshole game are you two playing at? Is this some kind of kinky role-playing shit you're into? 'Cause I'm not, so cut it out."

Dakar chuckled. "This is no game, Alex. This is recruitment."

"*What?*" Alex gaped up at him.

"You will join the army I am creating in order to defeat the vampire hordes that infest this city."

Alex stared at Dakar, his mouth slack with shock. "Are you nuts?" He gasped involuntarily. "Vampire hordes? Everyone knows there's no such thing as a vampire, never mind a horde of 'em. What the hell's the matter with you — with both of you?"

Alex's mind raced with all kinds of scenarios. Okay, these two were totally insane, or this was some kind of reality TV moment when some guy would step out of the shadows and yell "Cut!", or he was delirious and none of this was actually happening... But the cold, hard stone under his knees told him he wasn't hallucinating and when he looked from one sneering expression to the other, a real fear clutched at Alex's heart. These men, whatever they were, were dangerous — insanely dangerous — and he was in a shitload of trouble.

"Look around you," Dakar was saying. "You walk on this street every night, do you not? You are wondering why it is strangely darker than usual, why it is empty of other humans who might come to your aid. That is because I will it so — because I rule the night just as I now rule your future thoughts and deeds. You are mine, Alex Benson, mine to do with as I wish, to control you, to bend you to my will. You are young and strong. You will make a fine warrior, an ideal addition to my growing army — "

"You must be nuts!" Alex spat. "If you think for one minute that I'll — "

Dakar smiled down at Alex's defiant expression and laid his right hand on the young fire fighter's head, gently caressing Alex's short, dark-brown hair.

"I repeat, you are mine, Alex. Now, and forever."

And under Dakar's touch, Alex felt his will to fight slowly slip away. Gazing up into the demon's amber eyes, he whispered, "Yes, my Lord Dakar... I am yours."

Dakar nodded. "So it begins," he murmured.

Chapter Eight

"So what did you think of Alex?" Tommy asked as he and Andrew dismounted from Tommy's bike.

"A very nice man." Andrew smiled at his lover. "Even if his flirting is a little obvious."

Tommy chuckled. "Yeah, I won't have to ask him what he thought of *you*. Looks like I might have to stake my claim a bit more firmly."

"No need, *édesem*." Andrew slipped an arm round Tommy's waist and pulled him close while they walked up the steps to their apartment. "Although I'd rather you didn't bandy the word 'stake' around quite so freely."

"Huh?" Tommy stared at Andrew's smiling face for a moment or two before the penny dropped. "Oh, yeah..." He laughed. "Got it." He unlocked the door, immediately drawing Andrew into his arms as they entered the apartment. "*Szeretlek*," he murmured after kissing Andrew's waiting lips. "Sorry, I mangled that a bit. It's not the easiest language in the world, is it?"

"I'm sure my English is far from perfect, *édesem*," Andrew whispered, his full lips brushing Tommy's mouth. "I'm glad you remember the important words. I love you too. But there is something we need to talk about."

"Oh, oh…"

"Nothing that affects our relationship. Well, perhaps that is not exactly true — it could affect us both if what I suspect is reality." He led Tommy over to the couch and together they sat down, their arms comfortably around one another. "The men who were with Alex tonight… I sensed something strange about the tall one with blond hair. I think I know who he is."

"And he's not a good guy is he?"

"No. I think it is Dakar, the demon who inhabited your body."

"Jesus. You have to let Marcus know!"

"I already have."

"Oh, right, you can do that. But what makes you think it's him?"

"Demons exude a certain power. I sensed it from across the bar. Unfortunately, he disappeared before we got close enough for me to be absolutely sure. But that in itself made me suspicious. Why suddenly vanish because Alex was being joined by friends? Unless Dakar sensed my presence then recognised me, as of course he would, having been in my company the other night."

"Wonder why he was talking to Alex. You think he was just trying to pick him up?"

"Possibly. Your friend, Alex, is a very attractive man…"

"Hey…" Tommy tightened his arms round his lover. "None o' that."

Andrew chuckled and slipped his hand inside Tommy's shirt, gently teasing his left nipple. "Are you jealous?" he asked, his voice a near whisper.

"You bet I am. Even best friends don't get near the man I love." Tommy ran a hand through Andrew's silky hair and took his mouth in a long, demanding kiss. He felt his clothes fall away, and Andrew's naked body pressed hard against him. He moaned his satisfaction into Andrew's mouth as their tongues intertwined and Andrew grasped his erection, pumping it with long, measured strokes.

Tommy wasn't sure if it was that little spark of jealousy that had ignited his almost overwhelming need to know that Andrew was indeed all his—that his vampire lover wanted no other man but him. Andrew called him *édesem*—sweetheart—and had shown over and over again that he adored Tommy through his acts of love, his kisses, the long looks when they were in the company of others, the looks that promised so much when they would at last be alone.

And yet...and yet... Was he enough for Andrew?

His involuntary moan of apprehension was muffled by Andrew's lips and tongue that sent shudders of desire through Tommy's body, that heated his blood and made him want to cry out, "I love you!" for all the world to hear.

Hearing Tommy's silent cry, Andrew wrenched his mouth away from Tommy's to gasp, "I love you too, Tommy. Never doubt it for a moment. We are one, bound by love and blood—nothing but death can part us."

They fell back across the couch, Tommy's body covering Andrew's, his burning lips searing Andrew's cool flesh with the passion his lover's words had instilled in him. He kissed Andrew lips, the smooth column of his throat, lingering over his Adam's apple for a moment before nibbling on each tiny nipple already made hard by their mutual fervour. He traced his mouth in a hungry erotic pattern over the hard torso under him until he reached Andrew's raging erection and took it between his lips, sucking up the pre-cum, savouring the spicy essence that rolled over his tongue. Andrew writhed beneath Tommy, his hands alternately stroking Tommy's hair or clutching at his shoulders as Tommy began feasting on Andrew's balls, licking the soft skin, teasing them gently between his lips. Tommy lifted Andrew's hips, cupping his butt, giving himself access to Andrew's opening He slid his tongue over Andrew's perineum before lapping at the tight pucker in the cleft between the twin globes of taut, smooth flesh that tensed in Tommy's hands as he delved deeper, bringing his lover to the edge of ecstasy.

"Fuck me, Tommy," Andrew moaned out his need, lifting his legs over Tommy's shoulders, and Tommy raised his head and smiled at Andrew the smile that drove the vampire slightly mad with lust and wanting. "Gods, Tommy, want you so much. Fuck me, hard."

Tommy, his heart pounding and soaring as it always did when he made love to Andrew, guided his hard cock into the opening made slick with his saliva and pushed forward, his eyes zeroing in on the rapt expression on Andrew's beautiful face, on the ice-blue gaze that glazed with lust as Tommy drove himself deep into Andrew's core.

Yes…this is all I live for, Tommy exulted, *this moment when we are one. When everything and everyone else goes away and it's just Andrew and me — no one else, just Andrew and me…*

Andrew arched his body as he took all of Tommy deep inside, holding Tommy tightly to him with his arms and legs, his face upturned to receive all the kisses Tommy could give him.

"Oh, God..." Tommy's cry of frustration between kisses signalled his nearing climax. "Not yet, want this to last, forever. Oh, God, you're killing me, Andrew!"

Andrew smiled into Tommy's kiss, running his hands up and down Tommy's now sweat-slicked spine, soothing him, caressing him, using his power to let Tommy's orgasm recede for just a few moments more. He was rewarded by the sounds of his lover's rapture as he pounded Andrew's ass with a wild abandon, pumping his cock in and out of Andrew's hungry hole until he could hold back no longer.

With a groan that seemed to be wrenched from his very soul, Tommy came, flooding Andrew's core with his hot seed, thrusting deeper again and again in the throes of his ecstasy. Andrew held him clasped in a fierce embrace, riding the waves of pleasure and excitement along with his lover, his own climax exploding from him a few seconds later. Tommy collapsed over him, covering his face and throat with kisses, mumbling silly and some dirty words of endearment in Andrew's ear.

Andrew smiled, caressing Tommy's body with long, soothing strokes, nuzzling his neck, nipping gently at the smooth skin. He felt Tommy's body relax and grow heavier in his arms, then a gentle snore escape Tommy's parted lips. Gods, how he loved this mortal man. The earlier events of the evening pricked at his mind and instinctively he tightened his arms around Tommy, causing his lover to mutter in his sleep and press his lips to Andrew's neck.

He was sure the tall, blond-haired man talking to Alex in the bar had been Dakar, and that could only mean more trouble lay ahead for all of them — vampires and demons alike — but he would do everything within his power to prevent Tommy being involved again. Almost losing him once had been Andrew's worst nightmare. He would most definitely go along with Marcus and Joseph's plan to keep their mortals safe. For that reason he hadn't mentioned to Tommy the fact that Constantine had been in touch with Marcus. Constantine had learned that Dakar was rumoured to be gathering an army in order to challenge Marcus and his followers.

Andrew wondered at that. As a human, Dakar had been no match for Marcus. Perhaps he was more powerful in his demon form. He had, after all, overcome the champion Kardis had chosen to replace him. Yet, Andrew refused to believe that Marcus could ever be brought down. He was the most powerful of all vampires. Even the Dark Forces had failed in their attempts to vanquish him.

No, all would be well. Marcus would prevail and all of those near and dear to him would be kept safe. Andrew would not believe it could be otherwise.

* * * *

Tommy stared at the empty locker in front of him with disbelief. Alex's locker was stripped bare. Nothing of his friend's belongings remained.

"Weird, huh…" Tommy turned to find Fire Chief Brad Lambert standing behind him, his eyes also scanning Alex's empty locker.

"What happened?"

"He came in last night, grabbed everything out of his locker, left me a note of resignation on my desk and left. Didn't say a word to anyone here." Lambert gave Tommy a long look. "I'm guessing, from your stunned expression, he didn't say anything to you either."

"No, he didn't. I saw him last night. We had a beer. He was fine—never said a word about this. I don't get it."

"I called his apartment after I read the note," Lambert said. "No reply. Nothing on his cell either. No voice mail even."

"This is crazy," Tommy muttered. "Alex loved this job...*loved it*. He'd never quit." Tommy raked his fingers through his hair in frustration. "This makes no sense, Chief, no sense at all. Something's wrong. Something *must* be wrong for him to do this. Can I go over to his place? Maybe he's sick."

"He wasn't sick when he came in last night and stripped his locker. The guys who saw him said he looked okay. A little mad at the world, maybe, but otherwise okay."

"Mad at the world?" Tommy shook his head. "He was fine last night, joking and laughing like he always does. This is screwy..."

Lambert clapped a hand on Tommy's shoulder. "Okay, take an hour and go knock on his door. If he's there, I guess you're the only one he'll open up to. Find out what brought this on."

"Thanks, Chief."

"And Tommy, tell him if he changes his mind real quick before I have to file his resignation, he can get his job back."

* * * *

Good, he's home, Tommy thought as he left his bike next to Alex's car in the 'reserved for tenants only' parking area. On the short drive over to Alex's apartment he'd tried to understand the reasoning behind his friend's sudden decision to leave his job, but try as he might, Tommy just could not come up with a valid motive. Had something happened after he and Andrew had said goodnight and left Alex outside the Blue Moon last night? He'd seemed fine, and Tommy figured he knew Alex well enough to know when he might be out of sorts — or mad at the world, as Chief Lambert had intimated. No way had he been *mad at the world* when the three of them were having a drink. In fact, Tommy was sure Alex had really enjoyed meeting Andrew, had flirted with him even.

Damn, but this makes no sense at all.

He ran up the few steps to Alex's apartment and banged loudly on the door. He banged even louder when he got no reply.

"Alex! It's me, Tommy," he yelled.

Nothing.

He rattled the door knob and started in surprise when the door opened under his pressure. "Alex? It's Tommy," he said, stepping inside the darkened living room. "Are you home, buddy?" He scanned the room as he walked over to the kitchen and turned on the light.

"Alex?" He walked down the short hall to the bedroom. The door was open, and it was obvious the room was empty. No sound of the shower running. No sounds at all. "Shit..." Tommy glanced at his watch. Eleven. Too early for Andrew to be up and about, but he might just be awake. He pulled out his cell and punched in Andrew's number.

"Yes, Tommy?"

"Hi, sorry to bother you this early, but I got to the station and Alex quit his job. I'm over at his place and he's not here. His car is, but he's not."

"Are there signs of a struggle? Anything out of place?" Andrew asked.

"No, everything looks okay. Did you...did you sense anything wrong with him last night? I know you can pick up on stuff like that real easy."

"No, I did not. He seemed quite free of any kind of angst, or indecision. In fact, I would say he is a most uncomplicated man. Of course, you know him better, Tommy."

"No, no, I agree. Alex is kinda happy-go-lucky most of the time. This is just so *unlike* him, you know?"

"I understand your concern, but..." The hesitation in Andrew's voice drew Tommy to alertness.

"What? You did sense something, didn't you?"

"Tommy, I..."

"*Andrew.*" Tommy narrowed his eyes as he continued. "If you suspect something, you have to tell me what it is! Alex is my best friend and—"

"Yes, I know. It's just that, gods, Tommy—Marcus doesn't want any of our mortal friends involved in what might happen."

"What are you talking about?"

"Dakar, Tommy. Marcus has been informed by a fairly reliable source that Dakar is recruiting, or rather enslaving humans to help him usurp Lord Kardis, the ruler of the demon underworld. Then he plans to take on Marcus and his loyal followers."

"But what has this to do with Alex?" Tommy drew in a sharp breath. "You mean...? Oh, God, you think Dakar might have taken Alex?"

"Well, is it not a rather strange coincidence that we saw him in conversation with Dakar last night, then he mysteriously disappears after quitting his job?"

"Damn that fucking demon! I'll kill the son of a bitch if he hurts Alex."

"Tommy, calm down. We don't know for certain that's what happened. First, we have to find out just where Dakar is, and where he is keeping his recruits. I will contact Marcus. Perhaps his demon friend, Constantine, can be of some help."

"Yeah, another demon. How does Marcus know he can trust this guy?"

Andrew sighed. "Demons can never be trusted. They are inveterate liars, but Constantine owes his life to Marcus, and because of Marcus he has vampire blood in his veins. I have to believe that Constantine is as loyal as any demon can possibly be."

"You're not exactly filling me with confidence here," Tommy said, grimacing.

"Can you come home, Tommy? I can't go out yet, and the phone is not the best way to deal with this."

"Right. I'm going to root around for any kind of clue here, then I'll ask Chief if I can have the rest of the day off. Don't know how difficult it'll be with Alex gone, but I'll do my best."

Andrew closed his cell phone and fell back on the bed with a groan. The lethargy that all vampires endured until near dusk made it difficult for him to function at his full capacity. He could, however, move about the darkened apartment and he could communicate his fears to Marcus and the others.

If Constantine was indeed a reliable source—and at this point Andrew had no reason to doubt he was, given his and Marcus' history—then it might very well be that Alex had been abducted by Dakar and his minion, Arturo, along with who knew how many more humans. This would make things very much more difficult for Tommy, if his best friend was allied with the enemy.

He sent out a warning to Marcus and all vampires within reach of his mind. Jared, his once-time lover, would be returning soon to Los Angeles. He might even be able to pick up on Andrew's message.

"Andrew..." It was Marcus, always so quick to heed any warning or cry for help from his people. *"You are probably correct in your assumption that Tommy's friend is in danger. On no account must Tommy try to interfere. Use all your power to prevent this. Constantine tells me that Lord Kardis is aware of Dakar's plot to overthrow him and will use every tactic at his disposal to destroy Dakar and anyone who follows him."*

"But if Alex is among them..."

"It is regrettable, Andrew, but we must think first of those in harm's way—the unsuspecting humans who may get caught up in the fight."

"Alex is human."

"Not while he is in Dakar's thrall, if that is what has happened to him. Only Dakar, or Dakar's death, can free Alex now."

Andrew's cell phone rang seconds after he finished communicating with Marcus.

Tommy...

"Andrew, it's me. I can't get away from the station, darn it. There's an emergency on the 101 freeway so I'm needed."

"I understand, Tommy. In the meantime, I will talk with Marcus and see what can be done about finding Alex."

"Thanks Andrew. I love you."

"Love you too." Andrew was not about to tell Tommy what Marcus had said about the situation with Alex. His lover was not yet ready to hear that kind of bad news, and probably never would be.

Chapter Nine

Alex awoke to the sound of what seemed like hundreds of voices all talking at once. He sat up in the narrow camp bed he was lying on and stared about him, then gave his head a sharp shake in order to clear it of the fogginess he felt clouding his memory. How had he got here? Here, in this strange place surrounded by strangers, men and women in some kind of military uniform. He glanced down at what he was wearing and gasped. A dark green sleeveless T-shirt and camouflage pants. Where the hell had these come from?

He looked up, his surprised gaze taking in the cavernous space that soared above him. The place appeared to be a huge aircraft hangar, certainly big enough to house two or three jumbo jets.

What the hell? He searched in his pocket for his cell phone. He had to call Tommy or Chief Lambert and explain why he wasn't at the station. But how exactly was he going to explain this? The point was moot in any case — his cell phone wasn't in his pocket. He turned to stare at the man lying on the bed next to his.

"What is this?" he asked. "What's going on?"

"Damned if I know," the man replied, sitting up and rubbing his forehead. "I just woke up. Helluva headache…"

"Yeah," Alex muttered, acknowledging the dull throb between his eyes. "Only had a couple of beers last night."

"I didn't even have that much!" The man gave Alex a rueful grin. "Jason Bradley, by the way." He held out his hand.

"Alex Benson." Alex took the proffered hand in a firm shake. "So, maybe we should go find out what this is all about."

He stood, noticing that Jason was dressed in an identical uniform to his own. He also noticed the man was just slightly taller than him, with broad shoulders, dark, short-cropped hair and warm brown eyes. Despite the strangeness of the situation, Alex was never slow to appreciate a hot guy, and Jason certainly fit the bill.

"Guess you don't know anything about the fatigues either."

Jason stared down at what he wearing, obviously seeing the uniform for the first time. "Damn…someone's got a bunch of explaining to do."

Around them, other men and women milled about aimlessly, obviously all wondering why they were here—and where exactly *was* here? Their attention was suddenly and noisily drawn to a raised dais onto which strode a tall, blond-haired man followed by four other men, all in military gear, all shouting for silence.

Alex's eyes widened as he recognised the blond man. "Hey," he muttered at Jason. "That guy was talking to me in the bar last night. And, funny thing is I seem to remember seeing him again later."

"Oh, yeah?" Jason gave him an appraising look.

"Nothing like that," Alex said quickly. "I'm trying to remember, but it's like…just blank. Weird."

The tall man on the dais held up his hands indicating he wanted silence. "Some of you already know who I am," he said. "To you I say, the time draws near when you will be the fighting force that will end the reign of the man who has grown weak and worthless. I, Dakar, will replace him and all of you will be richly rewarded. To those of you who are new recruits, I say, come forward and be inducted into my glorious company. Today, you will join the ranks of those who will bring me to victory."

Dakar held out his hand again and beckoned. About thirty men and women moved towards the dais. Alex exchanged a glance with Jason and gripped the other man's arm.

"No, this isn't right. We don't belong here!"

But even as he said the words, Jason jerked his arm free and followed the others heading for the dais, and despite every part of Alex's brain screaming "No!" he found he could not resist the powerful force emanating from Dakar and the other men standing next to the — the *demon*.

Then he remembered. *Oh, God, last night! On the street, Dakar and Arturo. I was on my knees before Dakar, pledging my loyalty, giving myself to them for…for…*this.

Inexorably, he felt his will slip away again and he stumbled forward, reaching out to grab Jason for support. Jason turned to him and slipped an arm around Alex's shoulders as they walked together towards the men who now stared down at them with satisfied smiles.

"I don't care for the way those two men seemed to be outside your thrall at the beginning of the ceremony."

Dakar glared with annoyance at the demon who had spoken. "They were drawn in again quickly enough, Bazul," Dakar snapped.

"Yes, but it shows a weakness within the ranks that we cannot afford." Bazul looked around at the others. "I say dispose of them now before they cause us problems."

"We need every man and woman we have recruited," Dakar said.

"We need total subservience from every man and woman," Bazul retorted, his small eyes narrowing at Dakar. "What we don't need are men or women who are not completely under our control. At the moment of our strike against Lord Kardis we must be absolutely sure of our army. Any weakness of will cannot be tolerated."

Dakar snarled silently as he stared down at the mass of men and women comprising his 'army' now being put through rigorous drills in preparation for the first strike against Kardis. He didn't want to get rid of Alex—he was a link to the vampire he still lusted after. In his mind he'd hatched another plot, one he kept hidden from his supporters. He felt sure that Andrew, at Tommy's bidding, would try to rescue Alex and would fall into his trap. Once they were face to face, Dakar in demon form this time, Andrew would bend to Dakar's will and be only too happy to join him after he had taken the throne from Kardis. Together they would rule the demon underworld—demon and vampire—they would make history as the first bonding of its kind.

Dakar was forced from his reverie by Arturo muttering at his side, "Bazul may be right, my liege, and he is powerful enough to cause dissension among the others."

"There is a way to secure their loyalty," Dakar replied, turning with an arrogant pose to glare again at Bazul. *How dare this upstart even question my purpose?* "Give them both a dose of *ger*. It will bring them to heel, and take away any doubts as to why they are here. Arturo, see to it immediately."

"*Ger*?" Bazul raised a bushy eyebrow. "It has been known to drive humans to madness, Dakar."

"Only if taken in excess," Dakar snapped. "We will ration it carefully." He looked down to where Alex and Jason were engaged in martial combat, their sweat-slicked muscles displayed in superb definition as they strained against one another. "See how well they fight, Bazul. It would be foolish to dispose of these two fine specimens. The *ger* will only add to their skill and strength. Make it so, Arturo."

Dakar pointedly ignored the scowl Bazul threw his way as Arturo left to carry out his orders

Arturo wasn't too happy either with Dakar's decision to not dispose of the two humans who had appeared, for a short time, at least, to be free of his thrall. But Arturo's displeasure was of a more personal nature than Bazul's. Arturo suspected that Dakar had not given up on his desire to make the vampire, Andrew, his mate — something that would cause a great deal of conflict, if not downright mutiny when Dakar's intentions were discovered. Such couplings were forbidden, but Arturo was sure that when Dakar defeated Kardis and replaced him as Lord, he would change the law, at the very least for his own purposes, and place Andrew on the throne at his side.

Arturo sucked in a hissing breath at the thought. The vampire was handsome without a doubt, beautiful, in fact, but even if he acquiesced to Dakar's advances, which Arturo considered highly unlikely, he would never find acceptance among the demon populace. It could mean Dakar's ruin—could he not see that for himself? Arturo was tempted to expose Dakar's obsession to Bazul and the others. That would put an end to Dakar's dreams once and for all—and yet he felt he could not betray Dakar. A small part of Arturo still hoped that one day his liege lord would look on him as more than just an accomplice to his ambition, but as a friend, perhaps even as a lover.

Maybe, once the battle had been won, Kardis and his followers destroyed, Marcus Verano ground to dust, Dakar would reward him with more than just occasionally allowing him to pleasure his liege. Perhaps if he played his cards carefully, perhaps if he used the humans to his own purposes, he could both serve his lord and stop him from making a mistake that might cost him his leadership, and his life. Arturo wasn't quite sure how he could manage all this, but if the *ger* he was about to give the humans was not at full strength, if they were not completely numbed into obedience, and if he pretended to befriend them, especially the one named Alex, then perhaps he could use them to his own ends.

His plan was not without fault, not fully formed, and certainly he was putting his own existence at risk, but as he strode across the warehouse floor towards Alex and Jason he determined that it had to be done.

* * * *

Marcus surveyed the vampires gathered in front of him. He had called an emergency meeting to relay what he had learned from Constantine. He could, of course, have informed everyone by mind message, but he considered the situation important enough for them to meet and exchange ideas as to how to deal with the danger Dakar now posed. Jared, Andrew, Joseph, Micah, Jean-Claude, Carlos and his own lover, Roger, regarded him intently as he stood before them.

"I have informed our council leader Jacob Quince and the Vampire Council of the situation," he said, "and they agree we must be prepared for any threat from Dakar. Through Bernard in Rome, Quince questioned Constantine about the likelihood of a pre-emptive strike from Kardis against Dakar. Constantine had not heard rumours of that kind, but he is sure Kardis knows exactly what is going on and is prepared for an all-out fight to the end."

"Who has the advantage?" Roger asked.

"Well, Kardis will be fighting on his own turf with an army of those most loyal to him. Dakar, from all accounts, has raised quite a considerable force, but from what I understand from Constantine, his army is partly made up of men and women he has placed in his thrall."

"So they don't really know what they're fighting for, or who Dakar really is," Andrew remarked.

"No, and I'm afraid Dakar will not act in their best interests."

"You mean they'll be like cannon fodder," Micah said.

Marcus cast a wary eye at Andrew before replying. "Yes, I'm afraid that is exactly what they will be."

"Gods, we must stop him!" Andrew paced about until Jared caught him by the arm to try and calm him.

"Yes, we must," Joseph said quietly. "Such a mindless waste of humankind cannot be allowed. Those in government who know of our existence will put the blame squarely on our shoulders. They have always looked to us to control any threat from the Underworld. We were fortunate last time, but it seems this is on a much larger and more developed scale."

"What if we were to offer our support to Kardis," Jared suggested. "That might deter Dakar from his plan for a wholesale attack."

"Join forces with demons?" Roger almost yelled. "After what they tried to do to us in Rome? Why don't we just take on Dakar and his henchmen *before* they get a chance to attack Kardis? We have enough allies — Marcus can gather support from all over — Andorra in Spain alone can whip up dozens of vampires ready and willing to beat up on some demons!"

Marcus chuckled. "Calm yourself, Roger. Both you and Jared have made valid points. It wouldn't be a bad idea to approach Kardis with an offer of support as a deterrent to Dakar, and at the same time send out the call to rally our vampire allies. But our leader, Jacob Quince, should be the one to talk with Kardis. I'll see what he thinks of the idea."

Andrew stood to one side listening to the others, but formulating his own plan. He knew what Dakar wanted along with the leadership of the Underworld. He had seen the lustful expression on Dakar's face when they had been alone. Even though it had been Tommy's face at the time, the demon's mind had been open to him and Andrew knew Dakar wanted him. How badly, he was not sure, but there was one way to find out.

"I have an idea," he said in the lull that had followed Marcus' statement. "One of us should infiltrate Dakar's stronghold and break the thrall he has over his recruits. I volunteer for that task."

"*Andrew*," Jared said in protest, "Dakar would order your immediate execution if you went anywhere near."

"No, he would not. Dakar revealed something about himself to me when still in Tommy's body. He wants to bed me—"

"All the more reason to stay away." Jared gripped Andrew's arm. "Do you think for one moment you would be safe because the demon lusts after you? He would most likely have you chained and fuck you whenever he wanted release. Demons do not possess feelings that go beyond pure physical need—they don't *love*, Andrew."

"I don't want him to love me, Jared." Andrew smiled at his ex-lover. "I will not even allow him to touch me. What I will allow is for him to think I am willing to have sex with him, that is all, and it should be enough to let me gain access to his compound and his recruits. Once there I can free them of the power he and his followers have over them."

"Man, you make it sound so easy," Roger said. "But you can't go in there alone."

"Do we even know where *there* is?" Micah asked.

Marcus nodded. "A disused airfield between here and San Diego. Some corporation had plans to construct aircraft. They had even built a giant hanger, but they had to pull out when the economy collapsed." He stared long and hard at Andrew. "Your plan has many risks, but it is a way of getting inside without harming the humans. We would have to be there close by, however, if something should go wrong. Will you agree to that, at least?"

"Yes..." Andrew squeezed Jared's arm gently. "I will be careful, and knowing you are all within reach should I need you, will give me extra courage."

"Very well..." Marcus sent Jacob Quince a mind message informing him of this latest development. "Now we need a strategy to support Andrew."

"We also need to ensure our mortal companions are unaware of what we're doing," Joseph said. "Jean-Claude, can we put their safe keeping in your hands? Perhaps you could invite them over to Ron's restaurant until we let you know we have been successful, and Dakar is no longer a threat?"

Jean-Claude nodded. "I'd rather join you in the fight, but you're right, we need to keep them all safe."

* * * *

Tommy felt a little put out when he got home and found the apartment empty. He'd had a bitch of a day. The accident on the freeway had been a bad one with multiple vehicles involved, gasoline leaking all over the tarmac, people trapped inside their cars and SUVs. *Damn, what a mess.* And he'd been worried about Alex whenever his mind hadn't been fully occupied with the task at hand.

He stripped off his sweat-stained T-shirt, pulled a beer from the fridge and headed for the shower. He'd have loved it if Andrew had been home, ready to listen about the day he'd had, kiss him and make him feel better, get in the shower with him...

"Quit whining," he muttered, dropping his pants, his boxers and stepping into the shower. "Oh, yeah, feels good." He stood under the scalding hot spray and soaped himself vigorously. *Wonder where Andrew is. Did he find out anything about Alex's disappearance?* Chief hadn't heard any more since Alex's note saying he'd quit. *Jeez, but this is so unlike Alex!*

He had to admit to a certain amount of hurt feelings that Alex hadn't confided in him about his decision to leave—not just leave—*disappear*. They were buddies, after all, and even if Tommy hadn't come clean about Andrew, they'd always shared every other aspect of their lives with one another.

Sighing, he turned off the shower and grabbed a towel, rubbing his skin hard until it tingled. In the bedroom he pulled on a pair of shorts and a T-shirt then finished off his beer. A knock at the door surprised him. They didn't get too many unannounced visitors.

"Tommy, it's Alex."

Alex, thank God! He swung the door open and welcomed his friend with a warm hug. "Jeez, Alex, you had us all worried. Are you okay?"

"I'm fine." Alex stepped back and gave Tommy a cool smile that didn't quite reach his eyes.

"But you quit without telling me—" Tommy paused as something in Alex's expression warned him that his friend was not okay. "What's wrong?"

"You need to come with me," Alex said, his smile still cool and detached. "The Master needs you."

"What?" Tommy took a step back. "What are you talking about?"

"Don't resist, Tommy. It's easier if you just give in."

"Alex." Tommy knew now without a doubt that something bad had happened to his friend. His eyes widened as a tall, dark-haired man he didn't recognise stepped into the doorway. "Who's this? What's going on, Alex? Talk to me, dammit!"

"You have to come with Jason and me," Alex said softly, at the same time palming some kind of object in his hand. "Don't fight it, Tommy."

"The hell I won't!" Alex was his friend but Tommy was damned if he'd just go *wherever* without some kind of explanation. "You tell me first what's going on!"

"Jason." Alex turned to the tall, dark man now at his side who lunged at Tommy, taking him down so easily Tommy could scarcely believe it. His muscles strained to shove the guy off him, but it was as if he were powerless. He was aware of Alex leaning over him, then a sharp stinging sensation in his neck.

"*Alex*. What...?" He felt the pressure of the man's body leave him but he lay helplessly on his back, staring up at the two men standing over him. His vision blurred and darkness overcame him as he slipped into unconsciousness.

Chapter Ten

Andrew stood at one end of a maze of catwalks that led off in several different directions. His vampire senses told him that the main part of Dakar's stronghold lay somewhere beneath his feet. The scent of human bodies was strong but he could also detect a powerful force field blocking unauthorised entry. He needed Dakar to remove the power that held the force field in place—either that or end the demon's life, effectively destroying the force field by default.

He could also sense the presence of demonkind nearby—Dakar's accomplice, who'd been with Dakar the night Alex had met them in the bar. Andrew stepped out in full sight of the sub-demon.

"How did you get in here?" Arturo snarled.

Andrew returned the sub-demon's glare with an enigmatic smile. "Easily. Your human guards cannot detect the speed with which a vampire moves."

"What do you want?"

"I wish an audience with your leader, Dakar."

"Impossible!"

"Really? I think you had better find out from Dakar himself before you make such a statement."

Arturo advanced on Andrew, his face dark with rage. "You will stay away from him. He has no use for vampires!"

"I think he has a use for this vampire," Andrew said, chuckling softly. "And I repeat, I think you had better ask Dakar if he will see me or not."

"Why tell me? Why not go directly to him?"

"Because as you know, Dakar has placed a guarding ward around his quarters. I could destroy it, but I want our meeting to be cordial."

"*Cordial?*" Arturo snickered. "He wants more from you than cordiality."

"I know what he wants and I am prepared to give it to him."

"Why? You are vampire, and one of Marcus Verano's lackeys. You are our enemy!"

"I am tired of Marcus' weak-willed philosophy," Andrew said, hoping his words held the ring of truth. "I find that what Dakar can offer me is more appealing."

"I don't believe you." Arturo grabbed Andrew by the throat and tried forcing him back towards the catwalk railing. "I think you are here to destroy us — but I will stop you!"

"No, you won't." Andrew gripped Arturo's wrist and wrenched it to one side, snapping the bone. He cut off the sub-demon's howl of pain before it was heard by breaking his neck. The sub-demon's dead weight collapsed into Andrew's arms. Quickly, he pushed the body behind some nearby packing cases then hurried towards the area he sensed was Dakar's quarters.

There were two guards standing outside, both human. Andrew hesitated. He could release them from Dakar's thrall but that would leave them confused and in a place that would suddenly appear strange to them, throwing both men into danger. Instead, he approached them, smiling.

"Lord Dakar has requested my presence." He locked eyes with one guard who nodded and made to open the door.

"Just a minute, you didn't check his identification," the other guard started to protest and stood in front of Andrew, barring his entry.

"It's all right," Andrew said softly, his eyes boring into the second guard's.

"Oh, right. Sorry, sir."

The door was swung open and Andrew passed through into Dakar's rooms.

Tommy groaned softly and raised a hand to his head. *Jeez, but it hurts. Where the hell am I?* He blinked his eyes open and stared up at Alex who was hovering over him, his face a mask of concern.

"Tommy, you all right?"

"Alex!" Tommy sat up, cursing as the pain in his head worsened. "What the hell did you do to me, and why? And who's this guy?" He glared at Alex's companion, recognising him as the one who'd taken him down so easily.

Alex knelt by Tommy's side. "Man, I am so sorry. This is Jason. We don't know what's going on. All either one of us remembers is that we were under some kind of *trance* — I guess that's the best way to describe it — but it seems to have worn off. Remember that guy I was talking to in the bar when you and Andrew met me there? You said one of them was called Arturo," Alex continued after Tommy had nodded. "He's here, and he's been giving us something to drink, we're guessing to keep us in the uh, trance. But it hasn't worked this time around. After we drove you over here the effects started to wear off, and he hasn't been back to give us more."

Tommy struggled to take in all of what Alex was saying. "So, you didn't really quit, did you?" he asked. "You were acting under some kind of spell." *Andrew will know what this is all about – but how to contact him?* He sent out a silent call for help. Andrew had told him because of their blood bond he would always know if Tommy was in trouble. He only hoped that distance didn't matter. Of course, he had no idea where they actually were.

"Where are we, anyway?"

"It's some abandoned aircraft hangar," Jason told him, speaking for the first time, "but we're not sure of the location."

"Great."

"Hey, man," Jason added. "I'm really sorry for attacking you last night. I don't know what the hell brought all that on. I've never hit anyone in my life before."

"And I've never felt so damned helpless before," Tommy said ruefully. "So, all this has got to be the work of some supernatural force."

Alex and Jason exchanged glances. "Supernatural?" Alex gripped Tommy's hand. "Hey, that drug we gave you must still be playing with your brain."

"No. Okay, I guess I'm going to have to tell you what's really going on. Andrew is a..." *Oh shit, they'll never believe this. They'll freak and think I'm really nuts.* "Is a v...is *very* into the occult. I didn't know it until I told him about your sis, Alex. Anyway, when he saw those guys with you the other night, he pegged them for...uh, for demons."

"*What?*" Both men yelled at the same time.

"Demons," Tommy said again. "There are such things. I know it's hard to believe, but how else can you explain your behaviour? In a trance, you said, under some kind of spell, doing things you didn't want to do — being here dressed in fatigues like you're in some kind of army."

"There are dozens of other guys here, women too," Jason said. "You're right, it is like an army. We've been going through a weapons drill."

"See? What's normal about any of that?"

"But *demons*, Tommy?" Alex gave him a long, hard stare. "You're actually believing this, aren't you?"

"Alex..." Tommy tightened his fingers around his friend's hand. "Believe me, I am not shitting you. They exist, and so do a lot of other...uh, strange things, too. I only hope that — "

His words were cut off as the door to the small room they were in suddenly burst open and two armed men rushed in.

"What's going on?" one of them snarled, waving an AK47 at them. "You guys are supposed to be in formation. The portal's going to be opened any time now. We're on full alert."

"Portal?" Alex turned questioning eyes on Jason.

"The portal to the Underworld! What's the matter with you?"

"Fuck me," Jason whispered, visibly shaken.

The two guards gave each other knowing looks. "They're out of the thrall," one of them muttered, his finger tightening on the AK's trigger, but before either guard could fully react Tommy charged, head down, taking them both by surprise and slamming them into the wall with enough force to momentarily stun them. Alex and Jason jumped into the fray, grabbing the weapons and turning them on the shocked guards.

"You'll die for this!" One of them, his face now twisted with rage, lunged at Alex.

Jason swung the butt of the AK at the guard's head, laying him out cold. The other tried to turn and run from the room, but Tommy's quarterback frame was blocking the doorway. He delivered a punch that should have had the guard on his back, but the man merely staggered back a step and would have been on Tommy in an instant, if Alex hadn't cracked him over the head with the butt of the AK he was holding.

"Whatever they're doing to these guys sure makes them tough as nails," Tommy said, grimacing and rubbing his knuckles. "The guy's jaw was like a rock."

"We have to get outta here," Alex said. "If we're the only ones out of the thrall like this one said, we could be in a lot of trouble!"

Dakar whirled round as Andrew entered his quarters, his expression one of comic surprise, quickly overtaken by suspicion. Then, not to Andrew's surprise, a gleam of lust appeared in the demon's eyes.

Andrew gazed at the tall, imposing figure before him. Dakar was handsome without a doubt. His long golden hair framed a face that many would consider beautiful were it not for the malicious set of his mouth, which even when stretched in a smile, as it now was, retained an impression of evil.

"Well, well. To what do I owe this pleasure?" Dakar asked, unable to hide his smirk of satisfaction.

Andrew knew that demons had only a primitive form of mind reading, but he was careful to close off his thoughts as he replied, "I read your thoughts when last we were together," Andrew replied, his voice low and sensual. "I've had time to consider them, and must agree they are more than flattering. Of course, then I was not aware of your beauty, being as you were in the form of my mortal lover."

"Ah..." Dakar took a step closer to Andrew. "And what of your mortal lover?"

"I have left him. He no longer interests me."

"Is that so?" Dakar grinned and reached out a hand to brush Andrew's cheek. "Then you will not be upset to know he has joined my army."

It took all of Andrew's powerful self-control to not show his dismay at Dakar's words. He paused for only a split second to steady his voice. "Upset? Of course not. It was inevitable, I suppose. My being vampire was not enough for him. Being possessed by you gave him illusions of something he wanted more." Andrew wasn't quite sure where those words came from, but they seemed to please Dakar.

"Then he is a fool and unworthy of you," Dakar said, spreading his arms wide in an arrogant pose, "while I, as you can see, outmatch him in every aspect. In looks, in power, and as you will soon discover, my sexual prowess is without equal."

Andrew forced his expression to remain impassive even though he wanted to laugh out loud at Dakar's hubris. Did he really believe what he'd just said? The demon took a step nearer and slipped a hand behind Andrew's neck, pulling him in close. Their bodies touched and Andrew could feel the hard arousal at Dakar's crotch. He strove to control the shudder of revulsion it brought him and fought even harder to disguise it when Dakar's thick lips covered his in a hungry kiss.

He almost sagged with relief when a thunderous knocking sounded at Dakar's door and the demon sprang away from him with a snarling curse. Left alone, Andrew hurried over to a large plate-glass window and peered through it. Below him, he could see a huge area, with a large number of men and women in military uniforms. Some were engaged in some kind of weapons drill while others showed off their martial arts skills. Behind him he could hear voices raised in anger, and the name Arturo.

They must have found his body…

He turned away from the window as Dakar strode back into the room. "One of my men has been found murdered," he snapped with a deal of impatience. "I must confer with my officers. They expect it."

"Of course." Andrew stood motionless as if waiting for Dakar to say more.

"You will wait here." Dakar's smirk was back. "We will continue when I return."

Andrew nodded and smiled, the smile vanishing as soon as Dakar turned to leave. Tommy. Gods, but I must find him before I try to release the humans from Dakar's spell. He mind melded with Marcus. *"They have Tommy captive, and there is a strong force field surrounding the humans."*

"I think it's time we came in," Marcus replied. *"Keep Dakar occupied for as long as you can while I try to shut down the force field."*

Andrew shuddered. *"Marcus, you don't know what you're asking…"*

"I think I do."

Andrew swore he could detect a chuckle in Marcus' mind. *Surely not.* He flinched as Dakar strode back into the room, but the demon was too caught up in his purpose to notice.

"So now, Andrew..." Dakar stripped off his shirt, exposing his muscled torso, "I would like to see you naked."

"What about the murdered man? How did it happen?"

Dakar made a gesture of impatience. "My officers are investigating. I have no time for that—better things await me here."

"But he was one of yours—"

"Bah! He was of no significance. Now..." He reached out and tore Andrew's shirt open. "Yes, as I thought, perfection. I will enjoy fucking you, vampire, and you will enjoy my dominion over you."

"Sorry." Andrew placed his hands on Dakar's hard chest and pushed him back. "You are working too fast for me. I don't fuck within minutes of meeting someone—even someone as handsome as yourself," he added, thinking he should stroke the demon's ego, if not his body. "You could start by offering me a glass of wine or—"

"We have no time for that!" Dakar glared at him. "Tonight my army will stage an assault on the forces led by Lord Kardis. The plan to open the portal to the Underworld is underway even as we waste time here!"

Is it now...? "*Marcus, did you hear that?*"

"*I did. We are inside and have met with no resistance so far...*"

"*Any sign of Tommy or Alex?*"

"*Not yet...*"

"What's going on?" Dakar threw Andrew an ugly look. "You are preoccupied with something other than myself. How can that be? What are you up to, vampire?" He grabbed Andrew in a powerful bear hug, their bare chests slapping together with considerable force. "You think you can play me, eh? I know what you want, and there's no one who can give it to you better than I."

"So sure of yourself?" Andrew pushed his way easily out of Dakar's embrace.

The demon grinned at him. "While I had possession of your lover's body, I was privy to his thoughts—scrambled though they were I detected remnants of a conversation you and he had about immortality. You wished to reverse it, to live your life as a mortal man, to share that life with Tommy. Is that not so?"

"It was so. It matters not at all now."

"I think you're lying. What if I told you I know how this can be done?"

"Then I'd think you were lying. Even Marcus said it was impossible. How is it possible for you to know the secret, and not Marcus?"

"Marcus!" Dakar spat out the name with contempt. "He who thinks he knows all—yet in reality, knows nothing. He would keep this secret from you to keep you at his side, regardless of your wishes."

"Then tell me how it can be done."

Dakar chuckled. "The secret lies with the Talisman of Ardocan. Have you heard of it?"

Andrew shook his head. The Talisman of Ardocan? Surely Marcus would have heard of this if it existed...

"It has the power to reverse all things, even time itself," Dakar continued airily. "With it in your grasp you could become human again."

"*The Talisman of Ardocan is a myth...*" Andrew recognised the whispered words inside his mind as coming from Marcus. "*Do not believe Dakar, Andrew. He is merely trying to keep you at his side. Joseph and I are inside...stall him for as long as you can.*"

"And where is this talisman?" Andrew asked, side stepping Dakar's attempt to reach for him.

"After I fuck you, vampire," Dakar said, smirking. "After you suck my cock and give every part of yourself to me. After I have feasted on your blood and tasted the essence of the blood lust, then I will tell you the location of the talisman and how it will help you regain your mortality." He reached for Andrew, his mouth open in readiness to claim Andrew's.

Sorry, Marcus, can't do this!

Andrew wrenched himself from Dakar's embrace, this time showing his vampire strength, ready to beat the demon senseless if necessary. Dakar's growl of annoyance was cut off by the sound of a screeching alarm and once again there came a thunderous knocking on the door. This time, though, the room was suddenly filled with armed men—all of them demons—and all of them showing their amazement at Dakar's and Andrew's states of undress.

"Dakar!" One of them, a big burly demon with long black hair and wickedly small eyes, glared at his leader. "Our defences have been compromised, Arturo has been murdered and you—you are pleasuring yourself with this...this *vampire*! What are you? Our commander or a misguided fool?"

"You dare speak to me in that manner, Bazul?" Dakar grabbed his shirt and pulled it on quickly. "I will deal with your insolence later. Right now you will inform me how we came to be compromised and by whom!"

"We don't know by *whom*," Bazul yelled, his piggy eyes fastened on Andrew. "But who is this vampire? He could be a spy, someone who helped breach the force field."

"Impossible," Dakar snapped. "He was here with me when the alarm went off and when you reported Arturo's murder."

"Shouldn't you all perhaps be investigating this break-in?" Andrew said. "Suspicions and recriminations can wait, surely, until whoever has broken in has been captured." He moved towards the door as he spoke, the demons gaping at him with surprise.

So Marcus was right — demons are slow-witted.

Bazul pushed him out of the way as he blundered into the corridor behind Andrew. More men were running towards them. "Sire!" one breathlessly addressed Bazul. "There are three renegades among us. They overpowered two guards and are armed."

"This is your doing," Bazul yelled at Dakar, spittle flying from his lips in his fury. "Dallying with this vampire instead of staying alert and in command. You are not worthy of our support!"

He turned to stride away, but Dakar pulled a knife from his belt and flung it with deadly accuracy, the blade striking Bazul between his shoulders blades. The big demon screamed then fell forward and lay still. Andrew guessed the knife blade to be poisoned for it to have killed the demon so quickly.

"So die all traitors," Dakar hissed, glaring at the others who stood staring at Bazul's lifeless form. He bent to retrieve his knife from Bazul's body. "Now, we will gather our forces together and take the throne from Kardis. If anyone else wants to challenge me, let that" — he gestured with contempt at the fallen demon — "let that serve as a lesson to you all."

Silently the demons and human guards followed Dakar, Andrew tagging along behind. Earlier, he had been aware of Tommy's cry for help, but had been unable to respond without giving away the real reason he was in Dakar's stronghold. He knew without a doubt that Tommy was one of the 'renegades'. Now he had to make sure he could reach him before Dakar took his army through the portal.

"Andrew, the Vampire Council has been successful in gaining Kardis' cooperation. When the portal opens, Dakar has a surprise awaiting him."

Marcus' message was welcome. It looked like Dakar's plans would come to nothing, but uppermost in Andrew's mind now was finding Tommy, and hopefully Alex, and getting them to safety. For if Kardis' army surged through the portal, not only would Dakar's demon soldiers be in the line of fire, but the human recruits also.

Ahead of him Dakar's guards threw open two massive doors revealing impressive lines of uniformed men and women, human and demon, all armed and standing to attention, obviously awaiting Dakar's orders. He could sense vampire presence near him and new it to be Marcus and Joseph, cloaked in invisibility. Roger and Micah, not yet having attained that particular power, would be waiting somewhere nearby for the right moment to join them. As Andrew watched, a group of guards marched in escorting three men within their ranks.

Tommy, Alex and a man Andrew did not recognise were dragged in front of Dakar. Tommy must have put up a fight. His face was bruised and his arms bleeding.

Tommy! Marcus, they have beaten him...

"*Steady, Andrew...*" Marcus' warning sounded loud and clear in Andrew's mind and he forced himself to control his desire to smash Dakar's head to a pulp then rip out his throat.

Dakar turned and flashed a vicious smile at Andrew. "See, vampire, how your ex-lover scorns not only your affection, but also my commands." He waved a hand at the guards. "Kill them, all three."

"No!"

Any vestige of the control Andrew had steeled himself with disappeared as he launched his power at the guards, knocking all of them off their feet and sending them tumbling into the ranks of the waiting soldiers. Marcus and Joseph revealed themselves and were joined by Roger and Micah, the four vampires sending out waves of power that freed the humans of Dakar's thrall. Confusion erupted as the bewildered humans milled about trying to figure out where they were and why they were wearing uniforms.

Dakar screamed his rage, ordering his demon soldiers to take control, but already some of them were shaking their heads at him, unwilling now to face the army they knew to be waiting on the other side of the disintegrating portal. Any minute now, the portal would be fully open, Kardis would appear at the head of his loyal followers, and Dakar would be forced to either challenge him, or run.

"Andrew, have Tommy get the humans out of here. I'll send Roger and Micah to help him." Marcus' words spurred Andrew into action. He had momentarily been unsure whether to attack Dakar himself or leave him for his demon lord to deal with. Ignoring the furore around them, he ran to his lover.

"Tommy, you must lead the men and women away from what is about to happen. Roger and Micah will help you. Go quickly!"

"But what about you?" Tommy gripped Andrew's arm. "I can't leave you to deal with all this with just Marcus and Joseph at your back."

"Believe me, they are more than enough—now go, please!"

Reluctantly, Tommy turned to Alex and Jason who were staring at him slack-jawed with amazement. "Let's go Alex," he muttered. "Explanations come later. Follow those two vam...uh...guys. We need to get out of here."

"No argument from me," Alex said, grabbing Jason's arm. "Let's get the hell outta here!"

Chapter Eleven

At Marcus' instruction, the humans were herded away from the demons by Roger and Micah, and not a moment too soon, for with a sizzling blast the portal to the Underworld opened and Kardis, in full battledress, appeared at the head of his demon horde.

"Dakar!" he roared. "Surrender or die!"

Marcus and Joseph stepped between the two enemies. "Kardis," Marcus said, the power of his voice carrying over the chaotic noise that had erupted when the portal opened. "There are innocent men and women here, who are not part of your war with Dakar. Allow them to leave before taking your vengeance on Dakar and his followers."

"All here are my enemies!" Kardis' grating voice was filled with venom. "All will die! Stand aside, vampires, or be destroyed along with Dakar and his miserable cowards."

"That was not the agreement you struck with the Vampire Council," Marcus said quietly, now that silence filled the air and all seemed struck into immobility. "Renege on your promise at your peril, Kardis."

"I care nothing for the Vampire Council. Now stand aside—"

Marcus shrugged and gestured above him. "I was afraid you might be this much of a fool, so I arranged for some reinforcements to help change your mind."

From everywhere the air above them teemed with vampires led by Jared, Carlos, and Jacob Quince himself. Hovering overhead, their pale faces, set in hard, determined expressions, had some of the humans screaming with terror. Using this diversion, Roger and Micah swung the giant hangar doors open and the men and women streamed through to the outside and safety.

"You too," Roger said, seeing Tommy hang back.

"I'm not leaving Andrew! And don't go giving me the evil eye either, Roger, or you and me will have a falling out."

"Damn it, Tommy. Marcus will give me hell for this. Okay, but stay close to Micah and me—got it?"

"Got it."

"Okay, wait here while I make sure none of these people remember anything of this."

"How are we going to get them back to Los Angeles?" Tommy asked.

"There's a bunch of vehicles that I guess were used to transport them here," Micah told him. "They'll work it out, I'm sure."

When Roger returned they closed the hangar doors then hurried back to the main throng where a kind of impasse was in place. Jacob Quince, the head of the Vampire Council, had joined Marcus and Joseph at their position between the two warring factions. Kardis was conferring with two of his officers while

Dakar stood alone, his followers having seemingly deserted him.

Andrew regarded the demon without sympathy but with some curiosity. Had he been speaking the truth about the Talisman of Ardocan? Could it be possible that Marcus was wrong, and that it actually did exist? He was about to probe Dakar's mind for the truth of it when, startled, he saw Tommy accompanied by Roger and Micah running to his side.

"Tommy, you were supposed to leave with the others!"

"I told you I wasn't leaving you, and I'm not," Tommy said defiantly, slipping an arm around Andrew's waist. "So get over it." He jumped a little when the vampires who had been hovering silently overhead dropped to the ground as if as one, completely surrounding the perimeter of the hanger. "Jeez, there's a lot of 'em. Where did they all come from?"

"From everywhere," Andrew whispered as if that was answer enough.

"What'll happen, d'you think?" Tommy whispered back.

"Dakar will die, one way or the other."

"Oh."

"It will not be pleasant. That's why I didn't want you here to witness it."

"What? They goin' to chop off his head?"

"Something like that — eventually."

Tommy swallowed, hard. Eventually...

"So, Lord Kardis..." This time Jacob Quince was the one to address the demon lord. "What is your decision? The humans have been taken to safety. Dakar has been deserted by his so-called allies. There is no war to fight, unless you mean to take all of us on—something I really would not encourage."

After a moment or two, Kardis muttered, "Dakar and those who betrayed me must be punished."

"Absolutely," Quince said with a smile. "By all means, take them back to your realm and do with them what you will. But let this be over soon. The portal must be closed and sealed from this side—agreed?"

"Agreed." Kardis ordered his cohorts to start rounding up Dakar's men who put up little to no resistance. But when Dakar was led before Kardis, he roared his defiance.

"Kardis, you coward! I challenge you to fight me—show all here that you are not afraid of me. You think you can have me executed like a common criminal? That will never happen!"

Kardis, obviously only too willing to show his fellow demons that he was their rightful leader and Dakar nothing more than a rebellious upstart, threw aside his gun and started to pull his sword from its scabbard. But Dakar, moving with lightning speed before Kardis could arm himself, whipped out the knife with which he had killed Bazul. Leaping forward he plunged the dagger into Kardis' neck. The demon lord shrieked in agony and fell to his knees clutching at his bleeding neck. His eyes glazed over as the poison on the blade took effect.

Chaos ensued. Dakar's followers, suddenly inflamed with courage at the sight of their leader's action, turned on their stunned captors, wrenching guns and knives from them and striking them down before they could react.

Andrew grabbed Tommy and hustled him away from the fray. The vampires pulled back, watching in silence as the demons struggled for dominance, bodies on both sides falling from gunshot and knife wounds. Then, at a silent command from Jacob Quince, the vampires began to move forward, presenting a formidable wall of power that caused the demons to falter in their struggle and back up towards the open portal.

Dakar tried to rally his forces, yelling at them to stand and fight. A few hastened to obey but were thrown back by a mere gesture from any vampire they got too close to. Dakar was a vision of fury, his eyes blazing with rage at the line of vampires that moved inexorably towards him and his diminished army.

"You know you are beaten, Dakar," Marcus told the furious demon. "The only way out is through the portal. Go back to your world and face the consequences of your actions."

Dakar's gaze settled on Andrew. "You! Traitor! First you would betray your lover and your own kind. Now that the tide has turned you would betray me!"

"There can be no betrayal where there was no kinship," Andrew said quietly. "My coming to you was merely a ruse —"

"Then die!" Dakar screamed and threw his poisoned dagger straight at Andrew.

There was a blurred movement and the knife was stopped short, the blade a mere inch from Andrew's chest, the handle grasped securely in Andrew's hand. Then out of nowhere a figure sprang on top of Dakar, dragging him to the ground, punching him about the head over and over. Cursing, the demon threw his assailant off and jumped to his feet, his face a mask of fury. Then he laughed when he realised his attacker was Tommy, the mortal's face bone white with anger. Tommy rolled over onto the balls of his feet ready to attack again.

"You think you can best me, human?"

"Yeah!" Tommy yelled, raising his fists. "Stick your powers up your ass for a minute or two, and I'll beat the shit outta you."

"Well, that's not going to happen." Dakar grabbed a gun from a nearby demon and pointed it at Tommy. "You won't be able to stop the bullet!"

Without hesitation, Andrew hefted Dakar's knife in his hand and threw it with deadly aim at the demon. With a choking cry of agony, Dakar staggered back, his hands trying to pry loose the blade thrown with such force it had pierced his throat and protruded from the back of his neck. In a flash Andrew closed the distance between Tommy and himself and flung his arms around him. Together they watched as the demon who had plagued their lives, and endangered so many more, fell dying at their feet. As the other vampires gathered around, the remaining demons, both sides now leaderless, disappeared through the portal into the darkness beyond.

"Now it can be sealed shut," Quince murmured to Marcus. "But first we should make sure all evidence of the conflict is erased from this place." The vampires went about collecting the bodies of the dead demons, including Dakar and Kardis, dragging them into the tunnel beyond the portal. "Let their own kind deal with disposing of them as they see fit."

* * * *

It was long after midnight by the time Tommy and Andrew left the hangar. Tommy watched with awe as the vampires who had answered Marcus' call silently lifted off into the night sky and disappeared.

"Carlos and Jared are following the humans back to LA," Marcus informed Tommy. "I told Jared to make sure your friend Alex ends up in some familiar surroundings so he won't feel disoriented. The Blue Moon seemed like a good idea."

"Thanks, Marcus, that's his home away from home." Tommy's smile changed to a frown as he remembered. "Only problem is he quit his job and he's not going to remember doing that. It'll be a shock for him when Chief Lambert questions him about it."

"Then we must make sure Chief Lambert doesn't ask such questions."

"How're you going to do that? Everyone at the station will know by now."

Roger chuckled. "You would question the powers of the mighty Marcus Verano? It's already done, Tommy, my friend. No one at the station will remember Alex quitting."

"What? But how...?"

"Magic by Marcus." Roger rolled his eyes. "I swear he could take care of all these pesky problems caused by demons and vampire hunters and rogue vampires with the blink of an eye. He just likes to see us swing into action now and then. Keep us on our toes."

Marcus laughed and ruffled Roger's hair. "You do love to exaggerate, don't you?"

"But seriously, Marcus," Tommy asked anxiously, "Roger's right? No one will remember Alex quitting? He left the chief a note."

"Ah, yes. Thanks for reminding me." Marcus blinked an eye. "Gone."

Tommy gaped while the vampires laughed at his slack-jawed expression. "Oh. My. God!"

"Hey, you don't live for eighteen hundred plus years and not learn a thing or two, you know," Roger said, still laughing.

"Call your friend when you get home, Tommy," Marcus said smiling. "I am certain you will find he is just fine."

"Thank you, Marcus." Tommy hesitated for just a moment then flung his arms around the handsome vampire and hugged him tight.

"You are welcome, Tommy. Now let Andrew take you home, and um...take care of that black eye."

Tommy looked around for one of the vehicles Micah had said were there, and could see not one. "Oh no," he groaned.

"What's wrong?" Andrew asked with a little smile.

"There's no car or bus or anything left. That means—well, you know what that means. I can tell from the way you're grinning like a Cheshire cat, you know exactly what that means!"

"Tommy, édesem, you know I would never let you fall from my arms."

"I know that! It's just that, everybody laughs at me 'cause I keep my eyes closed the whole time."

"No one will see but me." Andrew leaned in and kissed Tommy's lips gently. "Besides, you're beautiful even with your eyes closed." He wrapped his arms around Tommy's muscular body. "Ready?"

Tommy held on tight. "Ready as I'll ever be." And together they flew off into the darkness.

Below them their vampire friends watched them speed upwards towards the clouds. Roger nudged Micah. "Wanna bet Tommy's got his eyes closed?"

Micah chuckled. "Not something I'd bet against—I'd be as well just giving you my money right now!"

* * * *

Andrew pressed a kiss to Tommy's cheek as they landed on the balcony of their apartment. "There, safe and sound," he murmured.

"Jeez, I always feel like such a wuss when we do that." Tommy shook his head ruefully. "And it's not like I think you'll drop me or anything. I don't even like flying in a plane." He slid the glass door open and they stepped inside. "Anyway, I better call Alex and make sure he's okay."

He pulled his cell from his jeans pocket and punched in his friend's speed number. "Hey, Alex, Tommy. You okay?" The sound of loud music and voices filled his ear.

"Never been better. I'm at the Blue Moon. You and Andrew comin' over?"

"No, it's a bit late. We're about to turn in. I'll see you later."

"Yeah, later, bro. Hey wait, did we ever meet a guy by the name of Jason?"

"Uh...can't quite recall, sorry. Why?"

"Well, it's the darnedest thing, but he's here. We started talking, y'know, and it was like we'd met each other before, but for the life of me I can't think where, and he can't either, that's the crazy thing, but Tommy, I swear I've spent time with him. I mean, not like that... I think I'd remember if we'd, you know, *done it*. He's hot, Tommy."

The rush of words made Tommy smile, glad Alex and Jason had connected again. "Well," he said, "that sounds like it's karma, Alex. Meant to be, that kind of thing."

"Yeah." Alex's voice sounded wistful.

"Is he there now with you?"

"He's getting us a drink. Oh, here he comes. I'll talk with you later, Tommy. G'night."

"'Night, Alex." Tommy closed his cell. "He's fine, just like Marcus said he would be. God, but that guy is amazing. I mean, you're all amazing, but he's like *super* amazing."

Andrew chuckled then drew Tommy into his arms. "Do I sense a rival for your affections?" he asked, nuzzling Tommy's earlobe.

"Absolutely not." Tommy tightened his arms around Andrew. "You gonna kiss my black eye better?"

"Already done, while we were flying home."

"I wondered why it had stopped hurting like a son of a bitch. I should've known..."

"*Szeretlek*, Tommy," Andrew murmured.

"Right back at ya, my vampire." He traced the outline of Andrew's lips with the tip of his tongue. "Sometimes I still have to pinch myself to make sure the time I've spent with you hasn't just been some kind of crazy, wonderful dream." He slipped his tongue inside Andrew's mouth for another long and hungry kiss.

"You know," he said when they paused and shared a smile, "when I think of all that could've gone wrong in the last few days, and especially tonight, my blood runs cold. That Dakar—are all demons such assholes? And the other one, Kardis, was no better."

"Demons are what their name suggests—demonic." Andrew took Tommy's hand and led him towards the bedroom. "There might be a few exceptions, but they lack skilled leadership, and their allegiances are easily swayed. Lord Kardis ruled for a very short span of time—something he had in common with his many, many predecessors."

"You mean they don't have the same kind of loyalty like you guys have for Marcus."

"Right. And don't forget Jacob Quince, the head of the Vampire Council. He was elected our leader before even I was born."

"So you guys are tight. That's good." Tommy leered at Andrew and began unbuttoning his shirt. "And speaking of tight…"

Andrew laughed. "Oh, my Tommy… I will never stop loving your one-track mind."

"Just never stop loving me," Tommy murmured, sliding his hands inside Andrew's shirt, caressing the smooth, cool skin that covered the sleek musculature of his back. "Mmm, you feel so damned good." He eased Andrew down onto the bed and began slowly stripping him. "Don't do that thing you do—you know, where our clothes just vanish. Great as that is, I want to take things slow tonight. I want to love every part of you, and thank whoever's in charge that after all we've been through, I still have you here in my arms…"

"Forever."

"Yeah, forever."

Tommy laid a kiss in the hollow of Andrew's throat then licked a trail over Andrew's jaw to his lush lips. Their tongues entwined, sliding, caressing, filling each other's mouths with a sensuality that drove the thoughts of 'going slow' from Tommy's mind. He tore at Andrew's belt, tugging it free. He yanked Andrew's jeans down, exposing the impressive bulge behind the sheer cotton of his boxer briefs. Tommy groaned and fell on it like a starving man, laving the outlined length through the flimsy material, shucking off his own shirt and jeans as he did so. Andrew's hips bucked upwards and he choked out a moan as

Tommy slid the briefs down and took all of Andrew's cock into his mouth, swirling his tongue up and down the hard, pulsing shaft.

Andrew gasped, his hands raking Tommy's thick hair. "You'll make me disgrace myself by coming too soon."

"No disgrace," Tommy mumbled, then raised his eyes to Andrew's and smiled. "Wanna taste you first anyway... Come for me." He swirled his tongue over the head of Andrew's cock, scooping up the pre-cum, sliding up and down the underside before he took it all back into his mouth. Gently, he teased Andrew's balls with his fingers, then dipped under to stroke his perineum. He inched one finger towards the ring of muscle around Andrew's opening, gently probing the sensitive flesh. He withdrew his finger and released Andrew's cock for a moment to moisten his fingers with his saliva, then slipped them back between Andrew's ass cheeks, continuing to circle his eager hole before pushing one then two in, gliding over Andrew's prostate.

Andrew's hips arched upwards in ecstasy then he bore down on Tommy's fingers, drawing them up inside him. The growl of pleasure that came from deep in his throat was both primal and electrifying, inflaming Tommy's senses, causing him to suck even harder, wanting, needing to feel the rush of Andrew's semen. Andrew cried out as he came, his creamy seed coating Tommy's tongue and the roof of his mouth. He gulped it all down, pumping Andrew's cock with his fist until every last vestige was drained from him.

After a few moments, Andrew eased Tommy up in his arms until their lips were level with each other, then took his mouth in a bruising kiss that had Tommy's already painful erection begging for release.

He gasped as Andrew flipped him over onto his back and reached for the lube they kept handily on top of the nightstand.

"You're hard again. You're so fucking amazing."

Andrew silenced him with another long, hard kiss and hoisted Tommy's legs on either side of his waist. The lube was cool on Tommy's pucker, warming as Andrew slid a finger inside, warmer still as another finger joined the first.

"Oh, yeah..." Tommy let his head fall back on the pillow and gave himself up to the ecstasy he knew would follow as Andrew withdrew his fingers and replaced them with the head of his cock. He raised his legs higher and Andrew pushed forward. He cupped his hands around Andrew's butt cheeks, pulling him in deeper, all the way to the hilt. His eyes rolled back in his head as Andrew moved inside him, a slow, rhythmic back and forth that made Tommy see stars with each pass of Andrew's hot, hard flesh over his prostate.

"Beautiful," he whispered. "Mmm, just like that..." Their bodies rocked together in unison, and Tommy felt himself edging towards a near delirious euphoria he knew only Andrew could bring him to. He clutched at Andrew's wide shoulders, locking eyes with him, turning his neck in invitation.

Andrew nuzzled the hot, slick skin, inhaling the aroma of Tommy's maleness and the sweet blood that pulsed beneath his lips. He bit down, tightening his arms around Tommy's body, blocking the initial pain he knew his bite would bring. The blood flowed over his tongue and his senses reeled from the infusion of the sustenance he craved, could not exist without. Beneath him, Tommy moaned, a sound that seemed wrenched from his very soul. Their bodies cleaved together as Andrew drank from his lover, their connection now transcending the physical, binding their hearts and minds together.

Tommy climaxed, his guttural cry one of triumph as his hot cum jetted between their writhing torsos. Andrew tore his mouth away from Tommy's throat, sealed the wound with his saliva then took Tommy's lips with a kiss that was almost brutal in its intensity. He gasped as his orgasm rushed through him, his scalding semen filling Tommy with such force that he arched upwards off the bed, clinging to Andrew as though his life depended on it.

* * * *

"Tommy…"

"Yeah?" Tommy stretched his sated body out, pressing and rubbing every inch of himself over Andrew's nakedness. "What's up?" he asked, nuzzling Andrew's neck.

"Something Dakar said has been rankling in my mind, although I think it was said only to make me want to stay by his side."

Tommy snorted. "Had to have been a lie then."

"Mmm. Most likely, but it was intriguing nevertheless."

"What did he say?"

"He said he knew of a way to give me back my mortality."

Tommy stiffened then sat up, swiping at the hair that had fallen over his forehead. He stared at Andrew long and hard. "Andrew, I thought we were finished with that conversation. Marcus told you it was impossible, that you would age quickly, even die."

"I know. It's just that I love you so much, Tommy, I want our relationship to be everything you want it to be, and you no longer fearing being left behind as the years go by. I know it still bothers you from time to time, and I understand the reasons. If I could find a way to be...*human* again, I would."

"But it's not possible," Tommy said. He lay down again and slid an arm under Andrew's shoulders, holding him close. "And I don't want you trying anything a fucking demon might think he knows. Marcus says they're all liars, slow-witted even, so how could any one of them know something like that?"

"You're right." Andrew sighed then kissed Tommy's cheek. "It will just have to remain an unfulfilled wish of mine. I love you, Tommy."

"Love you too."

They lay quietly again in each other's arms, their thoughts open to one another, Tommy wishing he could will time to stop and leave them forever like this.

Then he said quietly, "Change me."

"What?" Startled, this time Andrew sat up and stared at his lover with widening eyes.

"Change me. That way we'll both have what we want. You and me, together forever."

Tears stung Andrew's eyes. "Tommy, thank you for offering me your life, but as much as I want you by my side forever, I don't want you to make this sacrifice."

"I'll do it for you."

"And I love you for that, but everything would change for you, Tommy. Everything. You worry now about your friends and family noticing that you don't age, but as an immortal, as a vampire, it would be even more obvious to them that you are...*different*. It would put restraints on all your relationships, you could no longer be a fireman, something you love doing..."

"I love doing you more," Tommy said with a quirky smile.

Andrew chuckled softly. "Oh, Tommy my love, there's that one-track mind again."

"That won't change, ever. No matter how old I get. So..." Tommy stroked Andrew's silken hair, running it through his fingers, his smile now rueful. "...you don't want me to be like you?"

"There is nothing I would like more. To be side by side with you through eternity would be a dream come true."

"Well, then..."

"It's not something you should decide to do in the spur of the moment," Andrew said quickly, "or in the afterglow of our lovemaking. Only when you have given it a great deal of thought." He lay down again and rested his head on Tommy's shoulder, gently caressing Tommy's chest as he continued. "But the mere fact that you would even consider it, I think has made me happier than I ever thought I could be."

"That's good..." Tommy kissed Andrew's forehead. "And just so you know, I meant every word. I never thought I'd want to spend the rest of my life—never mind eternity—with any one guy, but you've already changed me in so many ways, so the next step is really a given."

"After you have *given* it a great deal of thought," Andrew said, tapping Tommy's chest with his forefinger.

"Yeah, after that." Tommy turned his head to grin at Andrew. "So, in the meantime, here we are, in bed, both nekkid. What d'you suppose we should do now?"

Andrew laughed softly. "Let's just follow that one-track mind of yours."

* * * *

Much later, while Tommy lay fast asleep, Andrew slipped from his lover's embrace and rose from the bed. Silently, he moved across the carpeted floor to gaze through the window at the moonlit sky. Somewhere out there, he thought, maybe, just maybe there is such an artefact as the Talisman of Ardocan.

And what if it could, as Dakar had said, reverse all things?

He could not only regain his mortality, live with Tommy as a human, love him for the rest of *their* lives, grow old with him — but he could also go back in time and save his brother Michael's life. Could these things really be possible?

Marcus had said the talisman was a myth, and Andrew felt he had to bow to the Master Vampire's knowledge — surely after all the centuries of his existence, if the talisman was real, Marcus would have some idea of its location. Then again, if he chose to believe it to be merely a myth, why would he even bother to find out?

Dakar had said he knew of its location, had dangled that tantalising piece of information in front of Andrew's mind, knowing no doubt that he would forever wonder as to its veracity. But Dakar was dead, Kardis too, the secret to be buried with them both, if indeed Kardis knew of it — if indeed *Dakar* really knew of it. Demons are consummate liars, he reminded himself with a wry twist to his lips. And even if the talisman did exist, where in this great wide world would he begin to search for it?

He turned away from the window and gazed for a long moment at the face of the man he loved with every fibre of his being. How could he ever leave him behind? How could he exist without him?

"Change me," Tommy had said.

And in doing so, he was offering to give up all he knew, to spend the rest of his existence, for what could very possibly be an eternity, with me. Andrew smiled and bent down to kiss Tommy's cheek. Whatever the outcome, whatever the Fates had in store for them, their love would last. *Of that I am sure...*

BLOOD TALISMAN

Dedication

My thanks to Sue Meadows, my editor, for her help in completing this story.

For Phil, always

Chapter One

The tall, dark-haired man stood outside the Los Angeles Central Library gazing up for a moment at the imposing Egyptian-themed edifice. Artfully illuminated at night time, each carefully carved symbol of the ancient world stood out in stark relief against the white-stone walls.

A wry smile touched his handsome, finely featured face as he contemplated the fact that the setting at least was appropriate for what he sought. The world of antiquity might just hold the key to unlocking the mystery he was determined to solve. Much of what he wanted for his lover and himself, might rely on the answers, positive or negative, he was convinced he would find within a certain tome housed somewhere in the archives of this building.

In just a few minutes the library would close for the night. He wasted no time, quickly passing through the main doors into the cavernous marble-lined entry hall. He smiled at the security guard, knowing that he was about to tell him, 'Sorry, we're closing'. Instead, the guard returned his smile — the power behind those ice-blue eyes immediately making the guard forget that the tall man dressed in a full-length black leather coat who now strode past him with purpose towards the door that plainly read 'No Admittance' had actually pushed it open and had disappeared.

The guard stood to one side as the library's employees and a few stragglers exited, then he locked the doors and walked over to the security desk. Apart from the routine checks he would make periodically he would stay at his post until he was relieved at midnight by the graveyard shift.

Andrew Berés descended the flight of stairs leading to the underground archives. It was dark, the power having been turned off in any unnecessary areas of the library. Not that it deterred Andrew. He could see in the dark better than any cat, or bat, for that matter. His vampire vision could pick out anything within the murky recesses of the basement.

If I were the Talisman of Ardocan – where would I hide?

If not the Talisman itself—and it did seem unlikely that it would actually be among the artefacts and documents piled high before him—at least some mention of it, be it myth or reality. Somewhere here, there must be some clue, a cross reference perhaps pertaining to its existence, or non.

Andrew's laser-sharp vision seared through the closed document boxes and crates, negating some as useless, pausing over others that looked as though they might be interesting, before dismissing them and moving on to the next box.

Marcus Verano, the most powerful of all vampires, had told Andrew he feared the Talisman did not exist, and at the time Andrew had been prepared to accept Marcus' scepticism, yet the demon Dakar had insisted that it was indeed real. If Andrew were to doubt either man's word, it would certainly be that of Dakar — a devious and treacherous demon, now dead. Dakar had inhabited Andrew's lover's body then had tried to seduce Andrew himself, all the while betraying his king by gathering a rebel force to usurp Kardis and take control of the Underworld region Kardis governed.

Yet hope, mingled with some doubt, remained in Andrew's heart.

His lover, Tommy, was a brave and beautiful man with whom Andrew wished to spend the rest of his existence. But Tommy was mortal and worried that as he grew older Andrew would leave him for someone younger. Despite Andrew's protestations to the contrary, he knew that in Tommy's darker moments that fear still existed, and with it a wish that Andrew, too, was mortal, and that they would grow old together. Something that, as the months had passed, and their love had become stronger, deeper, Andrew had longed for with all his heart.

Tommy had offered to give him his lifeblood, had pledged to accept the 'change' despite the fact he would be distanced from his family and friends, something Andrew knew tore at Tommy's heart and conscience. Because of his lover's willingness to sacrifice his closeness with those he held dear, Andrew was determined to at least try to find an alternative.

He had not mentioned his quest to anyone, not even to Tommy. Why build up hopes within him if the search should prove fruitless after all? Nor had he told his best friend Jared Lantos, although he knew Jared would not judge his actions. Jared also had a mortal lover. Although frowned on by certain segments of vampire society, it was not all that unusual for vampires' companions to be human. A regular infusion of vampire blood kept a mortal's youthful appearance, delaying the aging process and giving him or her many more years of life. But they were not immortal, and eventually a decision would have to be made...

Andrew paused in his search and a shudder ran through his body. The thought of losing Tommy was not something he could accept, nor the desolation he knew he would feel as keenly as a wooden, silver-tipped stake to his heart.

There must be an answer! Somewhere in all of this there must be a clue, however small, however remotely connected to the Talisman itself. Something to give hope...

Despair filled him as he neared the final row of boxes. Perhaps Marcus was right after all, and Dakar would be proven a liar, perpetuating the demon reputation for evading the truth at all costs. Or perhaps, his search — though fruitless here as it had been in New York and Washington D.C. — should continue in some other archive — in Paris or Athens or — He paused again, a flicker of recognition dancing before his eyes.

The word, Ardocan.

He strode towards a wooden box, securely bound with metal straps. A flick of his hand and the straps fell away. Quickly he delved inside and pulled out a file, tattered and yellowed with age. His fingers skimmed over the worn pages, his eyes scanning each one with supernatural speed.

There it was... *'The Myth of Ardocan. Findings of Arnold Metcalfe, July 1874'.*

Myth. Andrew's brow furrowed with a frown of disappointment. It was after all, only a myth?

"Lost in the mists of time, the existence of the legendary City of Ardocan has proven to be beyond discovery of even the most ardent explorers.

A city — not just a talisman.

The city was first mentioned in the Scrolls of Ashelak, one of the many Hittite princes raised to deity status, and it has long been sought without success, most of the research having been lost or destroyed."

Andrew's shallow breath caught in his chest, excitement flooding his powerful blood. The fact that men knew enough about it to actually search for it must mean that there were other writings, other theories, other possibilities. A smile touched his lips. That which had seemed out of his reach, a myth, now perhaps could become more of a reality. Yes, what he was reading described Ardocan as no more than a legend, but many legends were rooted in fact. Fact that could become less believable with time, for sure. The fabric of reality sometimes fashioned to suit a particular purpose. Yet now it was believed that the walls of Troy had been found. Troy, a legendary city that had existed and been destroyed before even Marcus Verano's existence. Was it possible then, that Ardocan could be uncovered, or at least the secrets it had once held — such as the Talisman?

The Scrolls of Ashelak. Would Marcus know of these scrolls? He'd said the Talisman's existence was rooted in myth. No doubt he'd point out that the city bore that same clouded history, but the Scrolls of Ashelak somehow had the ring of authenticity.

Something else to search for…

He concentrated his efforts now on a new search, but after scanning and rescanning the boxes and crates, he bitterly had to admit defeat. Nowhere here was there any sign of the scrolls.

Where then?

Carefully, he removed the several pages containing the reference to Ardocan, replaced the file in the box and sealed it again, making sure the metal straps appeared untouched. One day, he would return these pages to their rightful place in the library archives, but right now they just might be the means with which he could change his destiny. His slowly beating heart quickened with anticipation. He would show his discovery to Marcus and ask him about the scrolls. Yet, he knew, that should the Master Vampire try to dissuade him from any further research on the matter, he would have to ignore his advice. This was too important to both Tommy and himself to disregard, no matter what others might think or say.

Tommy. He glanced at his watch. His lover would be getting off shift at the firehouse right about now, and he wanted to be there to greet him when he got home. He rolled the pages gently like a scroll, then slipped them into his coat's inside pocket.

Moving like a silent shadow he climbed the stairs to the library's main floor and, again unseen by the dozing security guard, left the building.

* * * *

Andrew alighted on the balcony of the new apartment he and Tommy had moved into two months earlier. It had taken Andrew quite an effort to have Tommy okay the idea of giving up the smaller apartment he'd lived in for the past three years, but eventually Andrew had succeeded without using his 'other' powers of persuasion. Only some gentle loving had been necessary along with a deal of whining that Tommy's apartment wasn't big enough for two grown men. One of his 'selling' points was the fact the new apartment building sported a pool and a workout room, both high on Tommy's wish list. High on Andrew's list had been a room he could use as an office for his ongoing research. The apartment, being on the top floor, also had vaulted ceilings that gave it an open airy feeling, a welcome contrast to the busy, crowded streets of Los Angeles.

After discarding his leather coat, he retrieved the rolled-up pages he'd purloined from the library and quickly slid them into the bottom drawer of his desk. He'd tell Tommy about them later, after he'd talked to Marcus. He walked back into the living room just as the door in the entryway to the apartment opened.

"Hey..." Tommy's smile and husky voice always stirred desire in Andrew, and this night, though his mind was still filled with unanswered questions, was no different. Andrew strode into the young blond fireman's open arms, returning the deep, thrilling kiss Tommy placed on his lips. Tommy's hot breath filled Andrew's mouth, sending his senses reeling and his blood rushing south to his cock that pressed hard and proud against the erection he could feel behind Tommy's chinos.

Andrew inhaled his lover's scent, soap and clean sweat and the essence that was now uniquely Tommy—a combination of his own musk and the spicy overlay from the vampire blood Andrew had imbued him with.

Tommy broke off their kiss to say, "I showered at the station. Didn't want to waste time getting you into bed."

"I love the fact that your one-track mind is still firmly in place," Andrew said, teasing him. "But aren't you hungry?"

"Only for you." Tommy fisted Andrew's long, ink-black hair, drawing their mouths together again in another long, deep kiss. His muscles bulged as he lifted Andrew off his feet and carried him towards the bedroom.

Andrew chuckled. "What's this?"

"Oh, I know you can carry me with one hand behind your back, or no hands at all come to think of it." Tommy grinned as he deposited Andrew on the bed, then straddled his thighs. "But I've been sportin' this hard-on all day, just thinking about fucking you, so let me take control of this."

Andrew lay back and smiled up at him as Tommy pulled his T-shirt up over his head and unbuttoned his chinos. He hadn't put his briefs back on after his shower at the station and his impressive erection sprang free as he unzipped his fly. He leant down and ripped Andrew's shirt open, devouring first one of the pebbled nibbles on Andrew's smooth chest, then the other. Andrew groaned and started to ease himself out of his jeans but Tommy's big hands stopped him.

"Let me," Tommy whispered, hooking his fingers into the waistband and sliding the denim over Andrew's narrow hips. "Oh, yeah…" With one hand he gripped Andrew's cock at the base. Squeezing gently, he forced a glistening pearl-like drop from the slit then swiped at it with his tongue to savour the spicy pre-cum. "You taste so damned fine," he murmured between licks and before taking the rigid flesh into his mouth. He was rewarded not only by the sharp edge to the taste of Andrew's pre-cum but also by the soft moans of ecstasy that escaped his vampire lover's lips.

Tommy always got an extra sexual charge from the sound of Andrew's moans and the fact he was the one inducing them. Maybe in the years ahead he'd get used to it, maybe. But right now, the low hum that caressed his ears made him even harder than he'd been a moment before—and that had been hard. So hard it ached and Tommy couldn't wait to push that hardness inside Andrew, to feel that tight grip on his shaft, to plunge in and out and bring Andrew and himself to that state of near-delirium they experienced every time they made love. Tommy knew he and Andrew shared that ecstasy together because of the way their minds melded at the moment of climax. And Tommy loved that. There was no pretence, no faking in their relationship. After less than two years together, they knew each other's needs so well.

"Wanna fuck you," he whispered, raising his head to smile into Andrew's eyes.

"Want you to," Andrew said, raising his hips and presenting his ass to Tommy's eager mouth. "Want to feel every hard and wicked inch of you deep inside me."

Tommy tongued his way into the cleft between Andrew's cheeks, circling the hole with slow, rhythmic precision that had Andrew's moaning no longer soft, but harsh and demanding. Oh, yeah... Tommy added a finger, probing deep into Andrew's silken channel, finding the sensitive gland that had his lover clutching at the sheets in a near-frenzy.

Andrew grabbed him by the shoulders, pulling him up until he was kneeling between Andrew's muscular thighs. His erection throbbed in his hand as he guided it into Andrew's opening, filling him with the heat of his pulsing shaft. Andrew groaned, encircling Tommy's torso with his legs, his fingers teasing Tommy's nipples causing his breath to hitch in his chest. He leant down to take Andrew's mouth with his, their tongues tussling, caressing, gliding into the innermost reaches of each other's moist warmth.

The intensity of their lovemaking increased. The long, slow rhythmic thrusts Tommy had begun quickened as the need to release his pent-up ardour burned hot in his blood. The feel of Andrew's satin-smooth skin against the palms of his hands, the hard muscle under that smoothness, the silken heat that gripped his cock all combined to take him closer and closer to the brink of orgasm. His eyes rolled back in his head and he shuddered in the throes of his ecstasy.

"Andrew!" His throaty cry was muffled by Andrew's lips on his. Their arms tightened around each other as Tommy emptied himself into his vampire lover's depths. Andrew sucked on Tommy's tongue while his body spasmed and bucked beneath Tommy, his scalding release spraying over both their chests.

A long, shaky sigh escaped Tommy. He broke their kiss only long enough to say, "You're sensational, babe. Truly fucking sensational." Then he pressed his lips to Andrew's neck, nuzzling and nibbling at the smooth skin.

"You are quite good yourself." Andrew chuckled and patted Tommy's butt.

Tommy raised his head and gave him a mock glare. "Quite good? Lucky for you I know you're kidding. See, I can get into that mind of yours too at times. 'Specially these times. And right now, I know you're happier than a kid in a candy store."

"And because neither one of our erections has yet diminished." Andrew clenched his sphincter muscles round the base of Tommy's cock. "Perhaps I'll keep you in here forever."

"Sounds like a plan I could live with, except when I have to go to work, of course. Might look a bit peculiar."

They laughed together then fell into a contented silence, Tommy's head resting on Andrew's chest.

Chapter Two

Later, Tommy made himself a quick snack, then returned to the bedroom, with a glass of wine for Andrew and a beer for himself. Andrew took the glass with a murmur of thanks, but it was obvious to Tommy his vampire lover was mulling something over. Something he had not yet mentioned.

"So, what's on your mind?" Tommy put his beer aside and rested on one elbow. He stroked Andrew's hair gently, running the silken mane through his fingers.

Andrew looked at him with surprise, then quickly averted his eyes. "Nothing."

Tommy drew in a sharp gasp of mock dismay. "You just lied to me, Andrew Berés. Something's rankling around in that busy brain of yours—there's never nothing on your mind—but this something has you worried. So spill it."

Andrew sighed and laid his wineglass on the nightstand. "Have you always been this clever, or are you now learning vampire tricks of the trade?"

"I've always been intuitive," Tommy replied, chuckling. "And having doses of your blood doesn't hurt. So something is worrying you. What is it?" He placed a light kiss on Andrew's lips. "Come on, tell Daddy..."

Andrew cupped the back of Tommy's head and held him in place for a longer kiss.

"You're trying to distract me," Tommy mumbled.

"Is it working?"

"Mmm, yes. Wait—no." He lifted his head and gave his lover a hard look. "Come on, Andrew, tell me so I don't have to start worrying."

"I'm afraid that if I do tell you, you will worry unnecessarily, for I haven't yet decided whether or not to act on the information."

"Information?"

"From the library—about the Talisman."

"Oh, fer Saint Peter's sake..." Tommy let out a loud groan and slumped back on his pillow. "That again. I told you a hundred times you don't have to go looking for some old artefact that some dodo demon mentioned in order to get in your pants. Dakar was an asshole, and a liar. All demons are liars, according to Marcus, 'cept maybe Constantine, and as I don't know him, the jury's still out as far as I'm concerned. So why on earth would you believe anything that dick Dakar told you?"

"But..." Andrew took Tommy's hand in his and kissed it gently. "I found out that Ardocan exists—well, at least in legend. It was a city, Tommy. True there is no mention of a Talisman, but I thought if I took the information to Marcus, he might help me, and—"

"Didn't Marcus make it very clear that trying to change your immortality would be dangerous?

Andrew, I don't want you doing this. I don't want you putting your life in danger for me. Because this is what it's all about isn't it? You think I'm upset that I'll grow old and die long before you."

Andrew gave him a look of innocence. "So, you're not?"

Tommy sighed loudly and glared at Andrew. "Yes, all right, yes. But that's part of being in love with a vampire. I know that, and I've had to accept it, and I know there's an alternative. Don't think I haven't thought about it, talked it over with Roger and Micah and Ron. It's just not an easy decision, Andrew. My folks, my family back home in Portland. Hell, you and I have talked about this, and if you must know I still wonder why I let you talk me out of it all those months ago. We should have just done it, and damn the consequences."

"But I want you to be one hundred per cent sure." Andrew rolled onto his side and took Tommy in his arms. "*Szeretlek*, Tommy," he said, nuzzling Tommy's neck.

"Love you too."

"And I don't want anything to change that. Sometimes mortals who are changed, even willingly, can be resentful of their makers when they realise what they have become. My existence would be worth nothing if your love turned to hate."

Tommy snorted. "That's not gonna happen. Roger and Micah didn't end up hating Marcus or Joseph. And I can assure you" – he paused for a moment to drop a kiss on Andrew's mouth – "that my love for you is every bit as strong as theirs. Maybe even stronger."

"Mmm..." Andrew teased Tommy's lower lip with the tip of his tongue. "So all I'm asking is that you indulge me in this obsession of mine. Let me do some more research, talk to Marcus. If this time, my research leads to a dead end, and if Ardocan truly does not exist, I will never mention it again."

"Fine." Tommy tightened his arms around Andrew's hard body. "But I'm coming with you when you go talk with Marcus. Uh, uh..." He stilled Andrew's protest by touching a finger to his lips. "I want to know the risks involved in trying to find a lost city. I've seen that kind of movie, you know. Seems like there's always someone or ones out to throw a monkey wrench in the works."

Andrew chuckled. "Tommy, *édesem*, you live with a vampire. Most of your new friends are vampires. Not long ago your body was taken over by a demon, your best friend Alex was abducted into a demon army— and in addition, you're a fireman, putting yourself in the possibility of danger almost every day. You think my searching for Ardocan could be any riskier that all of that?"

"Well..." Tommy gave him a wicked smile. "Now that you mention it, I guess living with a vampire hikes up the risk factor, all by itself. However..." He kissed the tip of Andrew's nose. "I am going to be there when you talk to Marcus. I don't want to hear some watered-down version from you like it's no big deal. Okay?"

"As if I would hold anything back from you," Andrew said with mock affront.

"Right, as if..." Tommy stretched his muscular body against Andrew. "Mmm. I really need to get some sleep. I have to be up and at 'em early tomorrow, but you feel soooo good. Wanna go again?"

"If you have the strength."

"'Course I do." Tommy grinned, sat up and flexed his biceps for Andrew's benefit. "See? How can you resist?"

"I can't," Andrew said. He reared up and attacked Tommy's nipples, teasing them to hardness again, then threw him onto his back and covered his body with his own.

"Oh, yeah…"

* * * *

Andrew slipped from Tommy's arms, making sure he did not awaken his sleeping lover, and rose silently from the bed. After picking up his neglected glass of wine, he left the bedroom and walked into the living room, then onto the balcony, surveying the flickering lights of Los Angeles through the haze below him.

He frowned and sipped at his wine, deep in thought. Admitting to Tommy what he had discovered complicated matters. Tommy would want to join him in the journey to find the Scrolls of Ashelak and the city of Ardocan—even though at that moment Andrew wasn't sure in which direction Ardocan lay. The only clue he had was the mention of Ashelak being a god-like prince of the Hittites—one of a long line of royal princes raised to the position of a deity that the ancient civilisations of the Middle East worshipped. A minor god perhaps, but one important enough to be linked to Ardocan.

Even so, to involve Tommy in what might prove to be a fruitless search would not be a good idea. Of course, he could use his powers to make him forget all about their conversation. Vampires could manipulate human thought and memory, but Andrew was loath to tamper with Tommy's mind. He'd been through enough when they had battled Dakar's deviousness. Who knew what the long-term effects of such deception could be?

A night breeze nudged at his bare skin, sending a tingling sensation through his body. He shivered and stared up at the dark sky above him.

"I knew you would eventually believe me."

The words inside his mind startled him.

"You will not know peace until you have satisfied your curiosity."

Dakar! But how is it possible? "Dakar?" he said aloud, "I saw you die. How have you survived death?"

A mist-like wraith appeared before him, hovering a few feet away, the handsome features of the demon becoming clearer as his image solidified.

"You know so little of us, vampire. You should not place so much emphasis on what Marcus Verano tells you. Yes, you killed me, but my demon soul survives on another plane of existence—and regardless of your treachery towards me I am willing to forgive you and help you find that which you seek."

Despite the bizarreness of the situation, Andrew chuckled. "Forgive me? Come now, Dakar, in my dealings with you in the past, I saw no trace of a charitable spirit. What would make me think I could trust you now, even though you are dead and can do me, or Tommy, no harm?"

His chuckle was echoed by Dakar, but the demon's held a sinister edge. "You think not? There are those who would still do my bidding if I so desire it."

Andrew smiled. "You didn't succeed when you were in corporeal form, and when you had an army of demons behind you. I hardly think you are in a position now to threaten us."

Dakar shook his head impatiently. "So you say, but enough of that! Do you or do you not want to know the secret of Talisman and where to find it?"

"What I want to know is why you are so eager for me to have it. There must be something in this for you, Dakar, otherwise you would not be here now."

The demon's eyes glinted. "The Talisman can change many things. It can give you back your mortality—something you and your human lover crave. Don't deny it. I saw it in your expression when I told you of it before you sold me out."

"Very well, I won't deny it, but I repeat, what's in it for you?"

"The Talisman of Ardocan can turn back time. Something I think you already guessed at. If you find it and regain your mortality I would ask that you do me one favour."

"And what is that?"

"The Talisman demands a sacrifice—a blood sacrifice that binds it to the one who gives his blood willingly. In this case, that would be you." Dakar sniggered before continuing, "Once it has granted you your mortality, you must gift it to me so that I may use it to go back in time and live again."

"To wreak havoc on humanity, as you once planned to do?" Andrew's laughter was devoid of mirth. "I don't think so, Dakar. If that is the price of my mortality, it is far too high a price to pay. Apart from it being against my own conscience, every one of my friends would disown me."

"Bah! Conscience, friends," Dakar snarled, "all unnecessary obstacles that stand in the way of what you really want, vampire. Marcus Verano's philosophy has weakened you. If you truly loved your fireman you would renounce these foolish beliefs and follow your instincts—your vampire instincts. They served you well enough before your involvement with Marcus Verano and his sycophants."

"That's enough, Dakar." Andrew stepped back. "Return to your *plane of existence* and keep the knowledge of the Talisman to yourself. If it does exist, I will find it without your help, and without any need to grant you favours. The world does not need you in it trying to subjugate others to do your bidding. Go!" He turned away and walked back into the living room closing the sliding glass door. Through the glass he watched as Dakar's sneering image faded into the darkness.

"Who were you talking to?"

Andrew turned, momentarily startled by Tommy's voice. He stared at his naked lover who stood in the middle of the living room gazing back at him, with a questioning expression. For a moment all thoughts of Dakar and talismans were driven from Andrew's mind by the sight of Tommy's incredibly beautiful face and body.

Never did he tire of simply looking at him, or when he was alone, bringing the vision of Tommy's superb physique into his consciousness. From his impossibly wide shoulders, down over that sculpted chest, flat stomach, lean hips, muscular legs to his well-shaped feet, Tommy's face and figure would have been a feast for Michelangelo's eyes, would have graced the walls and ceilings of many a chapel in Italy, would have—

"Andrew?"

"Yes?"

"Who were you talking to?"

"Oh..." Andrew gave his head a little shake to clear his mind. "Would you believe me if I told you—Dakar?"

"Dakar?" Tommy gaped, his mouth slightly open in surprise. "But, I thought…"

"You're right, he's dead, but he was only too happy to let me know his spirit exists on another plane."

"Another plane?"

"Not Heaven, that's for sure," Andrew said with a soft chuckle. "Dakar wouldn't find a home among the angels."

"Wait, you're tellin' me that Dakar's ghost was here? I was sure we'd seen the last of him."

"We probably have. I turned his offer down."

"His offer? Damn…" Tommy's grin was rueful. "I'm beginning to sound like your echo." He stepped forwards and took Andrew in his arms, pressing his big warm body against Andrew's cooler skin. "What kind of offer?" he asked, his lips touching Andrew's temple.

"That he would lead me to the Talisman if I turned it over to him after I had regained my mortality."

Tommy sighed his exasperation. "Have you asked yourself why the hell he doesn't just go get it himself? If he can appear in front of you, why can't he go wherever the darned thing is? If it actually exists. "

Andrew tightened his arms around Tommy, relishing the feel of his lover's cock growing hard against his own rising erection. There really was no point in continuing with this discussion. When he was with Tommy, other things seemed more important.

"I have an idea," he whispered.

Tommy nuzzled Andrew's earlobe. "What's that?"

"We go back to bed and talk about this in the morning."

"You think I could sleep after you telling me all this?"

"Sleep wasn't what I had in mind."

"Ah. Now who's got a one-track mind?"

Andrew grinned. "Guilty as charged."

This time, Andrew moved them into the bedroom using his vampire powers. A surge of movement and Tommy yelped as in a flash his backside landed on the bed, Andrew on top of him. He laughed out loud with delight, crushing Andrew to him, arms and legs wrapped around Andrew's hard, lithe torso, their mouths meshed in a long, searing kiss. It could have been yet another bout of powerful, driving, exhilarating sex, but Andrew wanted to slow the pace this time, to take his pleasure in the feel and the sight and the scent of his human lover.

He let his lips linger over Tommy's, relishing the sensation of the soft, full flesh opening for him, responding eagerly to his kiss. He gently tweaked Tommy's nipples, and Tommy's rapid gasping breaths of ecstasy filled Andrew's mouth and warmed his blood. He traced an erotically hot trail of kisses over Tommy's throat, his chest, south over his firm, ridged abs before licking and teasing the flared head of Tommy's cock, savouring the pre-cum that glistened in the slit.

Andrew's senses reeled at the taste. He had to fight the urge inside him to bring Tommy to instant orgasm, to take pleasure in swallowing the seed of his climax and relish the full salty tang of his semen. He moaned, and Tommy, as if in response, bucked his hips upwards driving himself deeper into Andrew's mouth. Andrew took all of it, clenching his throat muscles around the head, massaging it while he listened to Tommy's ecstatic whimpers. He took a moment to lubricate his fingers with his saliva before slipping two of them into the cleft between Tommy's muscular ass cheeks. While he continued to suck on his lover's rigid shaft, he circled the ring of muscle around the hole, teasing slowly until a choking Tommy begged him, "Inside me...let me feel you all the way in there..."

Andrew pushed in, fingering Tommy's prostate, and was rewarded by a fresh surge of pre-cum over his tongue. He went deeper and now Tommy was frantically bearing down on Andrew's fingers, his body writhing wildly in total ecstasy.

"Fuck me please," Tommy groaned, grabbing at Andrew's shoulders. "Want you, need you..."

Andrew drew himself up between Tommy's legs and spread them wide. He paused long enough to lubricate Tommy again, then he guided the head of his cock into Tommy, penetrating him to the hilt with one stroke. Andrew plunged in and out of Tommy's silky-smooth channel, all thoughts of going slow abandoned. He reached for Tommy's erection, pumping the solid length to the rhythm their bodies had created. Tommy gasped, moaning loud enough to rock the rafters. He arched upwards to meet every one of Andrew's thrusts. and wound his arms around Andrew's neck, pulling him into a kiss that had them both instantly teetering on the knife edge of orgasm.

Their chests smacked together, Tommy's sweat-slicked muscles binding them in a crushing embrace. Words of lust-filled desire tumbled from their mouths, lost in intelligible meaning as their lips and tongues clashed in almost savage kisses.

Andrew felt the warm rush of Tommy's cum over his fingers and against his chest even as his own climax overwhelmed him. They shuddered in each other's arms then collapsed back on the bed in a sated tangle of limbs — Tommy's heaving breath filling Andrew's mouth as their kiss went on and on.

They lay silently in the afterglow of their mating until Tommy asked, "Was that a record?"

"Not quite," Andrew replied, chuckling. "We'd have to do it again."

"Oh God, I have to work tomorrow," Tommy whined. "So, no."

Andrew sighed deeply. "Tired of me already."

Tommy curled tight against him and fell asleep.

Chapter Three

The atmosphere at the home of Marcus Verano and his forever companion Roger Folsom was strangely sombre when Andrew and Tommy were ushered inside by Roger. After welcoming hugs were exchanged, Roger whispered the reason, the smile on his pale face more than a little strained. "Marcus has received news that his friend the Lady Andorra and her mortal lover, Tony, are missing."

Andrew had heard of Andorra and Tony, but had not as yet, met them. He had also heard that Andorra was a woman of considerable beauty and that Marcus and she had been one-time lovers, then friends for centuries. They had helped each other out of some very dangerous situations over time, and Andrew was certain that Marcus would now be planning some way of helping her. He was quick to express his concern for their safety to Marcus when the Master Vampire greeted them a few moments later.

"Thank you, Andrew." Marcus embraced him and Tommy, then led them through to the spacious living room where he entertained his friends. Roger slipped behind the long mahogany bar and began pouring red wine into crystal glasses.

"Beer for you, Tommy?" he asked.

"Thanks," Tommy said, taking the cold bottle Roger handed him.

"What worries me most about Andorra's disappearance," Marcus told them, "is the fact I cannot sense her presence anywhere. She and I have always had a close mental bond, but now it's as though she does not exist. I have contacted every vampire who knows Andorra and Tony, and they all tell me the exact same thing."

Marcus fell silent, his expressive, intelligent face serene, even though the others could tell he was deeply troubled.

"Do you think that they may...might have been, uh...you know, killed?" Tommy asked breaking the silence with some hesitation. "Maybe...maybe an accident or something?"

Marcus nodded gravely. "That has crossed my mind, Tommy, but if Andorra had suffered the final death I know I would sense that. When a vampire dies, those close to him or her feel the loss almost immediately, no matter the distance between them. No, I don't believe Andorra and Tony are dead. If anything, I think they might have been imprisoned somehow—locked away from all possible contact, physical or mental."

"But who would do such a thing?" Andrew asked. "Does the lady have many enemies?"

Marcus' smile was grim. "Together over the years, we have had many. I thought, however, that we had put those to rest, or at least in a position where they could no longer threaten us. My old foes, the Comte d'Arcy and the Dark Forces have been silent for a long time—but as you know, it seems there is always someone, either mortal or immortal, who wishes to do us harm."

"The last time Marcus heard from Andorra, she was doing some undercover work for the government," Roger said.

"Really?" Tommy couldn't keep the surprise out of his voice.

"Yes, really." Marcus chuckled before explaining. "We have a rather tenuous relationship with a few of those in power. Our ability to access places humans cannot so readily enter, and quickly ascertain who might be disloyal or an imminent danger to those present has proven beneficial to the more secretive departments of the government. Of course, our involvement along with our very existence would be officially denied, but we have proven ourselves to be very useful from time to time."

"Wow..." Tommy looked impressed. "Have you done any undercover work?" he asked Andrew.

"No, assignments like these are passed down from the Vampire Council," Andrew told him. He sipped his wine then turned to look at Marcus. "What, if anything, have you decided to do about your missing friends?"

"Until I can detect some sense as to where she is, there is little I can do," Marcus replied. "However, only tonight, I found out who it was that assigned her this covert operation. Of course, the man will not want to give me any answers, but—"

"That's not going to stop you," Tommy blurted. The others laughed while Tommy's face turned red. "Sorry, I just know that you, of all vampires, can get anything out of anybody. I've seen you in action before."

"You got that right." Roger grinned at Tommy. "Remind me to tell you sometime about our first night together."

"*Roger.*"

"Just thought we could use a little levity." Roger leaned across the bar to kiss Marcus' cheek. "Okay, ill-timed. I'll shut up for the time being."

Marcus sighed. "If only that were possible. Anyway, once I find out where it is she and Tony were assigned, I can begin my search from there."

"Marcus, if there's anything I can do to help..." Andrew gripped the Master Vampire's arm. "I would be only too willing to accompany you on your search."

"I may just take you up on that offer, Andrew. We'll see what Andorra's 'contact' has to say. Now..." He tapped the package Andrew had brought with him. "I believe you have something you wish me to see."

"Yes, although I hate bothering you with it when you are concerned for your friends' welfare."

"That's quite all right. Let me see what you have there."

Andrew withdrew the writings of Arnold Metcalfe he had 'borrowed' from the library and handed them over.

"Ah yes, the Scroll of Ashelak," Marcus murmured, after scanning the pages for a few seconds.

"You've heard of it then?"

"Indeed, yes. It's from the scroll that the myth of Ardocan first arose. First, a city lost in the sands of time, then the Talisman that Dakar told you about."

"You still maintain it's only a myth?" Andrew paused then said, "I had a strange visitor last night."

Marcus stared at him for a moment. "Dakar."

"Yes."

"What?" Roger yelped. "You mean that son of a bitch demon didn't die after you stuck him with that poisoned dagger?"

"He died," Andrew replied, "but he very smugly informed me that he exists on another plane. An alternate world if you will."

"Oh, for fuck's sake," Roger muttered. "Does that mean all those demons we killed off are still rolling around out there somewhere, ready to try and fuck things up again?"

"Dakar didn't mention any other demons," Andrew told him, "but that's hardly surprising as he cared for no one other than himself."

"And you," Tommy said abruptly. "Let's not forget that everything Dakar did when we went up against him had a lot to do with him wanting to get you in the sack, Andrew. And to me that means he'd tell you anything to get near you again. I bet even on this alternate plane he's fantasising about you and him doin' it—dirty-ass demon!"

"But fulfilling that particular fantasy would be difficult." Marcus chuckled and slid gracefully off his barstool. "Let me show you something that might help explain what is going on with Dakar and his ilk."

"There isn't a book anywhere he doesn't have a copy of," Roger said watching Marcus leave the room.

Andrew laughed ruefully. "I might have been better off searching Marcus' library instead of the world-famous ones."

"Getting back to what Tommy was saying about Dakar wanting to do it with you..." Roger had that wicked gleam in his eye they were so used to seeing when he had imbibed two or three glasses of wine. "What d'you think it would be like to have sex with a demon?"

Tommy screwed up his face. "Gross."

"I don't know. Constantine's pretty cute. Not my type of course," Roger added hastily, "but Gustav and he seem to be really into one another."

Tommy snorted. "In more ways than one apparently."

"Did I ever tell you about the time Joseph was stalked through time by a demon named Angelo?" Roger asked.

Tommy was now wide-eyed. "No! What happened?"

"Angelo—and no one deserved that name less than him—tried to take Joseph away from Micah—transported him through time, the son of a bitch. Anyway, he got Joseph in bed, and—here's the good part—" Roger allowed himself a chortle before continuing, "Joseph almost bit Angelo's dick off. That kind of slowed him down a bit."

"I bet," Tommy said, laughing.

"Then of course, we all came galloping to the rescue." Roger smiled, reminiscing. "Great days... Of course it made us really hate demons, until Micah and me met Constantine in Rome—but that's another story."

"Constantine has an advantage over other demons," Andrew said. "He has Marcus' blood in him."

"Yeah, we all do, even you, Tommy, indirectly." Roger waggled his eyebrows at him.

Anything Tommy was going to say to that remark was stalled when Marcus came back carrying a very large book. "Demonology," he announced, placing the book on the bar top. "There are several editions of this, but I'm fortunate enough to have one of the originals. I scanned one of the sections that deal with a demon's death, and you will find this interesting, Andrew. Look at this drawing."

He swung the book round so that Andrew could see, while Tommy peered over his shoulder.

"Looks like that creep, Dakar," Tommy muttered.

Roger snickered. "You mean Dick-ar, don't you?"

"But in fact, it is Azazel, one of the fallen angels," Andrew said, reading the caption under the illustration.

"Exactly." Marcus then pointed to the top of the page. "Azazel was punished for mating with human women and fathering many offspring. Some of his children were relegated to the Underworld and condemned to live as demons. Would the striking resemblance between Azazel and Dakar suggest to you that they were kin, perhaps through generations? And if that is so, it would explain why Dakar continues to exist."

Tommy shrugged his wide shoulders. "I don't get it."

"The legend says the fallen angels, known as the 'Fallen Ones', were rebels cast out of Heaven," Andrew said.

Marcus nodded. "That is correct. It is believed that their offspring gained a kind of immortality. If by some chance their existence on Earth is compromised, for instance Dakar's death at Andrew's hand, the part of them that is immortal cannot remain on Earth—that would account for Dakar telling Andrew he lives in an alternate dimension."

"How much trouble can he cause," Roger asked, "if he's stuck in another dimension?"

"Not very much—but what he wants is for me to find the Talisman and let him share in its power," Andrew said. "I already told him that's not likely to happen. Can you imagine it? Dakar allowed to wreak havoc again?"

"What do you mean by share?"

"The Talisman can be used to alter time. He wants to turn back the clock to before his death—"

"No way!" Roger slammed his hand down on the top of the bar. "No fucking way. We had enough of him last time."

"Calm yourself Roger," Marcus murmured, moving Roger's wineglass out of reach. "The existence of Talisman is still in doubt, and without it Dakar cannot be given back his life on this earth."

"Yet he was so certain of its existence, Marcus," Andrew said quietly. "And the mention of the Scrolls makes me wonder..."

Marcus sighed. "The Scrolls of Ashelak, yes, that is a different matter—and a very dangerous one. Many have died searching for the Scrolls, and to my knowledge they have never been discovered."

"The author of the manuscript I found in the library says a lot of the research has been destroyed." Andrew scanned the page quickly. "Arnold Metcalfe—do you think he meant deliberately destroyed or just gone with the passage of time?"

Marcus was about to reply when he suddenly narrowed his dark green eyes. He jumped to his feet, his body poised for action, his expression grim. "I have been given the whereabouts of Andorra and Tony."

"Where are they?" Roger demanded.

"In Iraq. Baghdad to be precise."

* * * *

Tommy looked around the locker area of the firehouse for his friend Alex. He needed a favour and needed it fast.

"Hey, Tommy." Alex was just coming out of the men's room, drying his hands. "You look worried."

"I have to ask the chief if I can take a few days off, starting now. Before I go in to see him, I wondered if you could cover for me on your days off."

"Oh, Jeez..." Alex frowned for a moment. "Jason just asked if I would go with him up to Big Bear for the weekend."

"Damn," Tommy muttered. "Well, that's okay, I don't want to bust up your plans."

"Is it real important?" Alex stared at him keenly. "You definitely look like you're worried about something."

"It's Andrew," Tommy said, sighing. "He's flying off to Iraq this afternoon. He doesn't want me to go with him, but—"

"But you're thinking of going anyway, right? What's he going over there for? Isn't it still pretty dangerous for tourists?"

"It's uh—more of a business trip, but I don't like the idea of him being there. You're right, it's still dangerous, and Americans are not very popular."

"I thought he was Hungarian."

"He is. You know what I mean."

"Well, lemme call Jason, see if he's okay with us taking the trip next weekend instead. 'Scuse me for a second." Alex grinned. "He gets kinda mushy on the phone." He stepped away to a corner of the locker area where no one was sitting, and Tommy watched as he called his boyfriend Jason.

Tommy was happy for his best buddy. A few months before, the demon Dakar had forcibly recruited Alex along with hundreds of other men and women to strengthen his demon army in his bid to take control away from their Kardis, the ruler of the underworld. Alex and all the other humans had almost been killed, but vampires had saved the day, and the upshot had been that Alex had met Jason who had also been 'recruited'. They'd been seeing one another regularly since then, and it looked like their romance was going well.

Alex was smiling ruefully as he walked back over to where Tommy waited. "He said okay, but only 'cause it's you. He knows how tight we are."

"Thanks, Alex." Tommy gave him a quick hug. "Tell Jason I love him. Well…" He winked at Alex. "I'll tell him when I see him next."

"Hey, 'nuff o' that!"

"Just kidding. Now I just have to get the chief to agree."

"He'll agree. You're his boy wonder!"

Tommy smiled ruefully. The chief might, but Tommy wondered if Andrew would still consider him his 'boy wonder' when he told him he was joining him in Iraq.

Oh, the air is gonna be blue, but I'm not backing down – not this time!

Chapter Four

The Lady Andorra drew herself up to her full height of five-foot-four and glared up at the man who towered over her, meeting his dark eyes with a fierce stare of her own. Though diminutive in stature, Andorra knew she still managed to exude an intimidating persona even while restrained and faced with a lethal enemy.

"Where is Tony, my companion?" she demanded in fluent Arabic. "What have you done with him?"

"You will not demand information from me," the man who had identified himself earlier only as Azid snarled at her. "Nor will you find me or my men threatened by your arrogant ways. We know what you are, and we know what daylight can do to you. Answer the questions I shall put to you again, or this time you will hear the screams of your companion as he has hot coals applied to his naked flesh."

Andorra strained against the silver chains that bound her to the wall of her cell—chains that weakened her and took away her vampire powers. Unbound, she could destroy this man in an instant and his cohorts with him, but unless by some miracle she was freed, she had no way of overcoming her captors and rescuing Tony from whatever hell these men had planned for him.

"Marcus!" Her silent pleas had so far gone unanswered and Andorra knew it had to be because of her weakened state. If Marcus had heard her he would have replied in kind and most likely would be on his way to help get her out of this mess.

She had been betrayed. Someone who knew of her mission had informed the terrorist group that now held her and Tony prisoner. They had also been informed of her powers for they had got to Tony first, using him as bait to lure her to their headquarters. Tony was human, and although made stronger than many men by Andorra's vampire blood, even he was no match for the five thugs sent against him.

Despite the fact that Tony was attacked in broad daylight and in front of several witnesses, no one came to his aid or alerted the police. Violence was an all too common occurrence in the daily life of Baghdad and for the most part people preferred to look the other way. The thugs had sent a note to Andorra's hotel room telling her where she would find Tony, and that if she wanted to see him alive, she should come alone, and without her vampire aggression. Andorra had at first thought she would be able to simply overpower the terrorists and rescue Tony — but now she blamed her own arrogance in thinking it would be quite so easy. The silver net that had dropped on her as she entered the building had weakened her enough to allow the men to use chains of the same metal that now bound her.

"What is it you wish to know?" she asked, her eyes never wavering from the tall man's sneering expression.

The terrorist heaved a long and exasperated sigh, his breath sour on Andorra's face. "I will repeat the questions I have asked for two days, but only once more. Who is it that you have been sent to protect? Where is the meeting place, and for when is it scheduled? You have one minute to tell us or your friend experiences the ultimate in pain, and you will have to listen to his cries of agony, his screams for mercy." Azid stepped back and folded his arms, his eyes sweeping over Andorra's face and body. "You know, you are a very beautiful woman. Too bad you are what you are, or I would have enjoyed having my way with you. It would bring me much pleasure to hear you scream your ecstasy as I fucked you. Too bad..."

Andorra laughed. "But good for you that you have not given in to your disgusting thoughts," she snapped. "Were I free of these chains I would rip your head from your body and give it to the crows for lunch!"

Azid's eyes widened with shock. "Women do not speak to men like that," he rasped, pushing his face close to Andorra's. "You should be lashed to within an inch of your life."

"This woman will speak to any man in this manner." Andorra turned away in disgust. "And take your stinking breath out of my face."

Azid scowled, then his expression of anger became smug as he sneered at Andorra. "Your man will feel even more pain to pay for your insolence. Perhaps you would like to reflect on that while you listen to his screams."

"Tony is more important to me than any other human being," Andorra said quietly. "He is also very strong and will not scream when you torture him. Nor would he wish me to be disloyal to those who sent me here. So even though I have been betrayed by someone paying you to do this, I will not tell you what you want to know. Tony will forgive me."

"Tony will die," Azid rasped. "He will not be around to forgive you." He turned to one of his henchmen and snapped, "Tell them to begin torturing the human infidel." He smirked at Andorra as the man left the cell. "We will see just how strong your man is. Not even the bravest can hold out very long when their flesh begins to burn and melt under the coals."

Oh, Tony, forgive me my darling. When this is over, I will heal you and give you immortality and invincibility so you will never have to go through this kind of pain again.

Andorra hung her head in sickening expectation of the sounds she knew would soon reach her ears. Azid was right—not even the bravest could withstand the kind of torture these vile men were about to inflict on Tony.

A few minutes crept by with excruciating slowness. Azid grumbled with impatience then growled out yet another order to one of the two men still with him in the cell. "Go see what is happening. Find out why they have not started the torture. I want to hear the infidel scream and beg for mercy, and I want to witness the effect of all that on his vampire mistress!"

Andorra raised her head and looked around her. Azid and only one man remained. If she could only break the chains she could deal with them both and rescue Tony. With all her mental will she strained against her bonds, then stiffened with shock as a terrible wail of terror erupted from outside the cell.

Tony.

The panicked cry was suddenly cut off. Somewhere a metal door clanged shut and an eerie silence permeated the air around them.

That was not Tony.

"Marcus!"

Azid and the other terrorist cried out and stumbled back from the cell door when it was flung open with such force it burst free of its hinges. The men's faces were etched in horror and Andorra watched with cold satisfaction as Marcus and Roger, in full vampire mode, strode into the cell, grabbed both thugs by their throats and slammed them brutally against the stone wall.

"Now you tell us who you are working for!" Marcus snarled, his fangs inches from Azid's sweating neck.

Another vampire whom Andorra did not recognise, rushed in, accompanied by Tony who immediately wrenched the silver chains from Andorra's body and pulled her into his arms.

"Tony—forgive me," Andorra murmured against his chest.

"For what? Nothing happened, Andy. Marcus and his buddies saved the day. This is Andrew, by the way."

Andorra acknowledged the handsome vampire with a nod of thanks, then slipped from Tony's embrace and stared at the two hapless men in Marcus' and Roger's grip.

She smiled. "Shall I tell you now, what you wanted to know—before we kill you?"

"But not before they vomit up the name of the man who betrayed you," Marcus said, letting Azid slide down the wall until he knelt in front of him.

"I do not know his name," Azid squeaked. "We were hired to extract information and pass it on, that is all."

"To whom would you pass it on?" Andrew asked.

"No one uses their real names—only codes."

"Then give us both code names, coward," Andrew said. "The one who betrayed the Lady Andorra, and the one to whom you would relay the information."

Azid hesitated long enough for Marcus to expose his fangs again and growl deep in his throat, while Roger squeezed the other terrorist's throat enough to make him croak—just barely, "Tell them, Azid, for pity's sake, tell them!"

"I only have the one code name to be used in dispatches—it is Krautman," Azid muttered, scowling. "That is all I know, I swear."

"I wonder why they needed this go-between," Andorra mused, with a speculative glance at Tony. "The government informant must surely have a direct link to this Krautman person."

"Perhaps he was afraid of a direct communication being intercepted," Tony said. "He could always say he was checking these guys out for future spy work."

"So what do we do with these jerks?" Roger asked.

"The same as we did with their friends before releasing them," Marcus replied. "Wipe their memories clean of all that has taken place here. Although what they planned to do to Tony merits stronger measures, too many dead bodies pose too many questions. Now, Roger!"

Andorra watched with grim amusement as the terrorists' faces, once twisted in fear and hatred now became calm, if puzzled, masks.

"You may go," Marcus said quietly, and without argument, the men shuffled away, not even giving him and the others so much as a backward glance.

Andorra stepped forward to embrace Marcus. "Thank you for this," she said, kissing his cheek. "I was beginning to despair for Tony's life. And you too, Roger." She smiled at the young vampire. "I see you've become quite the aggressor. And you have brought a new friend — Andrew?"

Andrew smiled, took Andorra's hand and laid a soft kiss on it. "Andrew Berés, my lady," he murmured, his old-world manners to the fore.

"He helped lay out those creeps that were looking forward to singeing my skin," Tony said, clapping Andrew on the shoulder. "You should have seen the looks on those bozos' faces when three mad-as-hell vampires came bustin' into the room!" Tony laughed, but Andorra could tell her human companion had been really shaken up by the whole experience. Perhaps it was time to give up this liaison she had with the World Council. Why should she needlessly endanger the life of the man she had loved for over a hundred years?

"How did you find us?" she asked Marcus.

"There are informants in every camp it seems," Marcus told her. "I could not reach your mind so I knew that whoever held you had weakened your powers somehow." He gestured at the silver chains now lying on the cell floor, and grimaced. "Whoever betrayed you instructed the men to take this precaution, but they had reckoned without our vampire network. I sent out a message for help to every corner of the globe, and as luck would have it, our old friend, Andre—you remember him of course—is here in Baghdad on business."

"Ah, yes, Andre." Andorra smiled. "The one whom no woman can resist. Or so he would like to believe."

Marcus chuckled. "Indeed. As you know, Andre can never conduct business in a city without sampling the, uh—local attractions. He had—shall we say—some early dawn delight with a lady who had actually seen Tony abducted by those thugs. Such things are not that uncommon here, but after they had pleasured themselves she complained to Andre about the violence that still goes on in the city, and cited Tony's kidnapping as an example. She told him she thought it was another kidnapping of an American for ransom."

"But what made him think it had anything to do with Andy and me?" Tony asked.

"He didn't, at first. But lying there, in the afterglow of their lovemaking—Andre's words, you understand—she asked him if he would take her away with him. He found himself curious about an episode serious enough to make her want to leave her homeland so as she lay in his arms, he searched her mind for details. That was when he recognised you, Tony, and immediately contacted me with the information."

"So, Andre and his impulsive philandering is to be thanked for saving us," Andorra said, laughing. "Remind me to thank him and his womanising next time we meet. Now, shall we get out of here? Our hotel at least has decent furnishings!"

* * * *

Later, seated in Andorra and Tony's more than decent hotel suite, enjoying some excellent red wine, and with the room sealed against any eavesdroppers, Andorra revealed the details of their mission.

"The President, the Defence Secretary and the Secretary of State?" Marcus didn't hide his surprise. "The Taliban and Al Qaeda all at one meeting place? Little wonder the Secret Service needed backup."

Tony nodded. "And total secrecy," he said. "If word got out that the President plus the Premiers of the UK, France, Israel, and Germany were all going to be here, chances are an assassination attempt would be too much for those extremist groups to pass up. This is big stuff, especially as China and Russia aren't on the invitation list."

"They were approached originally, but they declined," Andorra said, holding her wine glass up so that Roger could refill it. "I think they feel it wiser for them to simply sit back and let the other countries take the lead. Of course, if an accord is established with the Taliban and Al Qaeda, I am certain they will be very quick to accept the credit for it. Our job is to ensure the President arrives and leaves safely."

"Where is the meeting to take place?" Andrew asked.

"There is an underground bunker south of the city." Andorra paused to sip her wine before continuing, "Near the remains of the ancient city of Babylon as a matter of fact."

"Babylon?" Andrew threw a quick glance at Marcus. "Where it's believed the Scrolls of Ashelak are hidden."

"Scrolls of whosit?" Tony chuckled. "Sounds like a mummy joke comin' up."

"Well," Andrew said ruefully. "They could be a joke, I suppose, but I'd like to believe they are real. They are supposed to reveal where a talisman is secreted. A talisman that can change, uh – many things."

Andorra fixed Andrew with long look. "You mean the Talisman of Ardocan?"

"You've heard of it, then?"

Andorra switched her gaze to Marcus. "Heard of it enough to be sceptical as to its existence. It most likely does not exist. Right, Marcus?"

"Some pesky demon told Andrew is was for real." Roger cut in before Marcus could reply. "He also asked Andrew to share it with him when he found it."

"Which of course I would not do," Andrew said hastily. "Besides, as there is no actual proof the Talisman exists, it's all a foolish notion on my part."

"May I ask why you wish to find this Talisman?" Andorra asked.

Andrew grimaced. "Two reasons. It is said the Talisman of Ardocan can reverse time. I had hoped if that were true that I could change the past and have my brother, Michael, live again."

"And the other?"

"That there was a way to undo my immortality so that my lover, Tommy, and I would face the future together on equal terms."

"That is foolish indeed," Andorra snapped. "Such a thing has never been done – is impossible, probably dangerous!" Her expression softened a little as she gazed at Andrew. "You must love him very much."

"I do. I would do anything for him."

"Reversing time has been done," Andorra said. "Marcus can tell you all about that. The wish to bring back your dead brother is understandable, but whether the Talisman – if it does exist – has that power I do not know. However, there is no need to give up your mortality, Andrew. Tony is human, as I'm sure you know. He and I have been loving companions for over one hundred years, and see how young he still looks."

Tony chuckled. "Yeah, but I've been noticing some grey hairs recently."

"That is a concern for Tommy," Andrew said quietly. "About how he can explain away his ongoing youthfulness to his friends and family. It's like *The Picture of Dorian Gray* in a way."

"And we know that didn't end well," Roger remarked, rolling his eyes.

"Roger…" Marcus gave him a reproving look. "That isn't helpful."

Roger shrugged. "Just kidding. But maybe while we're here we could check out the ruins of Babylon. Maybe find some old writings on a wall."

"I don't imagine it would be that simple," Andorra said. "And from what I understand the excavation to install the bunker weakened whatever buildings were left. It's a 'no go' zone. Only military personnel and, of course, the VIPs will be allowed near once the meetings start."

"Which is when?" Marcus asked.

"Tomorrow morning. If you will excuse me, I have to make a full report to the Secret Service agents about what took place earlier—minus your involvement of course. They need to be on the alert for any further infractions of security." She rose gracefully from the couch and headed for the bedroom. "Will you stay, Marcus?"

"If you think we can be of use."

She paused at the doorway to the bedroom. "I will talk with the Secretary of State. She knows of you and under the circumstances might welcome your added muscle — figuratively speaking of course." She smiled ruefully. "I may have some opposition from Mr Hollingsworth, the Secretary of Defence. He isn't quite as on board with vampire involvement — he tends to be, if you will excuse the pun, rather defensive." She chuckled then closed the bedroom door quietly behind her.

Andrew left them a few minutes later and went down the hall to the room Tony had acquired for him at the front desk. Once there he pulled out his cell and quickly punched in Tommy's number. When Tommy answered there was a wall of sound almost drowning out his voice.

"Where are you?" Andrew asked, already dreading the answer.

"I'm in LAX. My plane for Baghdad leaves in a half hour. Phew... Talk about security. I thought I was going to have to spread my butt cheeks to get through."

"Tommy, I asked you not to do this. You promised me — "

"I didn't promise. If you remember I didn't say anything — I just kissed you — remember now?" He laughed seductively. "'Course, that kiss did hold a promise, just not the one you thought it did. I didn't hear you complaining at the time."

"Tommy, please, don't get on the plane. It's too dangerous here and — "

"Too late. I'm already in line. If I back out of here now there'll be an international incident, and you wouldn't want me arrested, now would you?"

Andrew groaned. "Oh, Tommy — what will I do with you?"

"You have to ask?" Tommy's sexy chuckle was warm in Andrew's ear. "You must be losing your touch. How'd it go with Marcus' friends?"

"They are safe. We got here just in time. Now look, Tommy—"

"You got a hotel room?"

Andrew sighed. "Yes, at the Saadoun. Don't forget there is a ten-hour time differential."

"I know. I'll get a cab to the hotel if you can't make it. Can't wait to see you."

And Andrew couldn't wait to see Tommy. Despite the man's recklessness, his stubborn refusal to stay behind and out of danger—or perhaps in a way because of those things too—Andrew couldn't wait to hold Tommy in his arms, and cover his face with kisses. He was hard just thinking about it.

"You've gone quiet," Tommy's teasing voice whispered. "Are you thinking of what you're going to do to me when I get there?"

"You know me too well," Andrew said, laughing in spite of himself.

"I'll see you soon. *Szeretlek*, babe."

"I love you too." Andrew closed his phone and sighed. He knew he had lost the battle of wills over Tommy's decision to join him in Iraq. They had argued about it long and hard with Tommy yelling that if Andrew was going to be fool enough to join Marcus and Roger in their attempt to rescue Andorra and Tony, well, then he was going to darn well be fool enough to go too.

"Because I saw your eyes light up when Iraq was mentioned," Tommy had said smugly. "You think that while you're there you can go see if what Dakar told you is true or not. Am I right? Of course I am, and if you're going to do that, then I'm going with you!"

Andrew had locked eyes with him but Tommy had looked away quickly.

"Don't even try that, Andrew," he'd said angrily. "You make me forget all this and I will never speak to you again. When I remember what I'm mad at you for, that is. You understand? You cannot manipulate me every time you think I'm sticking my neck out. I am not going to let you do this by yourself."

"But I won't be by myself — Marcus and Roger will be there — "

"I don't care!"

And on and on they had argued back and forth. Andrew had thought he'd extracted a promise from Tommy eventually that he would wait until Andrew had contacted him, but now when he played that scene back in his mind, there had been no promise spoken — only a kiss. A kiss that had led to an even more distracting and wonderful situation.

And he calls me manipulative!

Chapter Five

Andrew received a message from Marcus the following day that the Secretary of State had cleared them to accompany the Presidential contingent to the bunker for the first round of meetings with the Taliban and Al Qaeda leaders. Tommy's flight wouldn't arrive for several more hours, even if it was on schedule, so he felt easy about falling in with the plan. As luck would have it, a thoroughly pissed-off Tommy had called him from Frankfurt to let him know the layover there had been extended by four hours.

"If I didn't know better," Tommy had seethed, "I'd think you had something to do with this. Keeping me out of the way 'til you had a chance to look for the Talisman."

"Tommy!" Andrew had had to suppress a chuckle before answering, "You know even I couldn't do that."

"No, but Marcus could!"

Andrew had laughed then, but had quickly assured Tommy that nothing other than the airline itself had been trying to delay him, and that when Tommy did arrive, he would make very sure to make it all worth his long, long journey.

"Huh." Tommy had sounded placated. "Okay, then. I suppose."

"I love you, Tommy, and when you get here I am going to show you in every possible way just how much. There is not a part of you I will not hold, caress, lick...and suck."

Tommy groaned. "Oh, man—damn these airlines and their delays!"

* * * *

At dusk, they drove out into the desert in armoured vehicles. Andrew looked around with interest. Scattered here and there in the mostly barren countryside were silhouettes of blackened trees, the shells of bombed-out buildings, the occasional solitary man or woman trudging along the road, looking neither left nor right as the vehicles roared past them.

Andrew had lived through many wars in his two hundred years, had seen cities ruined, the results of massacres, yet here there was a pervading atmosphere of desolation, of hopelessness, the likes of which he had never before experienced. Surely there must be a way out of this seemingly never-ending war against the poor and oppressed. Governments might change, might rise and fall, corruption might go unchecked, but the status quo remained for most people. Roger and Tony sat beside him in the rear of the Hummer, both of them unusually quiet.

He stared at the back of Secretary of State Denise Harper's carefully coiffed head and found her mind blocked from his gentle probing. Hmm—working with vampires had increased the Secret Service's need for even more secrecy, he thought, smiling to himself. Roger nudged him and grinned then nodded to the back of the lady's head. He'd obviously had the same result.

Andrew nodded and pointed ahead as they approached a road block guarded by several soldiers. They were waved on after a momentary stop, then slowed again at what Andrew guessed must be the entrance to the bunker. Yet nothing was visible to the naked eye—absolutely nothing. They climbed out of the vehicle, a Secret Service man on either side of Denise Harper, and followed them to where President Metcalfe, Henry Hollingsworth, the Defence Secretary and the rest of their retinue, which included Andorra and Marcus, waited.

A low humming sound emanated from beneath the rocks and sand and a few seconds later a steel cage pushed its way up through the ground. No one showed any surprise or said anything apart from Roger who muttered, "Sweet." They were shepherded into the cage which was large enough to hold all of them except the soldiers who had guarded the convoy in armoured vehicles front and rear. The cage descended rapidly for several seconds before stopping at the end of a long brightly lit corridor flanked on either side by metal doors.

"The one second on the right there, Andrew..." Marcus sent a mental message to him. *"My senses tell me there are ancient artefacts stored there."*

Andrew could sense it too and was sure, from the tilt of Andorra's head in the direction of the door, that she had not missed it either. Whatever had been uncovered during the excavation lay behind that door, and Andrew was determined to find out what it was.

It was obvious President Metcalfe had been to this place before as he led the way down the corridor, his Secret Service men hurrying to keep pace. Security was at its ultimate level here. Cameras surveyed them from every corner and armed guards were stationed up and down the corridor. The entourage walked quickly to a set of double doors which slid open as they approached. A large room lay beyond the doors, in the middle of which was an oblong table. Several men and women were already seated at the table. There were barely suppressed gasps of surprise when Metcalfe entered.

So the secret Andorra had been entrusted with had not been leaked, Andrew thought, watching the expressions of the people in the room. It would have been far too much of a temptation for the terrorists not to have attempted an assassination attempt on the President if they had known of his inclusion in this meeting.

All but two people rose to acknowledge the President. Andrew didn't need to be told that the two who did not were the representatives of Al Qaeda, but he noticed that at least the Taliban members showed the President respect by standing and nodding stiffly in his direction. If they realised what Andorra and her companions represented they gave no outward sign of recognition, yet Andrew was sure that either the Taliban or Al Qaeda or perhaps both groups were responsible for Andorra and Tony's earlier captivity. Someone with a great deal of authority in a US government office was in collusion with them. The President greeted the group in passable Arabic, warmly acknowledged the other men and women representing various governments, then let the translator take over, getting down to business almost immediately.

* * * *

The meeting dragged on. Bitter recriminations were thrown at the allied representatives by the Taliban and Al Qaeda duos, but President Metcalfe fielded them well, reminding the four men of the atrocities committed by both terrorist groups against the people of Iraq and neighbouring countries, not to mention the threats against Europe and the US. That day, little was settled, but at least all the leaders agreed to meet again in the morning. As the room emptied, Andrew hung back, determined to find some way of entering the room he was sure held something useful in his search for the Scrolls of Ashelak.

A Secret Service agent appeared at his side and smiled. The man was handsome. Perfect teeth, chiselled jaw and bright shiny blue eyes.

"You with the Prez or Denise?" he asked, his hand touching Andrew's arm.

"Actually, neither," Andrew replied, wondering how he could get rid of him without seeming rude, or more to the point, suspicious. "I am a friend of the Lady Andorra's." He nodded towards the group walking slightly ahead of them. "We were…uh, called in, at the last moment."

"Ah…" The agent held out his hand. "Stan Walker."

Andrew took the big, warm hand offered. "Andrew Berés."

"You're Hungarian."

"Very perceptive, Agent Walker, but I suppose that's part of the job."

"Yeah, plus I spent some time in Europe." His smile widened. "I particularly enjoyed my time in Hungary. The people there are, uh — very friendly."

Gods, the man is coming on to me, Andrew thought, recognising the handsome man's overt flirtation. *And getting in my way – or could he be of some help?*

"This is quite an impressive place," Andrew said.

"Yeah. It's under what used to be the site of an old city."

"Babylon, it's believed."

"That's right. They dug up some interesting stuff. They'll ship it all off to some museum eventually, I expect."

"I would love to see what they found." He glanced at his watch. Another four or five hours before Tommy's plane was due. Enough time for... He met Agent Walker's blue gaze and smiled. *I hate having to do this, but...* He waited until the President and other dignitaries were far enough ahead, then said, "You can arrange that, right?"

Agent Walker looked a mite confused for a moment or two before he cleared his throat. "Yes, I can arrange that."

He walked over to the door that Andrew and Marcus had noticed earlier and waved a plastic card in front of a small panel set to one side. With a soft hiss the door slid open and Walker ushered Andrew inside. The room was immense, almost as large as some of the archives he had visited in his search for the Talisman. He immediately used his vampire vision and senses to quickly and efficiently scan the room for anything related either to the Talisman or the Scrolls of Ashelak. He sighed with disappointment as nothing relevant to his search was apparent.

Beside him, Walker stared about in silence. Andrew knew he wouldn't remember any of this in a few minutes, but right now he needed the man's memory intact.

"You say all of this was found while they were excavating for the bunker?"

"Yes," Walker immediately replied. "We were briefed on this before our first tour of the facility. There's more," he said, gesturing at a far wall, "but I'm not cleared for that area. Apparently they found some kind of deep pit that they're still trying to figure out what to do with. Choices are to fill it in or send some guys down to check it out. So far, no decision has been made primarily because of the meetings scheduled for the next few weeks. They've just shored it up until a decision is made."

Andrew nodded, then made his way to the door, Walker at his heels. "Thank you, Agent Walker, that was very interesting."

"No problem." Walker closed the door behind them. He met Andrew's eyes, and his smile was endearingly shy. "You seem like a really nice guy — cute too, if you don't mind my sayin' so — and I was wondering if you'd be free for a drink later when we get back to the hotel. I'm at the Hilton."

Andrew held the man's smiling gaze for the few seconds it took to have him forget what he had just asked, and that they had just been behind the door of a secured area.

"Hey, Walker!" Andrew's keen hearing picked up the call from Walker's Bluetooth. "What the heck are ya doin'? We're getting ready to leave."

"What?" Walker jumped a little and stared at Andrew for a moment. "Hey, we better catch up with the others. Sorry man, I don't know what I was thinking holding you back like this."

"That's all right," Andrew said. "My fault."

The agent didn't ask why Andrew considered it his fault, but rushed on ahead, leaving Andrew to follow behind.

Once they were at ground level again, Marcus asked quietly as they made their way back to the parked vehicles, "Find anything of interest?"

"Yes, and no. There is nothing in the storage room, huge as it is, but Agent Walker says there is a deep pit that is closed off until they decide what to do with it. That sounds interesting."

"How deep?"

"Deep enough for them to consider having experienced men go down to take a look."

"Or fill it in, perhaps," Marcus said. "Although I believe man's natural curiosity will win out."

"They are no more curious than I."

"Hmm..." Marcus turned a wry smile on Andrew. "I don't suppose I can talk you out of this exploration you are contemplating?"

"Marcus, if you would rather I didn't go through with this, I will respect your wishes."

"No, Andrew. I don't think you will be satisfied until you have investigated every avenue. Tommy will be here soon, though."

Andrew nodded. "He'll want to join me of course, and I'm not sure I'll be able to dissuade him."

Marcus gave him a knowing smile. "I would wager that once Tommy knows what you have in mind, you will lose that particular debate."

* * * *

Baghdad Airport was crowded, noisy and completely disorganised. There had been a bomb scare earlier resulting in the building being evacuated and all planes had either been diverted or were circling the area waiting for landing instructions. Now, the bomb had been found, declared a fake and the people were being allowed back in to meet their loved ones or to stand and wait in the long departure lines.

Andrew grimaced at the chaos around him, but he could already sense Tommy's presence in the terminal, his mind filled with colourful recriminations against every airline in the world. Andrew's frown turned to a smile as Tommy barrelled through the security barrier, a bag slung over his shoulder, his face lighting up when he saw Andrew waiting for him. Uncaring of the milling crowds they wrapped their arms around each other and grinned happily at one another, their lips touching as they exchanged hellos.

"Tell me you came by cab," Tommy said, "and that I don't have to travel vampire express to the hotel."

Andrew chuckled at Tommy's aversion to being flown around. His firefighter boyfriend had no head for heights unless there was a ladder under him. "We'll hail a cab, though it would be a lot quicker if—"

"Never mind quicker. As anxious as I am to get you naked and in bed, I'd rather wait for the cab."

* * * *

On the way to the hotel Andrew quietly told Tommy about the bunker, the storage room and the fact there was some kind of pit behind sealed doors.

"And you want to explore this pit, right?"

"Yes, but I'm afraid you won't be able to come with me. Apart from the fact it could be dangerous, getting you clearance to accompany the President's entourage would be impossible."

Tommy stared at him for a long moment before he said flatly, "You know, you must think I am really dumb."

"No, of course I don't!"

"Then why would you even say what you just said? You're a vampire, you can do just about anything — and that includes getting us both inside that bunker without being seen. Come on, Andrew, you know I'm right."

Heaving a laboured sigh, Andrew said, "Marcus was also right. Very well, but you must stay close to me every moment."

"I'll be glued to your side the whole time." Tommy stroked Andrew's thigh. He looked out of the taxi's window at the desolate city streets. "Are we nearly at that hotel yet? Doesn't look too hospitable around here."

The cab had turned a corner and was slowing as the driver drove down a narrow alley. Ahead of them they could see what looked like a half dozen or so men blocking their way.

"Uh-oh," Tommy muttered. "I'd bet this isn't a welcoming committee."

"I think you're right," Andrew said at the same time as he leant forwards and smacked the driver on the back of the head. "Reverse...now!" he snapped, meeting the driver's hostile eyes in the rear view mirror. The man's expression changed to one of fear and compliance. The taxi skidded to a halt, then immediately and rapidly backed up. The men gave chase, yelling at the driver to stop, but Andrew overrode their demands with mental images of what he would do to the driver if he did stop.

Once back on the main road, Andrew threw open the door and dragged Tommy out of the cab with him. "Sorry, but it's vampire express from here, my love." Wrapping his arms around Tommy he soared upwards leaving an astounded group of thugs gaping as he and Tommy sped away into the night sky.

* * * *

"Okay, I'll give you that one," Tommy said, opening his eyes as Andrew alighted on the balcony outside what he assumed to be their hotel room. "There was a definite need to get the hell outta there fast."

"I could have taken them." Andrew waved his hand over the glass door's handle. The door slid open revealing an opulently furnished room with an extremely large and enticing bed.

Once inside, Tommy pulled Andrew into his arms. "I know you could've taken them, but you were thinking the same thing I was — that it was only going to delay what we both really want — to fuck each other's brains out."

"Right, and why should we let some idiots get in our way?" Andrew ran the tip of his tongue over Tommy's lower lip, then pushed teasingly into the moist heat of Tommy's mouth.

A low, sexy rumble crept up from Tommy's chest as he pulled Andrew tighter into his embrace. "God, but that feels good," he mumbled against Andrew's lips. "I missed this."

"We were apart for only a day and a half," Andrew said, chuckling and grinding his crotch into Tommy's.

"A day and a half too long." Tommy grabbed the back of Andrew's head and planted a long and lust-filled kiss on his mouth. "Yeah," he breathed when they came up for air, "waaaay too long."

He backed Andrew up towards the bed where they collapsed onto it in a tangle of limbs, pulling at each other's clothing.

"Jeez, I'm so ready for this, but I should shower," Tommy muttered. "Been a long flight."

"You're not going anywhere." Andrew rolled Tommy onto his back and impatiently willed their clothes away. For a moment or two he was content to stare at the gorgeous but completely masculine body spread out so wantonly beneath him, then he lowered his head and licked Tommy's naked chest, nibbling on each nipple in turn as Tommy moaned and writhed against him.

"If I remember right," Tommy panted, sliding his erection over Andrew's in slow, sensuous moves, "last time we did this I was inside you, and terrific as that was, this time I want you to fuck me so hard I'll be walkin' funny for a week."

"Really?"

"Well…" Tommy chuckled, then grasped Andrew's cock and began pumping it. "Maybe not for a whole week. People might talk."

"Then I'd better slick you up first," Andrew said, returning the look of lust in Tommy's eyes. He lifted Tommy's muscular legs, exposing the twin globes of his beautiful butt and the quivering hole he knew was begging for his attention. Leaning in, he laved the cleft between the cheeks with his tongue, circling the opening with teasing licks. Tommy's legs trembled in Andrew's grasp and his gasping cries and moans echoed round the large room. Andrew hoped no one in an adjacent room would think Tommy was being tortured and call the authorities. He wove an erotic trail over Tommy's perineum, nuzzling his balls, taking each one in turn between his lips and sucking on them gently, causing Tommy to moan even louder. Tommy was never quiet during sex, but this night he was outdoing himself. Andrew shifted his attention to his lover's erection, the head of which was oozing pre-cum, and Andrew scooped up the creamy juice to savour the saltiness before taking the length of hard, engorged flesh into his mouth.

Tommy let out a long almost painful sounding groan. "Now, Andrew, please. Need you now, inside me."

Andrew raised his head and took in the incredible sight of Tommy's beautiful face, now flushed with desire and need. He settled Tommy's legs on his shoulders and guided his cock into the heat between his ass cheeks. Tommy grabbed Andrew's hips and pulled him forwards so that he slid inside him with almost no resistance, all the way to the base of his shaft, his balls brushing against Tommy's butt. Andrew pulled back then thrust in again, hard.

Tommy moaned. "Yeah, that's it, right there. So fucking good..."

Andrew slammed into him again and again. Tommy's body arched into Andrew's arms. He grabbed at Andrew's shoulders, pulling him down for a kiss that sent both men's senses reeling. They gasped into each other's mouths, Tommy's breath hot and sweet on Andrew's tongue. Andrew levitated them off the bed, holding Tommy in his embrace and driving into him at an ever quickening pace, their bodies meshed, joined together at mouth and core. Andrew felt the first hot spurt of Tommy's seed against his chest and he allowed himself release, flooding Tommy's silken heat with jet after jet of scalding semen.

"Fuckin' A," Tommy breathed out as they settled again on top of the comforter. "Love you, Andrew."

"I love you, too." Andrew traced Tommy's throat with his lips, then scraped gently at the tender skin with the tips of his fangs.

"Need some?" Tommy asked.

Andrew's voice was decidedly husky when he replied, "Perhaps just a taste?"

"Go for it." Tommy turned his neck towards Andrew. "You deserve it after that."

Andrew bit down, puncturing the smooth, vulnerable skin as gently as he could, but he knew he had brought unavoidable pain when Tommy stiffened in his arms and gasped out loud. He drank quickly, the heady brew of human blood joining with his own powerful vampire blood immediately sharpening his senses, increasing his libido. The pungent, coppery taste and scent lingered on his tongue as he pulled back, and licked away the bite marks from Tommy's neck. He placed a long kiss on the spot.

"Mmm..." Tommy smiled at him through sleepy eyes. "Good for you?"

"Very good. Sleep now, my love. You've had a long and busy day."

"I'm hard again."

"Sleep..." Andrew placed a gentle kiss on Tommy's forehead. "You and I have all the time in the world."

"Right." Tommy rested his head on Andrew's chest and in a second or two, began to snore.

Chapter Six

Marcus called their room later that night with an invitation to join them in Andorra's suite.

"There is a change of plan for tomorrow," Andorra informed them after Tommy had been formally introduced. "But first, I've had some wine sent up. Please help yourselves."

"Any chance of a beer?" Tommy asked hopefully.

"Right this way, my man." Tony led him over to the bar. "Just so happens they had some Bud Lite in the bar downstairs and I snagged us a few."

"Excellent..."

While Tommy and Tony enjoyed their brews and Andrew poured himself a glass of red wine Marcus told him, "The meeting scheduled for tomorrow has been cancelled. Apparently the Al Qaeda faction found it necessary to complain that they were not informed of President Metcalfe's involvement."

"So they're grandstanding," Andrew remarked. "How long do you think they will sulk?"

"Not for long," Andorra said with a wry smile, "particularly when they find out that the President has invited the Taliban members to his suite in the morning for private talks."

"Is that wise?"

Roger shrugged expressively. "Divide and conquer tactic, maybe."

"The US has had many secret talks with the Taliban," Andorra said. "There is already a division between the two terrorist factions. They rarely see eye to eye since the deaths of so many of their leaders. But they are a long way from any agreement with either the US or Europe." She took a delicate sip of her wine before continuing, "Anyway, tomorrow Andrew, you and your lover are free to do what you will. Tony and I are all the President requires at the meeting."

"Free to explore, eh, Andrew?" Marcus smiled across at him, already knowing from the expression on Andrew's face what had immediately filled his mind.

"I'm that obvious?"

Roger grinned at him. "You're chomping at the bit!"

Andorra frowned. "Is this about the Scrolls of Ashelak again?"

"I'm afraid so." Andrew assumed a suitably apologetic expression which apparently did not fool the lady.

"Andrew, please be warned. If you attempt to enter what is an extremely secret and well-guarded place, and if you are caught, there is nothing anyone could do to help you."

"Except Marcus and me," Roger said immediately.

Marcus sighed. "And I, Roger."

"Whatever…"

"I cannot involve you, any of you, in this obsession of mine," Andrew said in protest, with a wary glance at Tommy who was staring at them, listening to every word.

"How do you propose getting inside the bunker?" Andorra asked. "Even for a vampire, it will be tricky. The only way in and out is by the means we used — the elevator that is controlled by the guards."

"Actually, I have an idea that there just might be another way in," Andrew said, "avoiding the bunker completely. I have no proof as yet. I will have to go to the site of the Babylon ruins to test my theory."

"Which is?"

"The Secret Service man who showed me the storage room said there is a 'deep pit' sealed off and as yet not explored. I have a feeling that this pit could be accessed by means of an underground passageway from the ruins."

"That's quite a theory," Marcus said, but his tone suggested interest rather than dismissal.

"One I am going to test tomorrow night."

"One *we* are going to test tomorrow night," Tommy interjected.

"Uh, we still have to fully discuss that, Tommy."

"No, we don't!" Tommy's lower lip was set in a fiercely stubborn line. "We already fully discussed this, and where you go, I go — or you don't go!"

"Tommy!"

The tension was eased by Andorra's amused chuckle. "Why do I get the feeling that I am reliving an earlier scene from our lives?" She winked at Marcus. "Tommy sounds just like Roger when we went up against the Comte d'Arcy and the monster Gregory. Remember Marcus? Nothing we said could dissuade him from joining us."

"And look how that all turned out." Roger spread his arms as if for inspection and grinned so widely the tips of his fangs were exposed.

Marcus groaned. "Roger, this might not be the best example for Tommy, right now."

Roger pouted. "Excuse me, but I make an adorable vampire—or so you've told me many times. Usually in the heat of the moment, when you're having your way with me, of course."

"Roger…"

Tommy laughed. "You are too much."

"Isn't he though?" Tony weighed in. "Roger and his buddy Micah are a whole new breed of vampires. 'Course they're still young. They haven't lived for hundreds of years. They've still got a sense of humour, still like dirty jokes and banter. They've only been changed a few years and haven't had time to develop that whole broody, mysterioso thing vampires love to cloak themselves in. You know, from those clunky old horror movies Roger loves so much."

"Huh." Roger put his hands on his hips. "I think you just complemented and insulted me at the same time, Tony." He let his fangs fully extend and snarled at them.

Tony nudged Tommy with his elbow. "Ooh, that's our cue, so we should act scared."

Tommy was interested in Tony's story as the only other non-vampire in the room. "How'd you and Andorra meet?" he asked over their second beer together.

"First World War," Tony replied. "I was a Canadian living in London, hoping for a career as a musician, when they drafted me. I got shot when we were going 'over the top'. That's what they called leaping like idiots out of the trench and straight into German guns. Most of the lads I was with were killed that day. I lay there for so long I lost track of time, wondering why I didn't die, then suddenly this beautiful woman was there, looking after me, nursing me, giving me her blood."

"But didn't change you."

"No. When I recovered and found out just what she was, she told me the choice was mine. She went through the pros and cons of being a vampire and I figured what with her having to sleep in the daytime I could be more useful to her as a kind of bodyguard, you know."

"That's great," Tommy murmured. "So, you've never been tempted to make the change?"

"Tempted, yeah, but one of these days, I'm going to have to. The option will be taken out of my hands. Probably fairly soon."

"Why's that?"

"Because a mortal cannot live forever, even on vampire blood. I joke about finding grey hairs, but it really means it's a sign that my time is near. I either let Andorra change me, or I eventually will die."

"I see." Tommy fell silent as he thought over what Tony had told him.

"I can tell you've been doing some deep thinking about your situation," Tony said looking at him over the beer bottle he lifted to his lips.

"Yeah, something Andrew and I have to work out one of these days."

Tommy studied Tony's homely face and rangy physique. He didn't want to be unkind, the guy was nice, but he seemed like an unlikely match for a woman as beautiful as Andorra. He imagined her on the arm of some dashing, charming man of influence and power instead of —

"Know what you're thinking." Tony grinned at him.

"Huh? You do?"

"Yep. It's the blood. You've probably been getting some flashes of Andrew's mind now and then."

"Yeah. Jeez, I'm sorry, Tony. That was just way outta line of me."

"Hey, I get it. Don't think I haven't thought the same thing many a time. Andy could have just about any guy she wanted, so why'd she pick a putz like me?"

"You're not a putz. She probably sees the good guy in you. After all you've been together, what, a hundred years? How many couples can say that?"

"Not many. But remember, in vampire years, that's not such a long time!"

* * * *

Back in their room, Tommy wasn't about to let his and Andrew's earlier exchange go unresolved.

"I was serious about what I said, Andrew. You don't get to leave me behind and go diving underground and God knows where else without me. And just so you know, Roger's told me how to avoid those little mind games you guys like to play sometimes."

Andrew arched his eyebrows. "Oh, really? And just what did he tell you?"

"He said it's like when he was human and didn't want to come too soon when he was having sex, he would think of weird things, like his granny's underwear or his mom and dad doing it, so it would slow him down some. Now, of course, he can vampire control it, but he said if I fill my mind with other thoughts, not like those, but other things, any other things, you can't penetrate the jumble and I don't get zapped."

"How interesting." Andrew quirked the corner of his lips and took a step closer. He fixed his eyes on Tommy's. "Why don't we try it out now and see how it works?"

"Okay." He stared back into Andrew's eyes and tried to fill his mind with anything except—*Oh God, how beautiful those eyes are, how hypnotising they are, how quickly under their spell I could fall.*

"Whoa! Stop. Jeez..." With an effort he dragged his gaze from Andrew's. "Oh, that wasn't fair, Andrew. You did something before I could get ready."

Andrew drew him into his arms and kissed him tenderly. "Roger was pushing your leg, my love. No human can resist a vampire's will, especially up close like this." He kissed Tommy again. "Don't worry, I promise I won't zap you. You're right, we should do this together. I just ask again that you never leave my side for a moment."

"That's an easy promise to make." Tommy pressed his muscular body to Andrew's and held him tight. "By the way..." His lips vibrated sensuously on Andrew's as he murmured with a soft chuckle, "It's pulling your leg, not pushing."

"I knew that," Andrew said, laughing lightly. "Now shut up and kiss me."

Chapter Seven

Andorra and Tony made their way to the Presidential suite early next morning, before the sun was up. The Secret Service men had already swept the room for hidden 'bugs', cameras or any other electronic devices that terrorist spies had been known to use. Although the President's visit was still an official secret, there was no doubt that either or both the Taliban or Al Qaeda members who had attended the meeting the day before would have, by now, notified all interested parties as to the President's presence. This meeting had to be conducted swiftly, in complete secrecy, and hopefully with some kind of agreement reached.

Andorra scanned the room where the meeting was to take place. All seemed in order, but her senses went on full alert when Secretary of State, Denise Harper, signalled that the Secret Service agents should admit the Taliban contingent.

"Vampire," she whispered to Tony who stood at her side watching the men file in. "The tall young one in the tailored suit. He was not at the meeting yesterday."

Interesting.

She gave the vampire a knowing smile as he walked in with the other men who wore the traditional robes and *agals*. The vampire took his place at the table and narrowed his eyes at Andorra. He did not return her smile. Instead he looked decidedly uncomfortable and quickly averted his eyes from Andorra's searching stare. His mind was blocked to her, as she expected it to be, but she took pleasure in adding to his discomfort by keeping her gaze firmly fixed on his darkly handsome, though sullen face. A young vampire among the Taliban—and newly changed by the looks and scent of him.

Really interesting.

Andorra knew that just as there were those vampires who worked covertly with Western governments, some allied themselves to the 'other side', either for reasons of financial gain or in some cases, loyalty. Only one or two of the Secret Service agents on duty knew of Andorra's true identity, but now she wondered if they realised they had a Taliban vampire in their midst. She glanced around, taking in Denise Harper's calm expression and Hollingsworth's scowl. *He really does not like me being here.* Andorra knew there were many people, even those who employed vampires, who were wary, if not totally afraid of them. Andorra didn't think Hollingsworth was afraid. The man had a certain arrogance, a disdain for those he considered less than himself. Andorra had heard that he'd been furious when Metcalfe had passed him over as his running mate in the previous election.

And what could be the purpose of this particular vampire being at the meeting? Andorra sensed danger and kept a close watch on the vampire as the President rose to address his guests. Metcalfe had obviously discovered in his previous meetings with these men that they were not impressed with flowery words or promises they would interpret as worthless. He came straight to the point, warning them that their training camps in the Yemen were being closely monitored and that any planned insurgencies would be swiftly and decisively dealt with.

"Europe and the United States want peace, gentlemen," he said through an interpreter, "but it cannot be a peace at any price. You need to rein in Al Qaeda..."

A low rumble of discord rose from the throats of several of the Taliban and one man jumped to his feet, his anger reflected on his swarthy face. "We are not Al Qaeda's keepers," he spat, "nor are they ours. Peace will only be attained when all Americans leave our soil forever. You are desecrating the Holy Land, polluting it with your continued presence."

Metcalfe sighed and glanced at Denise Harper, shrugging his shoulders as he did so. It was obvious he had listened to this kind of rhetoric before, but Andorra saw it for what it was right then – a diversionary tactic. One to have the Secret Service agents focus their attention on the shouter, while the real danger moved with lightning speed, so fast the human eye could not catch his movement until he was upon the President, fangs bared, prepared to rip out his throat.

Andorra was quicker. Her speed blurred everything in the room around her, putting time at a standstill for the microsecond that it took for her to place herself between the President and his attacker. Her tiny, steel-like fist lashed out and smashed into the vampire's mouth, a devastating blow that broke his jaw and had him staggering back howling with pain. The agents, recovering from their momentary shock, sprang into action, guns spewing volleys of lead into the vampire's body.

The bullets could not kill him, but they had weakened him considerably. He fell to his knees, moaning and clutching at his jaw. Andorra knew he would heal in seconds and no doubt continue his attack. In that moment when he'd been temporarily disabled, she had read his mind. He had been programmed for this mission. There was no room for failure—for Krautman would accept nothing less than total success.

Andorra stepped forwards and grasped the vampire by his hair. He snarled at her just before she broke his neck. A collective gasp went up from the Taliban members and without a word they hurried from the room. The President stayed the agents with a gesture. Some had been prepared to go after the terrorists.

"Let them go. The meeting was useless anyway." He looked down at the vampire's body. "What do we do with him?" he asked Andorra. "Is he actually dead, or is he going to jump to his feet and have another shot at me?"

Tony knelt by the vampire and prodded him with a finger. "He's dead all right," he said. "He must be fairly young, Andy. He's not decaying."

Andorra nodded. "That is why he was so easy to overcome. He was recruited by Krautman."

"Perhaps he could've told us more if you hadn't— uh—broken his neck," Denise Harper said quietly.

"He told me enough." Andorra smiled at her. "Krautman is here with us in this room."

"What?" Metcalfe gaped at her, then at his Secret Service agents who stood surrounding them, guns still drawn, alert, ready.

"She's full of bullshit!" Henry Hollingsworth stepped forwards, his eyes cold, yet wary, and Andorra knew she was correct. The dying vampire's last thought had betrayed the traitor. "How can you believe anything this vampire bitch says?"

"Hey!" Tony grabbed Hollingsworth's arm and pulled him away from Andorra. "I don't care who you are, you don't talk to Andy like that."

Hollingsworth jerked himself free. "And you," he snarled at Tony, "what kind of man are you that lets a fucking vampire feed on him?"

"That's enough, Henry," Metcalfe snapped. "What the hell's got into you?"

The smile that crossed Denise Harper's expression was not warm or friendly as she turned away from Andorra and said to the President in a low voice, "I think the Lady Andorra is about to tell you something you never wanted to hear."

"She's full of crap, I tell you," Hollingsworth yelled, backing away.

"Henry…" Metcalfe's eyes widened with shock as he stared at his Secretary of Defence. "No…"

Denise made a small gesture and two Secret Service agents closed in on Hollingsworth. "Take it easy, sir," one said. "Don't give us a reason to shoot you."

* * * *

Later that night, Tommy sat on a bar stool in Andorra's suite, his eyes wide, enthralled by the story she and Tony related to them.

"Man, it sounds like something out of a movie," he said, when Andorra paused to take a sip of her wine.

Tony chuckled. "It kinda played out like one. I don't think I've ever seen a guy more thunderstruck than the President when Hollingsworth lost it. All that vitriol pouring out of the guy's mouth about how he could do the job better, and how Metcalfe was so low in the polls because of his stupidity, and that the rest of the world was laughing its ass off at his ineptitude when it came to dealing with the Middle East, the Taliban, Al Qaeda, and on and on. God, that Hollingsworth is a total arrogant jerk."

"But the vampire," Tommy asked, "where did he fit in?"

"That is something we must be very careful about in future." Andorra looked across the room at her fellow vampires. "It seems the Taliban has been experimenting. Sending vampires in to assassinate those they want to get rid of in places where they cannot bring weapons. The vampire needs no weapons. His or her strength alone will do the job. If I had not been there today, the President would most certainly be dead. The vampire was young, but extremely fast—a dedicated killing machine."

"But easily disposed of," Marcus said. "An older vampire would not have succumbed to a broken neck."

"Where are they finding these young vampires?" Andrew asked.

"They are, for want of a better word, breeding them," Andorra replied.

"But how?" Now Tommy's eyes were really big. "How do you breed a vampire?"

"Not intentionally, in the beginning. Two years ago a young man was attacked by a rogue vampire in the hills outside Kirkuk. The vampire fed upon him for several days and inadvertently changed him. He returned to his family, and well, you can imagine what happened. A local tribal leader had him captured and allowed him to feed on young men and women." A look of anger mixed with sadness clouded Andorra's face. "Some of them, of course, died, the vampire unable to control the blood lust, but some survived and mostly due to neglect, were changed. The Taliban heard of this, and some enterprising soul decided to experiment—the result was what we witnessed today."

"And Hollingsworth—how did he get mixed up in all this?" Roger asked.

"When Tony and I were assigned this operation, we were to be there simply as protection for the President," Andorra said. "The usual thing, as you know, Marcus. We remain unobtrusive in the background, but if there is any danger, our senses and mind-reading ability are alerted to it much more quickly that human bodyguards. Hollingsworth couldn't contact the Taliban directly with the fact the President was going to attend the top secret meeting—they expected only Secretary of State Harper. The terrorists, having failed to extract any information from us, forced Hollingsworth to move on to a secondary plan."

"That's where it gets really scary," Tony said, picking up the story. "Because the American and European governments have been using carefully selected vampires in covert operations, he got to hear about the fact that the Taliban had been experimenting with the exact same strategy, and saw it as a way to get rid of the Prez. Apparently, he didn't know that

Metcalfe had asked Andy to be at the meeting this morning."

"Which was why he was throwing me all those hateful looks," Andorra remarked. "He might have guessed at some point the vampire would have problems with me there, but he was thwarted in that he couldn't say or do anything for fear of exposing himself. I suppose he missed the fact that I would be able to read the vampire's mind. Although the vampire could close his mind to me in the beginning, the shock of my attack weakened him. I was able to penetrate hsi thoughts just before he died, thus discovering the truth of what he was involved in."

"Wow," Tommy muttered, after gulping at his beer. "You think this will ever be on the news?"

Andrew chuckled. "Doubtful. The President's Press Secretary would have difficulty explaining this particular episode."

"But what will they do with Hollingsworth?"

"That is under discussion, I believe, even as we speak." Andorra smiled. "I suggested severe memory loss, resulting in his having to resign. Denise Harper was quite keen on that idea." She put aside her wineglass and stood. "Now gentlemen, Tony and I must leave you. We have to fly to Washington D.C. and file a report, then I believe we have a meeting with the President when he gets back."

Tony grinned at Tommy. "'Course, we'll be there before him."

"Oh, yeah? How'd you reckon?"

Tony spread his arms out imitating a plane. "Andorra's really fast."

Tommy spewed out a mouthful of beer then clapped a hand over his mouth, his face reddening with embarrassment. "Christ, I'm sorry! But you guys are flying—flying—all the way to D.C.? Holy sh—! No way, no way could I do that."

"Hell, that's nothing," Tony told him. "We've flown much farther hundreds of times, right Andorra?"

"Right, Tony." Andorra smiled indulgently. "Now if you'll get your backpack ready we'll be on our way. And don't rumple that new dress I bought today."

Tommy did a double-take. "You bought a new dress on top of everything else you did today? You are truly amazing!"

"And you are truly adorable," Andorra said, kissing his cheek. "Andrew, I think you must take very good care of this young man."

"Oh, he does," Tommy said, then blushed again.

"And please..." Andorra's expression turned serious. "I know what you are planning on doing tonight, so please, please be careful. I would hate to hear something terrible has befallen you."

"Don't worry, Andorra," Roger butted in. "Marcus and I will be there to look after them."

Andorra rolled her eyes. "Well then, I needn't worry, need I?"

* * * *

Although Andrew was certain Marcus considered his quest a waste of effort, the Master Vampire had offered his and Roger's assistance when it came time to begin the search for the Scrolls of Ashelak. Andrew had purchased a rather poor map of the Babylon ruins, all that was readily available from a street vendor. At least it had the points of interest highlighted, though crudely represented.

Years before, Sadaam Hussein had begun work restoring Babylon, or at least the dictator's idea of what it should look like, but Andrew was not interested in anything that might be within the dead dictator's reconstruction. Lying in the ruins was the site of the ancient temple to the god Marduk. Andrew intuitively felt that, although the site had been excavated, what he was looking for, hoping for, would be found there.

"I don't know why I feel this, I simply do," he told Tommy while they were sitting side by side studying the map. "It's one of the most ancient parts of the original city, and somehow it makes sense to me that if there is an access leading to the pit the Secret Service man mentioned, it will be here."

"If you say so," Tommy murmured, stroking Andrew's back. "Let's face it, we're gonna be looking for something that maybe doesn't even exist, so why not take a shot in the dark — literally."

Andrew turned and smiled at him. "You know the only way to get there is by 'vampire express' as you like to call it, don't you? We can't very well take a cab or rent a car. The place is guarded by US military even though we're told they no longer have a presence in Iraq. And I have to warn you, to avoid being seen even at night, we will have to drop from the sky faster than at any time before you have ever flown with me."

Tommy gulped involuntarily. "I know — just don't drop me in the process."

A gentle knock on their hotel room door signalled Marcus and Roger's arrival. By mutual decision the men were dressed in black shirts and pants.

"How do I look?" Roger did a little pirouette.

"Fantastic," Tommy muttered.

"Are you nervous?" Roger asked.

"Why do you ask?"

"Because you look nervous."

"It's just the flying thing."

"Oh, not the wandering about in the dark under trillion-year-old ruins?"

"No, actually that doesn't bother me. It'll be like when I have to go into smoke-filled buildings." He smirked at Roger. "You should try that sometime."

Roger chuckled. "Point taken."

"So, are we ready to go?" Marcus opened the door to the balcony and stepped outside.

Tommy took a deep breath. "Ready as I'll ever be. Jeez, what I do for you, my vampire."

Andrew took his arm and they watched as Marcus and Roger lifted off into the dark sky, then Andrew slipped his arms around Tommy.

"Hold tight," he murmured.

"Like I wouldn't. Whoa!"

They were travelling faster than ever before in Tommy's experience, and it only took a few minutes for them to be hovering high over the ruins of Babylon. Below, Tommy could make out a few pinpoints of light he guessed to be a military outpost. His eyes widened when he saw two dark shadows plummet earthward.

"Ready, my love?" Andrew whispered.

"Yes," Tommy said, his voice sounding like a croak to his own ears. He closed his eyes and tightened his grip on Andrew trying not to let any weird noise, like some girly squeak, escape him as they went into freefall. The air rushed by them so fast that Tommy felt as if every breath in his body was being ripped out of him — then just as quickly it was over, his feet were on the ground and Andrew was already pulling him by his arm towards where Marcus and Roger were waiting. Tommy had no time to even reflect on what he'd just experienced. In the faint light cast by a shadowed moon he saw Marcus pointing at a pile of rubble.

That can't be anything, surely...

"I sense something under us right here," Marcus said quietly.

You do? Tommy could see only age worn bricks.

"Yes," Andrew murmured.

"Let's get rid of this debris," Roger said, sweeping his hand over the pile. Andrew and Marcus joined him in the sweeping motion and soon the bricks and rubble had been removed and a gaping hole exposed.

Tommy peered into the inky blackness. "How do we get down there? Shit—silly question. We're gonna jump, of course."

"Roger and I will go first." Marcus said to him, "To ascertain how safe it is for you down there, Tommy. There might be a lack of oxygen."

"Should have brought my breathing gear," Tommy quipped, in what he hoped was a couldn't-care-less jaunty tone.

Marcus and Roger stepped over the rim of the shaft and immediately disappeared from sight.

"How deep d'you think it is?" he whispered, his arm around Andrew's waist.

"Not so deep—and Marcus says there is breathable air. Let's go."

"Huh? Oh, right..." Marcus must have sent Andrew a message only he could hear. Tommy closed his eyes as Andrew grabbed him and jumped forwards. Would he ever get used to this? he wondered as they hurtled downward. *Probably not.* Their feet hit the ground and reluctantly he released Andrew from his death-like grip. "Just as well you don't bruise," he muttered. He reached for the flashlight he had secured to his belt.

"Dark as shit in here. I know you can see, but where are Marcus and Roger?"

Andrew pointed to a passage entrance. "Down there. Marcus says they have found something of interest."

"Already?" The beam from Tommy's flashlight picked out the remains of intricate brickwork lining the passageway's walls and roof. It was high enough for them to walk with their heads only slightly bowed. The passageway opened up into a large circular space lined with the broken remains of stone sarcophagi strewn around in disarray.

"A crypt," Andrew murmured, stepping inside.

"I'm afraid this is the work of grave robbers," Marcus said as they approached. "These tombs have been thoroughly pillaged over the centuries, and there are also signs of recent excavation. This does not look good for your search, Andrew."

Andrew nodded in agreement, and Tommy could see the disappointment evident in his expression. "There is still the pit," he said taking Tommy's hand.

"And there's another passage over there." Roger pointed to the far curved corner of the crypt. A doorway had been cut into the wall, flanked on either side by delicately carved pillars. "Let's see where that one goes."

This passageway was longer, narrower, making it necessary that they walk single file, Marcus leading the way. It was an accepted fact that his senses were more powerful than any other known vampire so that if there were obstacles ahead or—as in many ancient tombs and labyrinths—perhaps a booby trap or two set for the unwary grave robber, Marcus would be aware of them well ahead of time.

"Steps ahead," Marcus said, "going down."

"Going down? We must be several hundred feet below the surface already." Tommy wasn't nervous. At times he'd had to work in confined spaces, but he found it amazing that they could be descending even farther below the earth—and they hadn't even reached that pit yet. But Andrew had told him the bunker where the President had met with the Taliban was buried deep under the desert. Perhaps the architects who had designed the bunker had followed the paths of the ancient tunnels.

The steps led them even deeper and the air seemed thick and dank. Tommy really wished he had his breathing apparatus now. His flashlight beam picked out an unadorned ceiling, fallen bricks by the side of the steps, but nothing more. The silence was oppressive, the only sound Tommy could hear was his own breath rasping in his chest.

"Tommy, are you all right?" Andrew put a hand on his arm to slow him down.

"I'll be fine. It's just that the air's not so good down here."

"Sit for a moment or two..."

"No, I don't want to hold you guys back."

"Tommy, sit. I'll sit with you." He pushed a reluctant Tommy down onto the step and sat beside him.

"Sorry... God, I feel so weak all of a sudden."

"Don't be sorry. You're lacking oxygen."

Marcus climbed back up to where they had stopped. After staring at Tommy for a brief moment he pulled back his shirt sleeve.

"No..." Andrew moved closer to Tommy. "Tommy and I both thank you for offering, Marcus, but the blood he needs should be mine to give."

Marcus nodded and stepped back. Andrew bit into his wrist, then held the bleeding flesh to Tommy's lips. Their eyes met and held as Tommy first licked tentatively, then sucked hard, the spicy, potent essence coursing through his body, revitalising and oxygenating his blood almost immediately. Andrew kissed his forehead and the combination of the blood and the sensuous touch of Andrew's lips gave Tommy an instant hard-on that was clearly visible when, a few moments later, Andrew helped him to his feet.

A low chuckle came from an expected quarter — Roger. "Beats Viagra every time!" he snickered and received a look of disapproval from Marcus along with one of embarrassment from Tommy. "Nothing to be embarrassed about," Roger added. "Looks pretty impressive, even from here."

"All right, now that Tommy is fully recovered, shall we proceed?" Marcus grabbed Roger by the arm and hauled him down the last few steps.

"Just sayin'," Roger muttered as he was hurried away. "No need for everyone to get so uptight."

Andrew put an arm around Tommy's waist. "Feeling better?"

"Much. Sorry about the display."

"No need to be sorry. I'd have been surprised if there hadn't been that reaction. We all know vampire blood has aphrodisiacal effects. Roger just loves to tease."

"Doesn't he though? Uh, Andrew, you're stroking me. Nice as it is, you keep that up and I'll come in my pants."

"Right." Andrew nuzzled Tommy's neck gently. "It's your fault for being so alluring. Come... I mean, come with me." He chuckled as he took Tommy's hand. "I mean, follow me." His quiet laughter helped ease the tension that had surrounded them earlier.

"Wow, look at that," Tommy exclaimed. The steps had led them into a short passageway that opened up into another large crypt, again lined with plundered tombs, but this time it appeared they had come to a dead end. There was no opening other than the one they had used to enter.

"There's gotta be more," Tommy said. "Where's this pit the guy told you about?" He watched the three vampires spread out, tracing their fingers over the stone surface of the crypt. Tommy knew better than to break their concentration. If there was anything beyond this room, they would sense it.

But even if they do, how will they reach it if there's no other way out of here?

Tommy was about to find out.

"I feel something here," Marcus said, pressing against the wall in front of him. Andrew moved to his side and placed his hands alongside the Master Vampire's.

"Yes. A vibration—water perhaps."

"Water, way down here?" Tommy asked, striding over to join them.

"Artesian wells perhaps," Marcus said, studying the wall. "Or a water supply piped in for the bunker. We must be very close to it by now." He stepped back a few feet. "Roger, Andrew, concentrate on this spot in front of me. I think what we need is just about here."

The vampires stood stock still, their combined gazes focused on the place Marcus had indicated. Tommy gasped and stared with amazement as the wall began to crack and crumble, a large piece of the plastered rock crashing onto the crypt floor.

"Jesus..." Tommy gaped at the open space in front of him. "You guys..." Words failed him, for what could he say about having one more incredible feat of their supernatural strength revealed to him? "I'm so glad you're friends of mine," he quipped instead.

Now the sound of rushing water was louder and seemingly very close. Marcus stepped through the opening, the others following close behind. They found themselves in some kind of cavern, a gigantic dome-roofed space that soared over their heads to a dizzying height.

"Jeez, what is this place?" Tommy looked around at the fantastic rock formations that towered over them, at the water his flashlight revealed, pouring down the rock face, pooling in a huge subterranean lake that stretched as far as his eyes could make out.

"See, on the far side of the lake," Marcus said, pointing. "That large overhang of rock. There is an opening underneath it."

"But—" Tommy stopped himself from asking how they could get across the expanse of water. How else? He groaned softly as Andrew lifted him into his arms. "Here we go..." Well, at least this time they didn't have to be hundreds of feet in the air. No, this was more like when Andrew and he would go swimming and they would skim over the waves in each other's arms. This was actually kinda nice.

But what, he wondered, lay in wait for them on the other side?

Chapter Eight

The far side of the lake made way into what looked like the beginning of a labyrinth. There were far too many openings in the massive rock that loomed over them for Tommy to be sure that even Marcus would choose the right one. But the vampire didn't hesitate, and Tommy noticed that although Marcus had originally dismissed the idea of the Talisman's existence, now he seemed to be filled with a certain eagerness as he strode towards the opening, left of centre.

"Why this one?" he whispered to Andrew.

"Marcus knows the way," Andrew replied with what sounded like complete certainty.

"But he said the Talisman didn't exist."

Andrew smiled. "Even a vampire can change his mind."

They walked in darkness and silence for several minutes, Tommy praying that the batteries in his flashlight wouldn't give out. He knew his vampire friends could see in the dark and Andrew would guide him over any obstacle ahead, but he hated the idea of maybe not being able to see his surroundings—or something that might jump out at them from the shadows. *However, so far so good...*

Marcus and Roger stopped so suddenly that Tommy barrelled into Roger's backside despite Andrew's hand gripping his arm.

"Ow!" Tommy rubbed his crotch. "Christ, you really do have buns of steel!"

"We're here," Marcus said.

Tommy inched forwards as far as Andrew's grip would let him. "Holy crap," he muttered, gaping at the chasm that yawned at his feet. Even when he shone his flashlight downwards he couldn't even guess how deep it was.

Gotta be hundreds of feet deep at least... And we're going down there?

"You may stay here, if you'd rather," Andrew said quietly at his side.

Tommy jumped slightly, aware that right now his thoughts were an open book to Andrew. "No way," he muttered. "With the choices I'm given right now— go down there with you into that creepy place or stay here alone, in this creepy place—guess what I'm gonna choose?"

Roger chuckled. "There was a time when I'd have been saying the same thing. All right—" He waited until all four of them were poised on the edge of the abyss. "Let's go!"

Tommy gasped out loud as he and Andrew stepped off the rim together, Andrew's arms securely locked around Tommy's waist. This time their speed was controlled, not having the need to evade any observant eyes through night vision binoculars. Nevertheless, the rush of air around him took Tommy's breath away and the rock walls he saw in the beam of his flashlight sped by them at an alarming rate.

Just when he was beginning to think the pit was the bottomless one of legends he'd read about when he was a kid, his feet touched solid ground. He let out a long sigh of relief, and for a moment he was content to stay in Andrew's arms, resting his head on his lover's shoulder.

Man, but when this is over, I am going to write a book. Like anyone would ever believe this could happen. And it's not over yet…

"This way." Marcus' voice came from a long way off. It seemed he was impatient to move on. "There is an open shaft over here. It looks like it's the only way out of the pit."

"Oh great," Tommy groaned as Andrew released him. "Couldn't be stairs, could it? No, it had to be another freakin' hole in the ground."

They found Marcus and Roger standing by some rotting timbers over a gaping hole. Marcus bent and picked up a length of rusty chain. "I would hazard a guess that this might be the remains of an ancient lift that collapsed in on itself many years ago."

"You mean there were people here using this thing?" Tommy shone his flashlight on the broken remains. "But how did they get here? You guys broke through that wall up there. There was no entrance. Even the guys that built the bunker haven't been in here."

"This, I suspect, is the original entrance," Marcus said. "Everything else we have travelled through came after this."

Beside him, Tommy felt Andrew's body stiffen as if he had been alerted to — something.

"You hear that?" Andrew murmured.

"Yes," Marcus replied. "Someone approaches."

"What?" Tommy yelped. "Someone, down here?"

"Not in corporeal form," Andrew said.

Oh, for cryin' out loud... "What d'you mea—?"

"Dakar!" Andrew shouted. "We sense you nearby. Reveal yourself and tell us why you are here."

A low chuckle resonated off the rock walls that surrounded them, but Dakar did not appear. "He's here somewhere." Andrew gestured at the open shaft. "Shall we?"

Marcus nodded and he and Roger stepped into the darkness.

"Let's go." Tommy nudged Andrew towards the edge. Suddenly, dropping down into a deep, dark hole didn't seem nearly as intimidating as the alternative. "I definitely don't want to be up here with a dead demon!"

Andrew held Tommy tightly against himself as they dropped even farther beneath the earth. Gods, but now he wished he'd taken stronger steps to prevent Tommy from having to go through all of this. Tommy was brave, but he could sense the uncertainty, the fear of the unknown that niggled at his lover's mind each time they were faced with yet another obstacle, another plunge into the darkness. Truth be told, it was unsettling for all of them. He could also sense Roger's unease, and Dakar's presence brought a more sinister and dangerous element to their search.

The demon had decided to track them, and there could be only one reason for this. Dakar thought Andrew would give him the Talisman to restore his earthly life. That was not going to happen, and a confrontation with the demon would most likely be inevitable. Andrew wasn't sure what kind of powers

Dakar would still possess in his 'spirit' form, but he was sure some part of his devious nature would remain. Dakar had proven himself treacherous in the past—it would be foolish to think that his physical death had changed any of that.

Feet once again on solid ground, Andrew released Tommy from his embrace. "All right?" he asked.

"Right as rain," Tommy replied with a shaky chuckle. "But I can't help hoping we don't have to go any deeper."

"Hey, Tommy," Roger called out, "shine your flashlight on the walls over here. This looks interesting."

The space they had descended into was very different from the previous ruined crypts. Instead, the walls were lined with shelves on which rested urns of all different sizes and shapes. Some tall and elegantly fashioned of what appeared to be gold and silver, others small and made of plain clay. The orderliness gave the impression that nothing had been touched, nothing changed in many, many years—the thick layer of dust that coated the shelves and the urns adding evidence to that.

In the centre of the room stood what appeared to be a large stone sarcophagus, the top of which was heavily engraved in a language Andrew had no knowledge of.

"What d'you suppose this place is?" Tommy asked quietly.

"Some place even older than anything we have previously seen," Marcus said, eyeing the elegantly shaped vessels. "I would hazard a guess that these contain the ashes of some of the wealthier inhabitants, perhaps the ruling hierarchy—the smaller ones that of their servants—those who were chosen to die with their lords. It was a common practice in ancient times. And beneath this engraved stone is, I believe, what Andrew is searching for."

Andrew stared at the stone, surprised by Marcus' assumption. "The Scrolls of Ashelak—what makes you think that?"

"The language is Ancient Hittite. I am not completely familiar with the language, but I can see the words 'Prince Ashelak' engraved in the first line."

"Hey, let's move it out of the way then," Roger said eagerly. "We've come this far, why stall now?"

"No one is stalling, Roger." Marcus lifted a warning hand as Roger stepped forwards. "But remember, the men who built these tombs were masters of booby-traps. We might be impervious to flying shards of rock or a trapdoor in the floor, but Tommy is not. It would be wise if he stood well back when we move the stone."

"Sounds like a plan," Tommy said without argument. "Flying shards of rock don't exactly turn me on." He moved back to the far wall and watched as the three vampires moved the stone without actually touching it, using only the combined power of their minds. Nothing exploded, the floor did not collapse, the only sound was the disgusted exclamation from Roger.

"It's empty. The son of a bitchin' thing is empty. There's nothing in there but sand."

"What?" Tommy ran to stand by Andrew who could not hide his expression of disappointment.

"That's it, then," he said with despondence. "Someone must have removed it."

"If it ever existed." Tommy squeezed Andrew's hand. "Maybe it was just a ruse all along. Some practical joker from ancient times."

Marcus knelt by the empty sarcophagus and ran a hand over the sand. "Look. Bits of bone, and this finer, greyer sand—ash. The remains of Prince Ashelak perhaps?" Marcus stood and pointed at the rows of urns. "The writing on the stone is indecipherable to us, but perhaps contains a clue as to where the scroll is secreted. If so, the one marked with his name may just contain that scroll."

Andrew scanned the rows of urns with his vampire vision. "Not the one with his name engraved on it. The one next to it—the plain clay pot." He strode over and lifted it from its place on the shelf. "I'm almost afraid to open it. What if it turns to dust after being in here so long?"

"There's only one way to find out," Tommy said, in what was almost a whisper.

"And be quick about it!" The strident voice that filled the chamber and the rush of wind that accompanied it pulled the urn from Andrew's hands and sent it crashing to the floor where it broke into jagged pieces. A small roll of papyrus lay at Andrew's feet.

"Read it and see what is revealed!" the voice rasped again.

"Dakar," Andrew growled as he picked up the scroll. "You will not benefit from whatever is revealed, Dakar. I told you I would not share this with you."

"After I guided you and your vampire compatriots every step of the way? You owe me this Andrew, and I will hold you to our bargain."

"I made no bargain with you, Dakar, and I will not. You didn't guide us, you followed us. Not once did you mention the Scroll might be found in these ruins. Pure chance brought us here—that and vampire power, owed mostly to Marcus. Why are hiding anyway? Show yourself as you did before."

"I—I cannot..." Dakar's voice had lost its demanding edge. "My time in this alternate space grows short. I am not immortal like the Fallen Ones. That is why I need you to share the secret of the Talisman!"

Andrew glanced down at the writing on the Scroll. As on the stone, it was a mass of hieroglyphics he could not decipher.

"I'm afraid I cannot read this. We will have to take it to someone who can translate it for us."

"There is no time for that," Dakar screeched. "Marcus, he who knows all, or thinks he does, must surely be able to read it."

Marcus shrugged. "I can read only a few words, and it brings me no sorrow to inform you that I am unable to help you, Dakar. Perhaps Azazel, your forefather, can help. The writing is from a time of his existence on earth."

"He will not help me. He disowned me a long time ago. Now I find myself begging for help from vampires."

Tommy chuckled. "Yeah, and how's that working for ya?"

"Listen to me, Dakar," Marcus said, "there is no help for you here. We cannot decipher enough of the writing on the Scroll, and even if we could there is no surety that it would reveal the existence of the Talisman, even if it does exist. You must accept your fate, whatever it is..."

A horrendous wailing sound filled the air around them.

"What a drama queen," Roger muttered. "Can we get out of here now?"

"Fools!" Dakar screamed. "Don't you know what this is? This is the great burial chamber of the City of Ardocan, buried beneath the ruins of Babylon for centuries!"

Ardocan. Andrew remembered the text he had read in the library—the City of Ardocan that the Talisman was named after. Was it possible it was now within reach?

"No one has been here before you since the city disappeared in a cataclysmic earthquake thousands of years ago," Dakar continued, his voice tinged with panic. "All that remains is this chamber and the place where the Talisman was hidden. You cannot abandon the search now! Beyond these walls lies a labyrinth that may lead us to the Talisman. You are my last hope."

"We are not your hope, first or last," Andrew said. "Even if we find the Talisman, you cannot be allowed to use it to restore your life. Your treachery caused death and destruction when you were alive."

The wailing began again, reaching a crescendo that had Tommy covering his ears. "Jeez, somebody shut him up!"

"Come on." Marcus gestured to a small door at the far end of the chamber. "Best that we find out for ourselves once and for all if the Talisman exists or not."

The wailing ceased as they filed through the narrow door and into yet another long passageway. Andrew could sense that Dakar was following them. He would not give up quite so easily. Even though he knew Andrew was determined not to share the Talisman's power with him, Dakar would no doubt persist until the end, until whatever was giving him the power to pursue them ran out. Azazel, his ancestor, had refused to help, Dakar had said. Indicative of the low esteem in which even the Fallen Ones held him. If Dakar had proven himself a worthy adversary instead of the treacherous snake he was, Andrew might have felt some pity for him. As it was, the sooner the world was rid of the demon again, the better.

Ahead, the figures of Marcus and Roger were suddenly framed in light. The darkness of the passage had given way to a brightness that, though not a damaging sunlight, was almost blinding in its intensity.

"Wow." At his side, Tommy muttered his surprise. "Will you guys be all right in this?"

"Yes." Andrew stepped forward to stand beside Marcus. "It's reflected light, from these thousands of glass pieces." All around them, it was as if a million mirrors had been shattered in one devastating blow, the shards picking up and reflecting prism after prism of light. "But where is the source?"

"What's that?" Tommy asked, blinking against a dazzling beam emanating from a far corner. They approached slowly, all of them shielding their eyes from the powerful radiance ahead of them. "Too bad we didn't think to bring sunglasses," Tommy quipped. "Who knew we'd need them underground?"

"It's the Talisman," Andrew said, a sharp jolt of anticipation running through his body as he uttered the words. "It must be, Marcus. It does exist, after all. What else could it be?" He felt Tommy's hand grip his arm, slowing him down.

"Be careful, Andrew, please."

Andrew, his hand shaking with very un-vampire-like nerves, put aside the scroll and reached out to pick up the glittering stone. Large and heavy, it seemed to pulsate with an energy from deep inside it.

"It needs your blood," a voice whispered in his ear.

"I know."

"What?" Tommy asked, looking at him with surprise. "You know what?"

"It was Dakar," Marcus said, his expression grim. "The Talisman needs a blood offering. Andrew, this may be a trap."

"But how will we ever know if I don't go through with it?"

"Think carefully, my friend." Marcus put a hand on Andrew's shoulder. "What you do now will change the course of your existence forever. Is this what you and Tommy really want?"

"We've come so far," Andrew murmured. "It's all I've thought about for over a year."

"Andrew, you don't have to do this," Tommy said. "I will always love you, you know that. You don't have to sacrifice your immortality for me."

"Do it," Dakar's voice breathed ominously in Andrew's ear. "Do it, or I will!"

Andrew turned the stone over in his hands as if trying to see what lay inside, but all he could see was his own reflection cast a myriad times in the intricately cut prisms. Was it good, or evil? Was what he had obsessed over for so long really what he wanted? Now that the answer, was here in his hands, he was not sure. Tommy and he loved each other unconditionally. Did it matter that one would outlive the other? Was that not the way of most friendships, of nearly all loving relationships? It was possible that he, Andrew, could die before Tommy—a crazed vampire hunter, a moment too long in daylight, any of these things could end his existence. And if Tommy was taken, he would have these wondrous memories of their time together…

"Do it!" Dakar screamed, suddenly manifesting himself in their midst. "You vampires really are fools. You think my forefathers would actually refuse me this moment? I have this body for as long as it takes the Talisman to restore my life!" He grabbed for the stone – and Andrew and he began a tug of war over possession.

Tommy, momentarily caught off guard by Dakar's sudden appearance, yelled, "Fuck this shit!" then punched Dakar on the side of his jaw. The demon swung round, a snarl of rage on his lips. He picked Tommy up off the ground and flung him with supernatural strength against the wall where he hung impaled on a knife-like shard of glass protruding from the wall.

"Jesus!" Roger started forward to help Tommy but Andrew pushed past him.

"Tommy, oh Tommy, my love." Tears stung his eyes as he lifted Tommy down off the glass splinter that had pierced him close to his heart. Cradling him in his arms, he carried Tommy back to where Marcus held Dakar by the throat, his large hand slowly but inexorably squeezing whatever life had been given Dakar out of the demon's body.

"Stop," Dakar wheezed, struggling impotently against Marcus' powerful stranglehold. "There is your blood offering. Human blood – more sought after than any other. The Talisman will give you anything you desire. Don't be fools – use it!"

Andrew looked up at Marcus who flung Dakar away as though he were no more than a bundle of rags. He stooped to pick up the stone and handed it to Andrew. Tommy's breath was slowing as his life ebbed from him. His eyes fluttered open and locked with Andrew's.

"Sorry," he murmured. "I got in the way…"

"Andrew!" Roger gripped his arm. "Whatever you're going to do, do it quickly. He's dying."

Andrew covered the gaping wound in Tommy's chest with his hand trying to staunch the blood.

"He has only one chance," Marcus said. "It would seem the decision has been taken from you. You must change him or he will die."

A sob was torn from Andrew's throat as he gazed down at his dying lover's pale face. "Gods, but I would give anything to not do this without his consent."

Yes, Tommy offered to accept the change, to die in order to live with me forever, but I wanted to spare him that choice, to make my own sacrifice for him…

"The Talisman!" Dakar stood over them clutching his damaged throat. "Use it to save him and yourself," he croaked. "His blood and yours. Could there be a more potent combination? Let the Talisman's power decide your destinies."

Andrew knew he could no longer hesitate. He laid the Talisman on Tommy's chest then bit into his own wrist and let his blood fall on the stone and mingle with Tommy's. The Talisman turned red, absorbing both the human and vampire blood. It glowed, softly at first, then brighter and brighter, and Tommy writhed in seeming pain as the Talisman took on a shimmering, pulsating intensity. Instinctively, Andrew drew Tommy into his arms, holding him fast, the stone pressed between their bodies.

Andrew could feel Tommy's pain, a sharp excruciating sensation that made him want to scream out loud. Tommy reached around Andrew's neck and drew him in for a kiss that as he gave himself up to it, Andrew feared would be their last. Their lips and tongues meshed, and Andrew's body was flooded by a sensual heat he swore he had never before experienced, even in the most passionate moments he'd shared with Tommy. It was as though they had become one body, one soul, one entity, bound together for all eternity.

A strident voice invaded his consciousness. There were sounds of a struggle nearby. Andrew regained his senses immediately. He still held Tommy in his arms, the Talisman was pressed to Tommy chest, but all signs of blood and his wound were gone. His eyes were closed, his face pale as before, but serene, at peace. So beautiful — even in death.

"Give it to me, now," Dakar was screaming, or at least trying to. His throat, partially crushed by Marcus, prevented him from sounding like much more than a whining child. "You have used it to your advantage, now I need it before the Fallen Ones take away the last few moments of my life!"

Marcus lifted the stone from Tommy's chest and held it towards Dakar.

"No, Marcus," Andrew gasped. "He will only use it for evil."

"I know, and that we cannot allow." Marcus closed his hand around the Talisman and crushed it, letting the tiny glittering shards fall like dust through his fingers. At the same time, the scroll which had lain forgotten at Roger's feet, crumbled to dust.

With the Talisman destroyed, the light began to slowly fade from the chamber. The one constant source that had filled this space for thousands of years was no more.

"What have you done?" Dakar foamed at the mouth as the darkness closed in around them. He lurched towards Marcus, his once handsome face contorted with rage. "You have destroyed everything that could have helped me live again. You have deceived me once more."

"You have deceived yourself," Marcus told him calmly. "Your loathsome life ends now, for there is nothing here to sustain it any longer. Even the Fallen Ones have deserted you."

Dakar's mouth opened in a silent howl. In the dark his eyes burned with hatred, but the vampires could see his body begin to fade, become wraithlike, then a mere mist, before he disappeared altogether, blown away on the gentle breeze that had materialised, then just as quickly subsided.

"Good riddance," Roger muttered.

And Andrew could not disagree with that sentiment. Dakar was dead, really dead this time, yet Andrew felt a sadness wash over him. The Talisman was destroyed and could not now be used in an attempt to reverse time and space and bring his brother back to him. His eyes filled with tears as he lifted Tommy's lifeless body and carried him from the chamber.

Chapter Nine

Tommy could feel hands pulling at him, voices urging him to wake up, but oh, he didn't want to move from this incredible place, this haven in the arms of the man he loved, and could now love without fear of their ever parting. He'd dreamed he had died, but was brought back to life again by some strange miracle, and he'd never felt better in his entire life. It was all a dream, wasn't it?

"Tommy, wake up..."

Darn it – I guess I'm going to have to wake up!

His eyes fluttered open and he smiled as Andrew's anxious expression came into focus. "Hi," he murmured, still drowsy, still trying to cling to the fading vestiges of the dream he didn't want to let go. "Where am I?"

"We're back in our hotel room, *édesem*." Andrew stroked his forehead. "How do you feel?"

"Great. I had some kind of fantastic dream. You and me and the Talisman, and – Dakar? No that can't be right. Marcus and Roger were there though. I feel great, but different, somehow." He caught sight of

Marcus and Roger standing behind Andrew. "Oh, hi guys. You look so solemn. Did I do something to piss you all off?"

"Tommy..." Andrew held his hand tightly. "Do you remember anything of what happened when we were searching for the Talisman?"

"Uh, yeah...wait. We were in some kind of underground burial place, I think. Lots of glass all over in that last spot we ended up in. Oh, and yeah, before that I got short of breath and you gave me blood—then—Shit, Dakar was there, wasn't he? He tried to take the Talisman away from you. I decked him, then—uh, kind of a blank after that. Except...mmm... You and me, Andrew, having the greatest sex. Uh, wow, maybe shouldn't say that in front of Roger. He'll have some smart ass remark to make."

Roger chuckled. "Trust you to remember that part of the dream."

"So it was a dream?"

"Some of it." Andrew bent to kiss his lips gently. "But do you remember anything about the Talisman?"

Tommy nodded. "Yeah, it was on my chest. Fucking heavy and really painful for a while, but then it felt kinda nice, and you were there and I dreamed I died but I woke up, so I couldn't have died, could I?" He looked from Andrew to Roger and Marcus. Something in their expressions gave him pause. "What?"

"The Talisman saved you, Tommy," Andrew said. "But it changed you. It enhanced the power of the blood I gave you earlier. It made you immortal—like me, and Marcus, and Roger."

Tommy stared at Andrew, a queasiness gripping his stomach, while a nerve pulsed in his temple. "You mean I'm vampire."

"Yes."

"Oh, God." He shuddered and the sudden rush of tears behind his closed eyes burned as the realisation of what that meant flooded his mind. "Oh, God," he whispered again.

"I'm sorry, Tommy."

He blinked his eyes open, saw the tortured look on Andrew's face, knew he couldn't blame him. They'd talked about this. He'd even offered to accept the change. Hadn't it always been in the cards?

"Not your fault. You were hoping it would go the other way, right?"

Andrew drew his thumb gently over Tommy's eyelids, wiping away the tears. "The Talisman held both of our destinies when you were dying. The decision was out of my hands. If I could have saved you from the change, I would have. It was never my intention that it should happen without your permission."

Tommy sighed. "I guess I always knew it would one day." He paused, remembering. "It's coming back to me now. That bastard Dakar, he tried to kill me. Picked me up like I weighed nothin' at all and —"

"He's dead, Tommy," Roger blurted. "Gone for fuckin' ever!"

"Let's hope so." Tommy sat up, but held Andrew's hand clasped tightly in his own. "And the Talisman?"

"Marcus destroyed it rather than let Dakar use it to restore his life," Andrew said.

Marcus smiled. "It seemed like a good idea at the time."

Tommy attempted to return his smile. "Shit, we really went through it, huh. How long have I been out?"

"Two days," Andrew told him. "We felt it best to let you rest, let your body adapt to its — differences."

"Yeah, things sure are different. Everything's kind of, brighter, sharper. Oh, wait..." He ran a finger over his upper teeth. "Something feels funny up here."

"They're called fangs," Roger said, laughing. "They take some getting used to. I kept biting my tongue for days."

"Fangs." Tommy prodded them with the tip of his tongue. "Jeez, they're sharp!"

"All the better to bite with." Roger sounded like he was really enjoying this. He received a slap on the back of his head from Marcus.

"Roger, this is not the time to joke. Tommy has a lot to deal with right now and will need our support, not your usual flippancy."

"Sorry." Roger looked suitably chastened, but managed to sneak in a wink at Tommy, who grinned at him.

"Have you heard from Andorra and Tony?" Tommy asked.

Marcus nodded. "As you know, they had to go to Washington D.C. to give a full report on what transpired with Hollingsworth. It appears that there was more than one traitor involved in the attempted assassination of President Metcalfe. The Secret Service and the CIA are conducting a high-level investigation."

"And the talks with the Prez and the terrorists?"

"Suspended without any agreement. The Taliban are blaming the US for the breakdown in the talks."

"What a surprise."

"You and I have a midnight flight back to California booked for tomorrow," Andrew said. "That will give you a little more time to adjust. Marcus and Roger are leaving tonight."

Tommy leant back against the headboard and winked at Roger. "Would you guys mind if Andrew and me had a little time alone?"

"Not at all," Marcus said immediately, taking Roger's arm and leading him to the bedroom door. "When you are ready for company, you may call our room."

"Thanks."

"How come you don't correct Tommy's grammar like you do mine?" Roger demanded on their way out.

Marcus' retort was hidden by the closing of the door.

Tommy smiled and reached out to caress Andrew's face. "So, my vampire, do you still love me now that I'm going to be around forever? Here, by your side, to bug you for all eternity?"

Andrew chuckled softly and turned his face so he could kiss Tommy's palm. "I will love you through all the bugging you can throw my way. Nothing will ever change that, Tommy."

"Good to hear." He wrapped his arms round Andrew's neck and pulled him in for a long, long kiss. Oh, yeah. This was way more than a kiss. This was— exquisite. Not a word he'd ever used to describe anything, but nothing else seemed as expressive. Andrew's kisses had always been hot—those soft, luscious lips, the touch of them so quick to send every single nerve zinging straight to his groin.

"You know," he murmured when they paused for a moment between kisses. "I've always wondered what it would be like to make love as a vampire. To have no limits—and like then—not having to come up for air too soon."

"And?"

"And it's even more sensational than I ever imagined."

"Then you know what I have been experiencing from the first time we made love. How I wished so many times that you could have that same level of ecstasy as I."

"Andrew…" Tommy kissed the tip of Andrew's nose. "No one — no one — ever made love to me like you did. Every kiss, every touch, was like nothing I'd ever known before. Even before I knew you were a vampire, I was saying, 'Wow, but this guy is the best!' I just hope that now I can give you that same kind of thrill."

"You already do." Andrew kissed him again. "So, you really are all right with this? I know you must harbour regrets — your friends, family. But they need not know if you don't want them to. Our way of life can be adapted to theirs in some ways."

Tommy nodded. "I guess in a way, it was on the cards. I've thought about it a lot, talked it over with Micah and Roger — and with Ron, who hasn't made the change yet. It's all doable. Besides, I'm just happy I didn't really die, die. I'd have missed the hell outta you."

"And I'd have missed the hell outta you," Andrew said softly.

"There's just some things that kinda worry me."

"Of course there are. But I will be by your side every step you take into this new life."

"Like…uh — the first time I have to, uh…"

"Feed."

"Uh… Yeah, that."

"Don't worry. There are many different ways to drink blood. You will have my guidance in the beginning, but you will eventually work it out for yourself."

"Okay." Tommy looked around the room. "Amazing how everything looks and feels so different. Sounds, smells—your scent." He leaned in closer. "Mmm. I think I can even smell your blood...nice."

"Yes, every one of your senses has been heightened. That too you will have to get used to. It just takes time, Tommy. Something you now have plenty of."

Tommy nodded. Not only sounds and scents, but his vision was so much keener. And Andrew... God, he looked even more beautiful now, if that was possible. His eyes... Tommy had often thought them so unusually blue, like hot ice, but now when he gazed into them he could see shards of a darker blue surrounding the iris—amazing. The planes of his face seemed more sculpted, more perfect, and his mouth— oh, God—that mouth. So sensual it made Tommy's already hard cock ache at the thought of the kisses they would share.

He couldn't wait to make love to Andrew. Roger, always the one with the lewd comment, the wicked remark, had once told him in a more serious moment, that the first time he and Marcus had made love after he had been changed had been like nothing he could ever have imagined.

"It was like every single sensation, every touch and kiss had so much more. Every time I inhaled his scent, a scent I thought I knew from all the times we had made love, it was as if it was all brand new to me... Everything was new..."

Tommy had never forgotten the intensity behind Roger's words. At the time he'd just considered their conversation unusual because of Roger's sometimes tactless comments, but now he had a feeling he was about to find out what Roger meant.

"You know…" Tommy gave Andrew a slow, seductive smile. "I think the very next thing we should do is make love for the first time—I mean, as vampires."

"I'm so glad being immortal hasn't displaced that one-track mind of yours."

"With you around? How could that be possible?"

Andrew caressed Tommy's chest, and the slow subtle movements seemed to take on an even greater sensuousness than ever before.

"That feels, uh—amazing. I mean it always has—does—but now it's like my skin is even more sensitive to your touch." He groaned as Andrew brushed his fingers over his nipples. "Oh, my God, Andrew—it's all so much more."

Andrew leant forwards and kissed him, and Tommy opened to his lover, their tongues sliding over each other's in a caress that had Tommy seeing stars. With each passing moment it was if Tommy's awareness of every single sensation increased.

"Oh, wow," he murmured.

"What?"

"I can hear your thoughts, hear them as clearly as if you were saying the words." He leaned closer and kissed Andrew's parted lips. "You really do love me."

"Did you ever doubt it?"

"Not doubt, but sometimes I'd wonder why someone as fantastic as you, as different as you, would want Joe Blow Fireman, Mr Ordinary, you know?"

"You are far from ordinary, my love." Andrew cupped the back of Tommy's head and held him so their lips remained touching. "The moment I saw you, despite knowing I should go no further than drink from you, I think I was lost. Not for one moment did the memory of your sweet scent and taste leave me. If you were as ordinary as you think you are, why would I have sought you out, come to you that night and spent those incredible hours with you, making love to you, over and over?"

"Yeah, I'll never forget that first time with you." Tommy caressed Andrew's face with his fingertips. "I'd thought that you had forgotten me—then there you were at my door, in my arms—kissing me, driving me mad—God, it was fantastic."

"Yes, it was..."

"And of course, before that, you made me forget you. Well..." Tommy smiled wickedly. "You can't do that no more!"

"No..." Andrew kissed Tommy's lips gently. "But there are some other things you should know."

"Later," Tommy said, drawing Andrew into his arms and falling back against the mattress.

"Yes, later."

Their bodies and minds melded, taking them to a level of ecstasy no human could ever dream of experiencing. Tommy could hardly believe how different this all felt. Yes, he had relished every moment of their lovemaking before, but this—this was so incredible, so mind blowing, he wished Andrew had changed him after his Uncle Lazlo's attack. When he'd been drained of blood and hovered on the brink of death. But Andrew had saved him, had loved him enough to not change him. Tommy wondered now, if the situations had been reversed, if he had been vampire and Andrew human, would he have had the strength to ignore the call of the blood lust?

Andrew held Tommy's now harder than steel erection in his hand and smiled ruefully at him. "Strange thoughts to be having while I am pleasuring you."

"Right. It's just that everything is so crazy different now. Things I thought I'd never cope with, never really want, now I wish I'd always been like this, been like this from the beginning — with you."

"We have an eternity to experience all of it, Tommy. Just give yourself up to what I offer you."

"There's just one other thing."

"What's that?"

"You still have your clothes on. Naked or dressed you're still the handsomest man on the planet, but right now I want to see you, to feel you with nothing but your skin on mine."

Andrew smiled and Tommy knew he was about to will his clothes away. "No, not like that. I'd like to watch you take everything off...slowly...to see your naked body for the first time through my vampire eyes."

Without hesitation, Andrew stood before Tommy, toed off his sandals and began to unbutton his shirt. Tommy had always thought Andrew to be the sexiest man he had ever met, and now he made even these ordinary movements so sensual, so totally arousing. Tommy licked his lips in anticipation as Andrew's smooth, taut torso was revealed, his defined chest muscles dusted with dark hair, the small pale brown nipples still pebbled from the sensation of Tommy's kisses.

"Beautiful," Tommy whispered and stared in fascination as Andrew's shirt slid off his shoulders and pooled at his bare feet. He watched eagerly as Andrew unbuckled his belt and pulled down the zipper of his jeans. He eased the denim over his slim hips, pausing just slightly, teasing Tommy for a moment with a glimpse of pubic hair before letting his jeans fall revealing his cock, hard and proud, elegantly curved – the head already moist with pre-cum.

Tommy gasped. Of course he'd seen Andrew naked before, many, many times, admired his masculine beauty each and every time, but never like this. Through his enhanced vision that made everything sharper, clearer, brighter, Andrew's skin seemed to glow, every sculpted muscle was more defined, like warm smooth marble, every part of him more stunning, more… Tommy couldn't resist the thought, *more fuckable than before.*

"God, I never knew what I've been missing all this time," Tommy murmured, unable to tear his eyes away from the magnificent sight his lover presented to him. "I wouldn't have believed it possible that I could see you as even more gorgeous than you already are." He opened his arms and Andrew kicked away his jeans and lowered himself into Tommy's embrace. Their lips met and meshed in a long sensuous kiss, their hands tracing and caressing every contour and muscle of each other's body.

Sweet… Oh God, so much better than sweet…fucking unbelievable!

He whimpered as Andrew gently pulled away from their kiss, then moaned when Andrew began tracing an erotic pattern over skin that was so much more incredibly sensitised than before. It was almost too much – almost. When Andrew gripped Tommy's rigid shaft and swiped his tongue across the moist head Tommy's body bucked from the powerful sensation. He arched his hips, driving himself into Andrew's mouth. Andrew's hands slipped under Tommy's butt, holding him in place while he sucked long and hard, his tongue swirling over the blood-engorged veins beneath the silken skin of Tommy's pulsing shaft.

Tommy groaned, his hands fisting the sheets under him as Andrew's fangs scraped delicately at the base of his cock. He felt the slight flow of blood being sucked up into Andrew's mouth then those amazing lips were tracing a seductive pattern over his abdomen, his chest, his throat until they settled on his mouth and he tasted his own blood in their kiss. Andrew ran his tongue over the sharp edge of Tommy's fangs and they shared their blood, their breath, their very souls in the most mind-blowing kiss Tommy had ever experienced.

Their bodies moved together in perfect unison. Low growls were forced from their throats as they were inundated with sensation after sensation of total ecstasy. They crushed each other's body, writhing, straining for a closeness that was no longer close enough.

"Fuck me." Tommy was momentarily startled at the sound of his own voice—demanding, almost a snarl. "Inside me, now. I want to feel every fucking inch of you filling me up, making me come so hard I'll never forget it..."

The reply was silent but immediate. Andrew lifted Tommy's legs and pushed into him. There was no pain, only pleasure, exquisite rapturous pleasure that filled his blood with the liquid fire of a passion that had him again arching up off the bed.

"Oh, gods, Tommy." Andrew's voice shook from their shared emotion, their thoughts melding, the love and desire that enveloped their minds and bodies overwhelming them. Andrew lowered his head to claim Tommy's lips in slow, languorous kisses, nipping and sucking on his tongue. Each thrust of his hips, every long stroke deep inside Tommy's heat brought them both closer and closer to the edge. Every pass over Tommy's prostate had his cock jerking in response, the head slick with pre-cum, his balls pulled up tight as he teetered on the edge of what would be the most explosive climax of his existence – so far.

Andrew's balls drummed against Tommy's buttocks as the speed of his rhythm increased. Their eyes met and Andrew wrapped a hand round Tommy's hard throbbing flesh urging him on to the orgasms they both could no longer resist.

Harsh gasps and moans filled each other's mouths as they came together, their bodies rising off the bed from the force of the intensity of what they shared. White-hot heat enveloped them. Tommy's cum exploded from him, spilling over Andrew's hand, shooting over their chests. One more thrust and Andrew came, scalding Tommy's insides. Tommy clenched his sphincter muscles around the base of Andrew's cock, holding the power of that orgasm inside him as he buried his face against Andrew's neck, his new fangs scraping at the smooth flesh.

"Yes," Andrew murmured through a throaty breath as they settled again on top of the bed. "Drink from me…"

Tommy bit down, tentatively at first, then with more force, his fangs sinking into the pulsing vein. Andrew's body shuddered in orgasmic ecstasy at the bite, and Tommy moaned as the rich, powerful blood gushed over his tongue. He wrapped his arms even tighter around Andrew and his mind spiralled out of control as, for the first time, he felt himself become lost in the blood lust. He sucked hard, relishing the taste and scent of the sweet, spicy blood that flowed from the wounds he had inflicted on Andrew's neck.

And, oh God, it is…fantastic!

He was only dimly aware that Andrew had struggled free and now held him, his hand clasped firmly round Tommy's jaw. His ice-blue eyes glittered with a warning as they bored into his.

"Be glad it is me here with you now. I have the strength to resist—a human could not. You would have killed him, or her." Andrew paused. "I see remorse in your eyes. That's good, Tommy. Never take too much."

"I'm sorry." Tommy licked the wounds closed. "It's so easy to get carried away—and you taste so good."

Andrew nodded. "A lesson you have learned early, and one you will not forget." He kissed Tommy's lips gently. "*Szeretlek*, Tommy."

"I love you too," Tommy whispered, and knew without a doubt that it meant forever.

* * * *

Tommy lay quietly beside his sleeping lover. He still felt bad about what he had done earlier. Thank God, as Andrew had said, it was him and not some unsuspecting human he'd latched onto. Now, he totally understood what he'd only guessed at before. Just how strong, how almost uncontrollable the bloodlust was.

Jeez, but there was so much he needed to know.

Andrew had been right, there were a million questions buzzing around in his brain. And a couple of situations, that when they returned to the States, could no longer be avoided. Mainly what to tell his family, his friends, particularly Alex? Would he still be able to be a fireman? He loved his job, hated the idea of giving it up. Maybe he could corner the night shift. But what if they called him out on an emergency, like for a forest fire, when all the divisions got together to act as one team, day and night? Maybe Andrew had some ideas how he could handle all of this. After all, Andrew had gone through similar circumstances when he'd been changed. He hadn't been a fireman though, and he'd had his brother, Michael, for support.

Michael. Although he had never met the man, knowing him only through images on faded photographs and Andrew's poignant memories of him, Tommy felt a deep sorrow that Andrew had not been able to bring him back. The destruction of the Talisman and the Scrolls had ensured there would be no way back for Dakar, but also for Michael.

He must have been a helluva guy...

One who had stood by his younger brother when their evil uncle had changed them against their will. One who had nurtured him, had protected him as they had entered this strange new life together.

Well, I got Andrew. And who could be better really?

Uh-oh. Something he hadn't thought about until now. He sat up.

"Hey, a thought has just occurred to me," he said, nudging Andrew awake.

"Only one?" Andrew smiled up at him. "I would imagine there will be many thoughts, and many questions. Fortunately, we have lots of time ahead of us for you to ask as much as you like."

"Okay, but here's a really pressing one. Being vampire means I can fly, right?"

"Yes, that is correct."

J.P. Bowie

"But how am I going to do that when I have no head for heights, unless—"

"Unless there's a ladder under you? Yes, I've heard that one many times, Tommy."

"Hey." Tommy poked him in the ribs. "That's a little unfeeling you know."

Andrew chuckled and sat up. "Tommy, your fear of heights was a human failing. Now that you are no longer hu—well, let's say mortal, that vulnerability will no longer be a part of you. You won't get sick, you won't grow old—and you won't close your eyes when we go soaring into the night sky together. Although, I have to admit, that was a rather endearing eccentricity of yours."

"You're jerking me around, aren't you?"

"Never."

"Huh. Well…" Tommy laid his head on Andrew's shoulder, and snuggled against him. "I guess I'm gonna find out the first time I try it."

"I'll be right there with you, don't worry." Andrew chuckled. "By the way, I thought it best when we leave tomorrow not to subject you to the flight Marcus and Roger are taking tonight."

"You mean…?"

"That's right. They are flying vampire express back to LA."

"Shit. I can't believe that at some point I'm going to be okay with this."

"You will. Of that, I have no doubt. It's just a part of your new life, after all."

"Huh." Tommy was quiet for a few moments then he said, "At least it means I can take my niece and nephew on the Ferris wheel next time I see them. They always want to go to the fairground, and I've always chickened out taking them on it. They never could understand why a fireman wouldn't go up there."

"One thing about that, Tommy."

"What's that?"

"Just remember to take them to the fairground at night."

"Oh, right."

Epilogue

Tommy walked into the firehouse and made his way to the chief's office. Chief Lambert looked up and gave Tommy a nod then indicated he should sit.

"Nice vacation?" he asked then looked at Tommy though narrowed eyes. "You sure didn't get a tan while you were in Iraq."

"Not really the kind of place for sitting round the pool."

Tommy gave him a tight smile. He was still a little uncomfortable smiling at humans, a tad worried he might show the tips of his fangs. Sometimes, they seemed a little long, even to him.

"Anyway, Chief, I wondered if I could have the night shift on a permanent basis."

Lambert arched an eyebrow. "Really? First time I've been asked that. Most guys like to avoid that shift if they can."

"It just kinda suits my purposes for the time being," Tommy said, reciting the line he'd rehearsed earlier.

"And what might those 'purposes' be, if you don't mind me asking?"

"Uh, I'd like to go back to school, earn a degree in Sociology."

"Is that a fact?" Lambert looked impressed. "Well, looks like I won't be losing you for a few years."

"No, sir." Tommy allowed himself a half grin. "It'll take a while, but I have to think of the future."

"Of course. Okay, I'll schedule you for the eight o'clock shift starting tomorrow night, how's that?"

"Terrific, chief. Thanks a lot."

"No problem, Tommy. And…" Lambert shivered a little as he shook Tommy's hand over his desk. "You should try and get a bit of sun on your days off. You look a mite pale."

* * * *

Alex was waiting for him when he left the firehouse. "How'd it go?"

"Fine. He was surprised, but as there are always plenty of guys waiting to transfer to other shifts he was okay with it."

"Jason's waiting for us at the bar," Alex told him.

'Things are good with you and him then?" Tommy asked.

"Yeah, real good," Alex said happily. "We're talking 'bout moving in together."

"I'm glad to hear that, Alex. Glad you've finally found the one." Tommy didn't add that now they might not see each other as much in the future. He was happy that his best friend had found someone to share his life.

"Is Andrew joining us at the bar?"

"Yes. And a few of his friends — well, our friends now — his and mine."

"Oh, yeah? Cool."

"Yeah, they're a great bunch. Kinda different, but you'll like them." Tommy put his arms round Alex's shoulder and hugged him close. "Once you get to know them."

About the Author

J.P Bowie was born in Scotland and toured British theatres in numerous musical shows including Stephen Sondheim's Company.

Emigrated to the States and worked in Las Vegas, Nevada for the magicians Siegfried and Roy as their Head of Wardrobe at the Mirage Hotel. Currently living in Henderson, Nevada.

J.P. Bowie loves to hear from readers. You can find her contact information, website details and author profile page at http://www.total-e-bound.com.

Total-E-Bound Publishing

www.total-e-bound.com

Take a look at our exciting range of literagasmic™
erotic romance titles and discover pure quality
at Total-E-Bound.